WITH THESE RINGS...
who will they wed?

Rick knew he should get up and leave.

Soon, he thought.

There would be too many complications, too many expectations, if he stayed.

He didn't need that.

But he needed Jill. He needed her warmth, her sweetness. Just for now. He'd leave in a little while, he promised himself.

Just for a while he'd pretend he was the kind of man who could stay. The kind of man who deserved the love of the woman in his arms.

The kind of man she—and her child—could rely on.

Don't miss the next exciting installment in Patricia Thayer's WITH THESE RINGS miniseries. Look for *Her Surprise Family* in Silhouette Romance, coming in September 1999.

Dear Reader,

Welcome to Special Edition...where each month we publish six novels celebrating love and life, with a special romance blended in.

You'll revel in *Baby Love* by Victoria Pade, our touching THAT'S MY BABY! title and another installment in her ongoing A RANCHING FAMILY saga. In this emotional tale, a rugged rancher becomes an instant daddy—and solicits the help of Elk Creek's favorite nurse to give him lessons on bringing up baby.

And there's much more engaging romance on the way! Bestselling author Christine Rimmer continues her CONVENIENTLY YOURS miniseries with her thirtieth novel, about an enamored duo who masquerade as newlyweds—and brand-new parents— in *Married by Accident.* And you won't want to miss *Just the Three of Us,* Jennifer Mikels's tender love story about a high-society lady and a blue-collar bachelor who are passionately bound together for the sake of an adorable little boy. Then an estranged tycoon returns to the family fold and discovers unexpected love in *The Secret Millionaire* by Patricia Thayer— the first book in her WITH THESE RINGS series, which crosses into Silhouette Romance in September with *Her Surprise Family.*

Rounding off the month, Lois Faye Dyer will sweep you off your feet with a heartwarming reunion romance that results in a surprise pregnancy, in *The Only Cowboy for Caitlin.* And in *Child Most Wanted* by veteran author Carole Halston, a fiercely protective heroine hides her true identity to safeguard her nephew, but she never counted on losing her heart to the man who could claim her beloved boy as his own.

I hope you enjoy these books, and each and every novel to come!

Sincerely,

Karen Taylor Richman
Senior Editor

Please address questions and book requests to:
Silhouette Reader Service
U.S.: 3010 Walden Ave., P.O. Box 1325, Buffalo, NY 14269
Canadian: P.O. Box 609, Fort Erie, Ont. L2A 5X3

PATRICIA THAYER

THE SECRET MILLIONAIRE

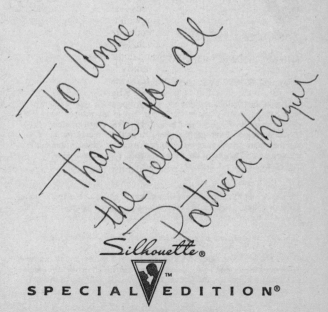

To Anne,
Thanks for all
the help

Patricia Thayer

Silhouette®

SPECIAL EDITION®

Published by Silhouette Books

America's Publisher of Contemporary Romance

To Daralynn
I couldn't have picked anyone I'd want more as my daughter-in-law. My son truly found an angel.

Thanks to Dr. Mario Ficarola for sharing your Italian culture with me. And to Millie Caggiano, for the long phone calls filled with wonderful stories about your large family. I couldn't have done this series without you both.

 SILHOUETTE BOOKS

ISBN 0-373-24252-2

THE SECRET MILLIONAIRE

Copyright © 1999 by Patricia Wright

This edition published by arrangement with Harlequin Books S.A.

® and TM are trademarks of Harlequin Books S.A., used under license. Trademarks indicated with ® are registered in the United States Patent and Trademark Office, the Canadian Trade Marks Office and in other countries.

Look us up on-line at: http://www.romance.net

Printed in U.S.A.

Books by Patricia Thayer

Silhouette Special Edition

Nothing Short of a Miracle #1116
Baby, Our Baby! #1225
*The Secret Millionaire #1252

Silhouette Romance

Just Maggie #895
Race to the Altar #1009
The Cowboy's Courtship #1064
Wildcat Wedding #1086
Reilly's Bride #1146
The Cowboy's Convenient Bride #1261

* With These Rings

PATRICIA THAYER

has been writing for fourteen years and has published nine books with Silhouette. Her books have been nominated for the National Readers' Choice Award, the Holt Medallion, Desert Dreams's Golden Quill and the prestigious RITA Award. In 1997, *Nothing Short of a Miracle* won the *Romantic Times Magazine* Reviewers' Choice Award for Best Special Edition.

Thanks to the understanding men in her life—her husband of twenty-eight years, Steve, and her three sons—Pat has been able to fulfill her dream of writing romance. Another dream is to own a cabin in Colorado, where she can spend her days writing and her evenings with her favorite hero, Steve. She loves to hear from readers. You can write her at P.O. Box 6251, Anaheim, CA 92816-0251.

All underlined places are fictitious.

Prologue

"Tell me about Grandpa being a hero," eight-year-old Rick Covelli pleaded.

His grandmother, Vittoria Covelli, smiled. Every time she looked at the boy she saw a mirror image of his namesake, her late husband, Enrico.

"*Si,* my grandson. But I've told you and your brother the story many times."

Dressed in his pajamas, young Enrico had stayed home from school because of an asthma attack. "Please, Nonna," he begged as he bounced on the bed. "I want to hear about Italy and how Grandpa flew an airplane in the war."

Vittoria gave him a stern look. "You must be still—remember your asthma." It saddened her to know this sweet boy couldn't play like other children.

Rick's small chest struggled for each breath as he lay back down on the bed. "I'll be good," he promised, his ebony eyes wide with excitement.

Vittoria sat on the edge of the mattress. The same wrought-iron bed she'd shared with her beloved husband for more than forty years.

"Many years ago in Italy, my family, the Perrones, lived in a small village. When I was a young girl it was a bad time. There was war devastating our country and people, but our village in Tuscany fortunately did not see much of the trouble. Not until your *nonno*'s airplane crashed not far from our home."

"That's when you met Grandpa Enrico and saved his life," Rick offered.

Vittoria raised a hand. "You go too fast."

"Sorry," Rick said. "Please tell me more, Nonna."

"At night, I could hear the airplanes in the sky. I lay in bed and prayed for everyone to be safe. Then one night I heard a plane that didn't sound like the others. Something was wrong with the engine.

"It was Grandpa's plane, wasn't it?"

She nodded. "Yes. It was an American plane. It had been hit and was trying to make it back to its base, but it crash-landed in a field a few miles from our house. The next day, I found U.S. Army Sergeant Enrico Covelli hiding in our barn. He'd managed to free himself from the wreckage, even with a leg wound and loss of blood."

Vittoria remembered it as if it were yesterday. Though battered and bruised, Enrico had still been the handsomest man she'd ever seen in all her seventeen years. He was also the enemy. But she was afraid he might die, and she couldn't let that happen in a prison camp.

Hearing her grandson's voice urging her on, Vittoria continued the story. "I knew that I should turn him in, but I ended up secretly caring for his wounds and staying while he fought his fever. Then after a few days, he began to get his strength back. He spoke to me in Italian. I was shocked when he told me his name was Enrico Covelli, an American. His parents had come from Rome. I could not turn him over to the soldiers."

"No, Nonna," Rick said, shaking his head, "you had to hide him."

"But I was afraid that he'd be discovered." Vittoria had known she was falling in love with the American. Then came the night Enrico confessed his love for her. He didn't want to leave her, but he had to find his way to the Allied lines. They'd both be in danger if he was caught.

Vittoria began again. "I'd heard about the underground. A group who helped get people to safety. The next night, before your nonno Enrico left, he promised that he would return after the war. He said he wanted to marry me and bring me to America. I told him I loved him, too. Then he kissed me goodbye and disappeared into the night."

Young Enrico reached for the case on the nightstand and opened the box to display the medal.

"My grandpa got the Purple Heart for being wounded."

"*Si,*" Vittoria agreed. "I didn't know if he ever even made it out of the country. Another year passed, and then the war ended." Tears filled her eyes at the memory. "I thought he must have died, because he'd promised never to forget about me."

"But he didn't die," Rick encouraged.

Vittoria took her grandson's hand. "No, but I had no word from him. I waited for months, but nothing. By then my *padre* had an offer from Giovanni Valente for my hand in marriage."

"Your father wanted you to marry a mean man."

"No, Rick, Giovanni wasn't mean," she explained. "I just didn't love him as I loved my Enrico. But my *famiglia* urged me to marry him because of his wealth. Even during the war, the Valentes managed to hold on to their vineyards, and my father saw that someday they would be prosperous again. We had nothing left of value except the ruby rings that were to go to the firstborn daughter when she married. That was me.''

It still saddened her to remember it. She had used the yards of white silk from Enrico's discarded parachute for her wedding gown. At least she'd have something of her true love with her.

''My padre gave the rings to Giovanni as a betrothal gift.''

''But Grandpa came to rescue you?''

Vittoria smiled. How many times had she told this story to her children, and now her grandchildren? ''*Si,* he returned the week I was to marry Giovanni.''

She remembered the day so clearly. She had nearly fainted when Enrico came for her, but when he took her into his arms and kissed her, she knew she wasn't dreaming. After he'd finished his time in the army, he'd come back as soon as he could. Just like he'd promised.

''Your *nonno* asked for my hand, but my *padre* insisted that I was already promised to another. That didn't stop Enrico. We went to the Valente family to explain that I couldn't marry Giovanni.''

''Were they angry?''

''What do you think? Giovanni was furious! He soon realized that he had no choice except to release me, but he swore he'd never love another and refused to return the rings.''

''Oh, Nonna, what did you do?''

''How could I leave my inheritance, my betrothal gift, with a man who wasn't going to be my husband? Enrico stood up to Giovanni and argued that the rings were to be used as wedding bands. Finally Giovanni conceded, but he only gave back the groom's ring. He slipped the bride's ring on his little finger as a symbol of his stolen bride. Then Madre Valente placed a curse on the rings, stating that until the two were joined again, the Covellis will not have an easy road to love.''

All these years, Vittoria's heart had ached deeply. She got up and crossed to the dresser. Trembling, she opened the drawer, pushed some clothes aside and pulled out a small black velvet case. Although Enrico had never believed in the power of the curse, Vittoria knew that something had shadowed their love over the years.

''Can I see it, Nonna?'' Rick asked.

She returned to the bed. Carefully she opened the case to display the large bloodred ruby with a circle of diamonds embedded in the ornate gold band. When the two rings had been side by side, they were a perfect pair. The last time had been more than thirty years ago. Now at fifty-two, Vittoria still prayed for the rings to be reunited, especially after losing her beloved Enrico this past year.

''Wow! I bet it's worth about a million dollars.''

''Oh, my Enrico, it will be worth so much more than money if you find the love that will break the curse.''

Chapter One

Coming home was the hardest thing Rick Covelli had ever done.

It had been a long time since he'd called Haven Springs, Indiana, home. Six years to be exact. He just hoped his family was willing to welcome the long-lost son back into the fold.

Rick walked into Maria's Ristorante, inhaled the familiar aroma and happy childhood memories. Pushing his way through the dinner crowd, he suddenly grew anxious. He glanced around the converted storefront that now resembled an intimate European café. There were hand-painted murals on the walls, and the gleaming hardwood floors were framed with brick tiles. Judging by the number of people waiting for a table, lack of customers wasn't a problem.

A waitress appeared. ''How many, sir?''

Rick looked at her. She was a young woman with thick honey-blond hair that was pulled back and fell in long curls to her shoulders. A light sprinkling of freckles were scattered across a straight nose and creamy skin. When his gaze locked with her big deep-blue eyes, recognition dawned. Although her looks had changed considerably, he'd never been able to forget Jill Morgan. He managed to swallow his startled reaction and find his voice. "I don't need a table. I'm looking for Maria."

Jill's eyes widened, and he knew she was remembering, too. "I'll go…and get her." She turned and rushed away.

Painful memories from two years ago threatened to engulf him—the day of his father's funeral, and later that evening at the house when friends and family came by to pay their respects. Rick hadn't been able to handle even one more word of sympathy, no matter how well-meaning, and went outside to get some air. That was where he'd found the blue-eyed angel—Jill Morgan.

Rick heard his name being called and was pulled from his musings. Across the room he saw his mother come rushing toward him. The short, gray-haired woman greeted him with a forgiving smile and a huge hug. "Oh, Rick, you've come home!"

He stood back and grinned. "Does that mean you're glad to see me?"

Tears streamed down Maria Covelli's cheeks as she reached up and planted a kiss on each of his cheeks. "You are my son. Of course I'm glad you're here."

Rick's throat clogged with emotion. No matter what, he could always count on his mother.

There was more commotion and he looked up to see his grandmother, Nonna Vittoria, and his sister, Angelina, hurrying over to greet him. After exchanging hugs all around, they moved the reunion into the corner of the bar that was reserved for family and employees.

"Oh, my, you must be hungry!" his mother exclaimed.

"Look at you, skin and bones." Before he could protest she headed for the kitchen, followed closely by Nonna.

Rick smiled at his sister. "It sure is good to be home."

He'd driven down Main Street as if he owned it, Jill thought, remembering the black-and-chrome motorcycle that had raced past the restaurant window while she'd waited on a customer. But never in a million years had she expected the rider to be Rick Covelli. The son who'd walked away from his family and broken his mother's heart.

And then, as big as life, he'd strolled in dressed in black, a big grin on his handsome face, forcing every woman in the place to take notice. His hair was cut short enough to be civil, yet long enough to be wild. But the real threat was in those piercing black eyes, which could mesmerize you into thinking things you had no business thinking.

Jill drew a deep breath as she took in his broad shoulders and muscular chest covered by a formfitting black T-shirt under a leather jacket. Jeans tapered to fit his long legs, and when he sat down at the bar, she got a view of his nicely toned backside.

She jerked her gaze away and headed to the kitchen. She'd met Rick Covelli before, and he was like no one she'd ever known. She'd never expected to see him again.

"Jill," Maria called over the noise in the busy kitchen, happiness sparkling in her brown eyes.

Jill hurried to her side. "Yes, Maria?"

"Would you take this food out to Rick and tell him I'll join him in a few minutes?"

"Sure." Jill smiled, even though it was the last thing she wanted to do. She took the plate and carried it through the double doors and around the maze of tables to the bar. By the time she reached her destination she was shaking.

* * *

Rick took a sip of his Chianti and began to relax for the first time since he'd ridden his bike across the state line into southern Indiana and past the Haven Springs city-limit sign.

He'd had a lot of regrets over the years, some while he'd lived here, more after he'd moved to Texas. The biggest was that he'd never managed to have a comfortable relationship with his father, that he hadn't reached out and tried to resolve the turmoil between them.

Although Rafaele Covelli, Sr., had been dead for two years, Rick's feelings of guilt hadn't faded, especially now that he'd finally found his way home.

"Excuse me."

A soft feminine voice caught Rick's attention and he looked across the bar at Jill Morgan. Her beauty still caught him off guard. That her fresh scrubbed look appealed to him was a surprise. Usually his tastes went to older, more sophisticated types. He met her gaze and saw wariness in her sapphire eyes.

"Your mother asked me to bring you dinner," she said.

She was holding a plate of Maria's famous fettuccine *alla marinara.* His mouth watered. "Thank you." Rick reached out to help her with the plate and their hands brushed. She jerked back, nearly knocking over his wine.

He managed to catch the glass. "Whoa, I didn't mean to scare you. I'm harmless."

They both knew that was a lie.

He rubbed his day-old growth of beard and grinned. "Okay, let's say I'm housebroken."

Her gaze danced away from his. "I forgot the bread," she said, and quickly disappeared before he could stop her.

In the mere hour he'd been home, Ms. Morgan had run away from him twice. Rick thought back to the first time they'd met. The day of his father's funeral.

They had all arrived back at the Covelli house, a crowd

of people hovering in the family living room. Everyone dressed in black, murmuring words of sympathy about Rafaele Covelli's fatal accident. Rick had had to get out of there, and fast. He made his way through the kitchen and found more people. More apologetic people. He grabbed a bottle of wine and a glass and headed out the screen door. He raced down the steps into the backyard, past his grandmother's roses, to the bench he and his father had built years before. Rick had only been eight years old, but Rafaele had wanted his sons to share his love for carpentry. The garden bench was their project.

Rick's body was soon racked with sobs and he collapsed on the weathered bench. God, it wasn't fair. His dad wasn't supposed to die. Not this young and not in a stupid accident.

Guilt overwhelmed Rick. If he'd been here—if he'd been the son he was supposed to be and worked alongside his dad—maybe he could have discovered the problem before his dad got trapped in the collapsed building. Now he was never going to be able to tell his dad that...he was sorry.

A sound caused Rick to glance up. A short distance away, in the rose arbor, stood a woman. In the moonlight, he could see her long blond hair curled around her pretty face. Her expression was a mixture of concern and embarrassment.

"I'm sorry. I didn't mean to intrude.... I was just taking a walk." She started to leave.

Suddenly Rick didn't want to be alone. "You look like an angel standing there."

"I'm not an angel, Mr. Covelli." Her tone was sad.

"Good. Neither am I," he joked, then grew serious. "And the name is Rick. What's yours?"

"Jill. Jill Morgan."

"Well, Jill Morgan, I'm not very good company, but...maybe you could just stay with me awhile."

She looked panicked as she rubbed the chill off her arms. "I should go in."

He stood and removed his suit jacket. "Here, this will keep you warm." He went to her and placed the coat over her slim shoulders, practically covering her loose-fitting dark print dress. She was even prettier up close. "Please, just sit with me." He took her hand and led her to the bench.

They sat there for the next two hours. They talked about his father, a conversation interspersed with long periods of silence, but what he remembered most about that night was how Jill Morgan had never judged him. Maybe that was why he'd never forgotten her.

"Well, if it isn't the prodigal son come home."

Rick dragged his thoughts back to the present, glanced up to see his older brother, Rafe, approaching. He stood up, and they embraced.

Rick drew back. "I see you're still as ugly as ever."

"And you're still jealous of my good looks."

Rafe laughed. "That'll be the day."

The sturdily built six-footer settled on the bar stool next to Rick's. Rafe was the oldest of the three Covelli children, and more like their father than either of the other kids.

Rafe had been the one who jumped in and took over things after their father's death. He'd worked hard, but his efforts had barely succeeded in keeping the family construction business afloat. Rick was the middle child, and the baby of the family was their beautiful and spoiled sister, Angelina. She was barely out of college and was working in the Covelli and Sons office. Their cousin, Tony Covelli, who was like a brother to them, had come to Haven Springs to attend college. Since graduation he'd made his home with the family and worked as their financial adviser, keeping the books and a tight rein on the budget.

Now, after a six-year absence, Rick had returned. Was

it too late for him to reclaim his place as a member of the Covelli family?

Jill appeared and set down a basket of bread. She smiled and quickly moved away. Rick couldn't help but enjoy the view.

"You're wasting your time," Rafe said.

"What are you talking about?"

"Don't bother asking Jill out."

"And just how am I wasting my time?"

Rafe cocked an eyebrow. "Read the writing on the wall, buddy, or should I say on Jill?" He nodded toward the waitress taking an order from a corner table in the dimly lit restaurant. "It says Hands Off."

Rick eyed Jill again. She was tall, and although her skirt nearly covered her knees, he could still see that her legs were long and shapely. She had a look that made a man think about sultry nights and satin sheets. Rick reached for his wine and took a swallow, hoping to calm the effect she had on his already overheated body.

"So, bro," Rick asked, "Ms. Morgan already turned *you* down?"

Rafe made a snorting sound. "To our mother's chagrin, since Jill arrived in town two years ago, she's turned down everyone who's asked her out," he said. "Did you ever meet her? At Dad's funeral?"

Rick hated to remember that time. The shock of his father's accident, his mother's devastation, the years he'd missed by not coming home to settle things.

"I don't recall her as a shapely blonde." He remembered her as the quiet young girl who'd sat with him, who'd kept him from drinking away his misery. Most of the evening was a blur, except for the angel who'd appeared out of the shadows.

"She's changed a little since then," Rick said.

Rafe nodded. "She'd only arrived in town a month before and was going through a rough time herself. The restaurant had just opened and Mom hired her.''

"She looks different somehow."

"And she still isn't your type."

"Oh, and what is my type?"

Rafe gave his brother a sidelong glance. "Let's just say she doesn't play by your kind of rules." He looked thoughtful. "I believe when you went off and joined the Marines years ago, there were no less than three girls in town with broken hearts. Unless you've changed, bro', I don't think you want anything permanent. Besides, have you been gone so long that you've forgotten about the *maledizione?*"

Rick grinned. "The family curse. You're right. I haven't thought much about it over the years." Their Italian-born grandmother had always believed her marriage to Enrico Covelli had been cursed. She'd wanted a large family, but she'd had a rough time having two sons and was never able to have more. The troubled courtship between her son Rafaele, Sr., and Maria was due to the curse, as well.

Rick glanced at his brother. They were both thinking about some of the other things that had happened to the family.

"Does Nonna Vittoria still talk about the missing ring?" he asked.

"It's been worse since Dad's death," Rafe replied. "I think she tries to make a connection between the curse and the structure falling on Dad."

Rick swore under his breath. When he was a kid, he'd wanted to go to Italy and beat up that Valente guy for stealing the ring that meant so much to his grandmother. Now he had the financial resources to find the man, but it had been so many years ago Signore Valente was probably dead by now.

"It probably doesn't help matters with my surprise visit," he said.

Rafe grinned. ''Are you kidding? You're her husband's namesake. She's always adored you.'' He reached out and tickled his brother's chin. ''You were such a cute kid.''

Rick smacked his brother's hand away. All he could remember was being sick and his grandmother telling him stories. ''Yeah, well, I love Nonna, too.''

''Then hang around awhile.''

It felt as if a vise was gripping Rick's heart. ''You know me, bro, I'm not good at staying in one place for long.''

''Could be the curse.''

''Ah, the curse. I haven't had any complaints in the love department.''

''Conquests in bed don't count,'' Rafe said. ''You ever thought about why you're not married?''

Rick nodded. ''I know exactly why I'm not. No attachments for me.''

''You may feel that way now, but what happens when you find the woman you want to spend the rest of your life with?''

Rick's gaze searched the room until it fell on Jill Morgan's sweet face. She glowed with innocence. That alone should have had him running the other way. But for some reason he was drawn to her. ''I'd run like hell.''

Rafe cocked an eyebrow, then followed Rafe's gaze. ''Then Jill's not for you. I don't want to see her get hurt.''

Rick shook his head and sighed. ''Don't you ever get tired of playing the protector? Trying to save everybody?''

His brother's back straightened and he looked away. ''Only when I fail.''

Rick saw the pain in Rafe's eyes and felt like a heel. ''Hey, you've been working your rear end off trying to keep things together around here. No one's blaming you for the problems with the business.''

''Oh, sure. Dad expected me to keep the business going. We were close to bankruptcy when you—'' Rafe stopped, looked around and lowered his voice ''—came through with the money.''

Rick shrugged. ''What's the big deal? I had it to give.'' He recalled the many all-nighters he and his partner, Leo Tucker, had pulled down in Texas, just waiting for an oil well to come in. It had all paid off, though, big time. Now he and Tuck let their foreman and crew do the manual labor while they planned the next dig. No, money was not a problem. There was certainly enough left over for Rick to help the family.

''Isn't it about time I started acting like a Covelli?'' Rick asked. ''Or have I been excommunicated?''

Rafe gave him one of those big-brother looks. ''You were always a part of this family, Rick. You just chose a different road to travel.''

''Dad could never understand that.''

''In his own way he did. But it was hard for him to let you go. You know how he was about family. He wanted both his sons to stay in the business. Especially you.'' Rafe smiled. ''He always said that you were the master carpenter—like Nonno. Your hands were gifted.''

''And I disappointed him by taking off.''

''I thought you were finding yourself.''

Rick poured more Chianti into his glass, then filled a glass for Rafe. ''I guess you could say it was a little of both. I just knew that I couldn't fit into Rafaele Covelli's tight, restricted world. I wanted to see more and do more.''

Rafe took a sip of his wine, then said, ''You two were nothing alike. I'm more like Dad was. I never had any urge to leave Haven Springs or to do anything else but be a carpenter. I used to hate it when we had to go as far as Louisville to bid on a job.''

''You'd rather stay here, even if Covelli and Sons is limited to restoring homes and storefronts?''

Rafe shrugged. ''Hey, you know I want to get the busi-

ness back into the black, no matter where I have to travel.
But it's more important to clear the Covelli name of any
wrongdoing. This accusation about Dad being responsible
for the building's collapse has been eating away at my gut.
Hell, our father was buried in the rubble.'' Rafe's jaw
clenched as he struggled to get the words out. ''If Dad
hadn't started bidding on larger projects like that strip mall
and hiring men he knew nothing about, then maybe he'd
still be alive.'' Rafe paused and swallowed hard. ''Everyone knows that Rafaele Covelli, Sr., would never have used
substandard materials like they found on that job site.
Someone has to know the truth.''

Rick nodded in agreement. ''I'll do whatever I can to
help you.''

''You already have, by giving us the loan.''

When Rafe had called describing the family company's
dire financial situation, Rick had jumped at the opportunity
to help out with a loan. He'd never told his family how
wealthy he'd become in Texas. Anything surrounding his
leaving seemed an off-limits topic where his family was
concerned. Besides, they never asked, and he didn't want
to sound as if he was bragging. They knew he'd done well,
but they had no idea he'd become a millionaire virtually
overnight.

''I hope I can talk you into sticking around a while,''
Rafe said. ''You know Mom and Nonna would love it.''

Rick glanced over to where his mother was talking with
a group of patrons. Then his attention went back to the
blond waitress exiting the kitchen, carrying two large plates
of spaghetti. Jill moved between the tables, her hips sway-
ing as she maneuvered through the crowded room. His
body responded to her delicious curves. Stick around?
Maybe he would.

''I'll think about it.''

"Don't think about *it* too hard, bro. You'll be disappointed."

"You still trying to warn me off Jill?"

"No. I'm just trying to tell you she doesn't have the time or the desire to go out with you."

"Why? She have another man in her life?"

A smug look appeared on Rafe's face. "You could say that."

Rick had dealt with other men being around before. "Shouldn't be a problem," he said confidently.

"Oh, I don't know. She's pretty stuck on the guy." Rafe leaned back and folded his arms across his chest. "He's been with her for over a year."

Rick chuckled. "This reminds me of high school, when you bet me I couldn't get a date with Mary Ellen Anderson." He picked up his fork and took a bite of food. "We all know how that turned out."

"We're not in high school anymore and Jill is not your ordinary challenge. She's shot down every man in town."

"I bet I can get her to go out with me," Rick said.

At Rafe's laugh Rick insisted, "I mean it. I can get Jill Morgan to go out with me. Anything you want to wager?"

Rafe looked thoughtful. "If you're serious, how about this—I win, you stay around until the historical-district renovation is completed. Say, three months. I could really use an expert carpenter. Not to mention that you work real cheap." Rafe grinned. "Oh, come on, we're working on Maple Street, with all the Victorian homes. We won the bid for facade renovations. It's keeping us busy. Like I explained on the phone, we're working up a bid for the new convention center planned here for next year. So what do you say, Rick? I know you're busy bringing in all those oil wells, but we sure could use you around here for a while. And not just for your money, either," Rafe rushed to add. "We want *you* here."

Rick was touched by the offer. He could call his partner and let him know he wanted to stay awhile longer. Leo Tucker could handle things in Texas for now. Rick had learned that one advantage of running his own successful business was the freedom it allowed.

And of course, Rick had no intention of losing the bet. "Sure. I have a bet to win. What do I win by the way? What do I get?"

"Name it."

Rick studied his older brother. They were the same height and build, with maybe ten pounds difference between them. Rafe's eyes and skin were dark, his hair black and short. He was one of those straight down the middle, play-by-the-rules guys. It was time to change that, at least a little. "Okay. If I win you have to get a tattoo."

"What?" Rafe said incredulously. "No way. I would never get—"

Rick grinned. "What's the matter, big brother? Worried that my charm will win over the fair lady?"

Rafe opened his mouth to say something when the lady in question came over to the bar. "Rafe, I'm really sorry to bother you," she said. "But I need to get home to Lucas, and my car is at Turner's Garage. Your mother said you were going out to the shop, anyway, so maybe you could… Do you think you could drop me off at my house?"

Rick watched as his brother touched Jill's hand, and he tensed at their familiarity.

"Sure, Jill. Go get your coat and I'll take you home."

"Thanks." She smiled at Rafe.

Suddenly Rick wanted to be the recipient of one of those smiles. Before he could offer to fill in for Rafe, Jill took off.

Rafe stood. "Well, I'd better get the woman home to her man. Wouldn't want to keep him waiting."

"Traitor."

His older brother laughed.

"Wait," Rick called. "How much time do I have to fulfill this bet?"

Rafe glanced at the anxious woman standing at the back door. "Take as much time as you need. Remember you're working with a disadvantage."

Rick frowned. "What?"

"The Covelli curse."

Thirty minutes later Rick was still nursing his glass of wine. The restaurant's dinner crowd had diminished, but some patrons were obviously reluctant to leave. Many of them had come up and welcomed him back home. Rick graciously thanked them, but felt awkward knowing that he was only going to be around temporarily. He had a business and a life back in west Texas. That was where he belonged. Haven Springs might have been his home once, but that was before…before he turned his back on it and took off.

At least this time he could help the family. Getting the call from Rafe had been a surprise, but not as surprising as his older brother's asking for money. Even though Rick knew Rafe could get the money from their mother, Rafe didn't want to put her restaurant in jeopardy. Besides, Rick was thrilled he came to him. He could have sent a check, but instead, he'd hopped on his Harley-Davidson and ridden straight through from Texas.

When he'd hugged his mother, he'd felt ashamed that he hadn't been home since his dad's funeral. But Maria Covelli didn't hold a grudge. She'd told Rick many times that she loved him, that the past didn't matter. She only cared he was home now.

But the past mattered to Rick, especially when he couldn't change it.

"*Famiglia* Covelli," Rick murmured into his wineglass. All his life he'd heard about the importance of family.

Rick wished he could blame the curse for his strained relationship with his father. They'd been butting heads since Rick turned fourteen. No matter what he'd done, he couldn't conform to what Rafaele Covelli, Sr., had expected of his sons. Maybe it was because growing up he'd been sick a lot. His childhood asthma had kept him inside, or in bed, when other kids were out playing. When he finally outgrew it, there was no stopping him. He went out for every sport in school. And he was pretty good. Then he'd taken a liking to cars, fast cars.

He was also a good carpenter. He'd been taught by the best. His father. But Rick hadn't been sure he was ready to join the family business just yet. Needing time to think things through, he'd joined the Marines.

Although Rick called and wrote, his father never had much to say to him, and when he came home after he got out of the service, their strained relationship hadn't improved. Since he still couldn't bring himself to join the family business, the two continued to fight until finally Rick left again. Rafaele, Sr., just couldn't understand his middle child's not wanting to follow the same path he and his father, Enrico, had chosen. Rick glanced around the warm inviting atmosphere of Maria's Ristorante. A lot had changed in six years. He was happy his mother had kept busy after her husband's death, and with Nonna's help, had turned her cooking skills into a profitable business venture. And Rick had to say he was happy to be home. At least for a while.

But he knew there was lots of work ahead. The failing carpentry business, his eccentric family. His mother would try her best to find him a wife, and Nonna Vittoria would offer up her prayers for the domestication of her wayward grandson.

Rick shook his head. He needed to set them all straight. He planned to remain single for a long time—he just liked it that way. He'd never heard any complaints from the women he'd been with. He'd made sure they all knew the rules.

His thoughts turned to Jill Morgan. The shy girl he'd met two years ago in the rose arbor was still present, but she now had a certain strength and self-assuredness. She still wasn't his type, though. Too young and innocent. The type who believed in knights in shining armor and happily-ever-after. He was definitely not knight material.

Rick watched his mother walk across the restaurant and head straight for him. Maria Covelli was nearly fifty-three, but she looked a lot younger, even after the strain of losing a husband and trying to run a restaurant. Since his last visit, she'd cut her hair short, and Rick noticed more streaks of gray. She was only five feet two inches tall, her figure still trim while her curves were generous. His father used to tease his wife by saying he liked having something to hold on to.

"Enrico." She kissed both his cheeks. "Do you know how wonderful it is to have you home, son?" Tears came to her velvet-brown eyes. "Oh, I've missed you!"

"Mom, I missed you, too." He took her hands in his. "I called and wrote you."

She gave him a stern look. "You sent postcards with your name signed on the bottom. That is not writing your mother. You should have come home more," Maria continued. "Look at you. You are so thin. You need a wife to take care of you."

"Mom, don't start," Rick warned, loving all the attention. "I didn't come home to have you find me a wife. I came home to help with the family business."

She clasped her hands to her breast. "So you're going to be staying. At least for a while?"

He nodded, pleased he was the cause of the joyous look on her face.

"I pray that Rafe will fix things. I'm so happy all of my kids are together. Rafaele would have wanted it that way." Tears flooded her eyes. "Oh, Rick, what's been done to your dad's name and his company."

Rick stood and pulled his mother into his arms. "We'll find a way to keep the business going. I promise."

Maria blessed herself. "God rest my Rafaele's soul. He worked so hard to build his business. It was his life. Now after his death they're telling lies about him. Nonna Vittoria has been lighting candles to St. Anthony that this will be all cleared up soon."

"Don't worry, Mom. Rafe and I will get to the bottom of it."

She hugged her son again. "I knew I could count on you."

Rick realized he'd never be able to leave town before fulfilling his promise to his mother. Just then one of the busboys came out of the kitchen carrying a book. "Jill left this."

Maria took the textbook. "Oh, my. Jill will need this for her test tomorrow."

"I can run it by her house," Rick volunteered, pretending a nonchalance he didn't feel.

Chapter Two

Jill carried her eighteen-month-old son, Lucas, up the stairs to her apartment over the garage. He'd been running a fever most of the day, and she didn't want to be away from him any longer, even though her landlady, Karyn—who lived in the main house—was willing to keep him through the night.

Karyn Ashmore had been a lifesaver after Lucas's birth. Since Jill had come to Haven Springs two years ago, both Karyn and her husband, Bob, had been there for her. There weren't many people who would take in a pregnant stranger whose car had quit on her out on the highway. Bob was an experienced police officer; still, people couldn't be too careful these days. The Ashmores had become Jill's landlords, and her best friends, too.

"C'mon, honey," Jill said to Lucas as she walked into the small apartment. "I'll get you something to make you feel better." She set the toddler on the kitchen counter and reached into the nearby refrigerator for his medicine. She poured some of the pink liquid into a spoon, and he opened his mouth wide and swallowed it. "That's my boy."

"Hurt, Mommy," Lucas said as his chubby hand touched his throat.

"I know," she crooned as she gently brushed his curly blond hair off his warm forehead, then smiled into his trusting blue eyes. "You'll feel better in a little while."

She moved Lucas into the bedroom they'd shared since she'd brought him home from the hospital. Her double bed was against one wall, the secondhand crib against the other. Carrying Lucas to her bed, she pulled back the blanket and laid him between the cool sheets.

"Mommy's going to read you a story."

That usually brought a cheer from her son, but not tonight. He lay quietly in the bed, his cheeks flushed, his eyes only half-open.

Jill quickly changed out of her uniform and into a faded sweatshirt and pants. She took a book from the bookcase, sat down next to Lucas and began to read. Before she'd made it to the second page, he was sound asleep. She picked him up and cuddled him against her as she carried him across the room and carefully put him down in his crib.

There were so many things Jill wanted for her son. She knew that Lucas would never have his father around. Keith Dillon didn't want anything to do with marriage or fatherhood. He had only been interested in his music. Too bad she hadn't discovered that about Keith before she foolishly fell in love. It would have eliminated a lot of the pain she'd suffered over Keith's desertion. Then came his death, when his bus crashed outside Chicago. Jill couldn't even go to her parents. She had disappointed them by leaving school and falling in love with an unworthy man. There were times when she'd just wanted to give up. But then Lucas was born.

Jill smiled down at her sleeping son. He had made it all worth it. Everyday she counted her child as a blessing. She didn't need another man in her life. She had her hands full with this little guy. Bending down, she placed a kiss on Lucas's cheek.

Jill switched on a night-light, then went into the living room. With a sigh, she sat in the old brown recliner and glanced at the rickety TV tray on her right, stacked with college textbooks. Most nights she studied right here. But tonight she couldn't seem to gather enough concentration to cram for tomorrow's test. Not after seeing Rick Covelli walk into the restaurant. He'd been the last person she thought would come back to Haven Springs. And after their evening together two years ago, she wasn't anxious to see him again. Not after their night together. A time when she'd been vulnerable, alone and pregnant with another man's child. Worse, she knew that she couldn't let herself fall for someone like Rick Covelli.

During their hours together, they'd talked, a lot. She could still hear the sadness in his voice as he poured out how he'd let his father down. She'd known the wine had loosened his tongue, but she'd stayed with him and listened, worried he'd drink too much if she left him alone.

In the protective darkness, she'd sat while he'd talked, wishing she could help in some way. Besides, she was the expert on disappointing parents. Her father still hadn't forgiven her for quitting school and having a no-account musician's baby.

A soft knock on the door drew her attention. It was probably Karyn checking on Lucas. Jill got up, crossed the small room and pulled open the door.

Her mouth fell open when she saw Rick Covelli standing on her stoop. He was still dressed in black, his leather jacket speckled with beads of water from the misty rain. His dark hair was damp and falling across his forehead. He smiled, and Jill's heart started racing.

"Rick…"

He smiled and held up her book. "My mom thought you might need this tonight."

"Oh," was all she could think of to say. Why did this man have her so tongue-tied? Rafe and Tony didn't affect her this way. "Thank you," she said, reaching for the book.

He pulled it back. "It'll cost you."

Jill felt a strange nervousness take over. He must have sensed it.

"It was a cold, damp ride over here. I could use a cup of coffee."

"Sure," she said, and opened the door wider. As he moved past her, she caught a whiff of his scent, a mixture of leather and woodsy aftershave. All at once she was light-headed.

Rick set the textbook down on the table, removed his jacket and laid it on the edge of the sofa. "Thanks. It's getting a little wet out there."

He brushed his hand over his hair and his face to wipe away the drops of rain. Jill couldn't help but notice how the muscles in his arms bulged with every movement. His black T-shirt fit tightly over his broad shoulders and chest. She had difficulty catching her breath. When she looked up at his face and saw his smile, she knew she'd been caught staring.

Jill glanced away. "Well, that's Indiana weather for you. Just wait a minute and it'll change. I'll get you a cup of coffee," she said, then turned and walked to her small kitchen alcove. She put water on the stove, then got a jar of instant out of the cupboard.

Rick swung one leg over the stool at the counter and sat down. "Mom said you're going to school."

"Yes. I'm a senior at Bedford College." Jill shivered. He was too close. Except for Bob Ashmore, she hadn't had a man in her apartment before. And she liked it that way. Her gaze went to Rick's jeans, stretched over muscular thighs, and her blood warmed. Finally the water boiled and she poured them both a cup of coffee.

She set the mugs on the counter, then excused herself and went to check on Lucas. Seeing that he was still asleep, she closed the bedroom door so they wouldn't disturb him. Then she came back and sat on a stool next to Rick.

He held her gaze. "I'm glad you decided to go back to college."

She looked at him. "Then you remember what I told you about school?"

He smiled. "I remember quite a few things from that night." He looked sheepish. "As I recall I spilled my guts, too."

"You needed to talk to someone."

"And you were a good listener, Jill Morgan. I was in pretty bad shape. I never thanked you for holding me to- gether."

"Your father had just died. It wasn't good for you to be alone."

He smiled. "So I was sent a blue-eyed angel."

"I'm no angel." She wished he'd stop staring at her.

"You helped me a lot. I just hope I didn't do anything to upset or offend you."

Jill took a sip of her coffee. "No, of course not."

"Good. I wouldn't want that on my conscience, now that I'm going to be hanging around for a while."

She froze, then seeing his puzzled look, she forced a smile. "I bet your family is happy." She envied him that.

He grinned. "It won't be long before they get tired of me."

Rick sat back and studied the pretty blonde. In baggy

sweats she still looked sexy. Would she miss him if he were to pack up his bike and head out of town? Hell, what was he thinking? She was too young for him. Why had he gotten involved in that stupid bet with his brother?

"I promised Rafe I'd help with the historical restoration." He held up his palms. "Seems he needs these."

Rick watched as Jill's gaze lowered to his hands. All at once his roughened fingers tingled, as he remembered what it had felt like to touch her. "I'm good at the close, intricate work. I take the time to do the job right."

His eyes held hers for a long moment just as the rain began to fall in earnest, pounding on the roof. Finally she glanced away.

"I'm sorry if I've been staring," Rick said. "I was just thinking about the night in the rose garden. You seem different now."

"It's been two years. My hair is longer."

Rick knew it was more. The girl who stood in the moonlight that night had turned into a woman. A beautiful woman. Slowly more memories came back. Jill's soothing voice. The tenderness in her gaze. A surge of heat raced down his spine. Her touch, and then her sudden disappearance into the darkness.

The ensuing awkward silence was broken at last by Jill. "It seems like everyone is happy to have you home," she said.

"Yeah, Indiana is one of those places you always want to get away from, but it's good to come back to once in a while. I guess that's where the song came from. You know, 'Back Home Again in Indiana.'" He raised an eyebrow. "Are you from around here?"

She shook her head. "No. Chicago area."

"How did you end up in Haven Springs?"

"It's a long story."

He shrugged. "I have the time."

She paused a moment, then began. ''My car broke down just outside of Haven Springs. Bob Ashmore found me and brought me into town. I stayed:'' She stood up. ''Look, the rain's stopped, and I need to study.''

Rick watched her gaze dart to the bedroom door. Damn! Was that where her boyfriend was sleeping? A surge of jealousy went through him. It was definitely time to leave.

Rick got up, walked across the room and reached for his jacket. ''Thanks for the coffee.''

''Thanks for bringing my textbook.'' She pulled open the door.

''Good night, Jill,'' he said, and walked outside.

''Night,'' she answered, shutting the door behind him.

Rick stood on the stoop for a time and studied the now starry sky. Then he looked down at the street. Old maple trees lined the sidewalks, and the big Victorian houses cast monstrous shadows under the streetlights. Pulling on his gloves, he started down the steps.

Jill Morgan intrigued him, maybe even more than she had two years ago. He wondered what kind of secrets she kept hidden behind those blue eyes.

Pulling on his helmet, he climbed onto the Harley-Davidson and turned on the ignition. He moved slowly down the driveway, but once he hit the street he gunned the throttle, and the bike started to fishtail. Feeling a rush of excitement, he quickly brought the powerful bike under control and raced down the street, counting on the cool night to wash away his desire and banish any more thoughts of Jill Morgan.

But later, even after a thirty-minute ride around town, Rick still had Jill on his mind.

Hell, there had been other women who had given him the cold shoulder, and he'd just walked away. But there was something about Jill that drew him, and he'd swear she'd reacted to him, as well. He downshifted, then turned onto Elm Street as thoughts of her inviting mouth and her lovely eyes followed him.

Hell, he didn't need this. What was he doing thinking about a woman who was involved with another man? Yet he knew that, bet or no bet, he wasn't about to retreat.

Finally he pulled into the narrow alley behind the restaurant and parked. After removing his helmet, he unlocked the back door and went up the stairs to the two rooms he was using as an apartment. He tossed his helmet on the shelf in the tiny closet where he'd stowed his duffel bag.

His mother had wanted him to stay at the house, but Rick preferred to have his own space. He went to the refrigerator and pulled out a beer. He sat down on the sofa, picked up the phone and dialed Texas.

The phone rang several times before it was answered with a brisk hello from his friend and business partner, Leo Tucker.

Rick grinned as he checked his watch. "Tuck, don't tell me I got you out of bed?"

"Covelli, you ugly son of a gun, what the hell is going on?"

"Not much. Just getting settled in. Sorry I didn't call sooner."

"No problem. I've been working 'round the clock, anyway."

"I take it this well is a stubborn one."

"She's takin' her sweet time paying out."

"You know, Tuck, you don't have to be there to personally see it come in. We still get paid." It never did any good to tell his friend this, because Tuck was superstitious.

"And paid pretty well at that, don't you think?" Tuck chuckled. "Say how's that good-looking mama of yours?"

"She's just fine. She said to say hello and get a promise from you to come and visit."

"Can't wait."

"There's something else, Tuck. I need your help."

"Sure. Just tell me what I can do."

"I need some discreet investigating done on an accident that happened a few years back. Think you can get that PI friend of yours to work on it?"

"Sure. Billy Jacobs is the best in the business. What do you need done?"

"I need my father's name cleared."

For three days Rick had been working steadily on Mrs. Kerrigan's house. Rafe had woken him up the first morning at five to get him going on the renovation job; he was to start by rebuilding a porch and replacing the rotted posts. Rick was suspicious of Rafe's motives, assigning him to this job, as Mrs. Kerrigan just happened to be Jill's next-door neighbor.

Another worker, Charlie Wilson, was in his forties and had worked for Covelli and Sons for years. Charlie was finishing up putting the plywood on the roof, and later that day they were to start replacing the termite-damaged window frames. Last week Rafe had salvaged a dozen double-hung windows from a house over on Third Street that was being torn down.

But Rick was lagging behind today. His mind wasn't on his work. Not with one eye on the house next door. He'd been here since 6:00 a.m., and as far as he could tell, no one had come or gone from the premises, except for Officer Bob Ashmore, who'd driven off in his patrol car.

Mrs. Kerrigan came out of the house, carrying a plate of cookies and two glasses of lemonade. "You boys could use a break."

She set the tray on a metal table and glanced around the large porch, now sporting the new flooring and roof. "You're doing such a wonderful job. I can't tell you how ashamed I've been of the run-down condition of this place. But since my Henry passed away, I just couldn't afford to keep it up. Now with the federal grant money, at least the facade is repaired."

"This is a fine house, Mrs. Kerrigan." Rick looked up to the new gable roof above the third floor. He took a long drink of lemonade as he sat down on the new porch railing and propped his booted foot against the turned post. He still had to build the spindlework supports, which meant long hours in the shop tonight. But he was looking forward to it. Must be his creative nature. "It's been a pleasure to restore it."

The old woman smiled. "Watching you work out here reminds me of my Henry." Her gaze went to Rick's upper arm. "Oh, my, your scar. Were you wounded when you were in the service?" She looked concerned. "My Henry was wounded at Normandy in the Second World War. We were lucky he made it home. A lot of men didn't."

"That was quite a battle." Rick was embarrassed to say that he hadn't seen any action, except in a few rough bar fights while stationed in South Carolina. "I was never in combat in my four years in the Marines. This happened during a training mission."

Rick glanced at his arm. The scar had been there so long that most of the time he forgot he had it. While training some new recruits, he'd had to go in and help one of the boys who'd frozen up. The kid ended up tangled in barbed wire and Rick tore his arm while pulling the boy free.

"Henry was in the Marines, too. I have his medals."

"Maybe you'll show them to me," Rick said, then out of the corner of his eye, he caught sight of Jill coming down the driveway next door. "But right now I better get back to work. Thank you for the wonderful cookies and lemonade."

Smiling, the gray-haired woman also glanced in Jill's

direction. "Jill's so pretty, and very sweet. Always stopping by to see me. Last Christmas she and Lucas came over and spent the afternoon with me." She sighed. "He's such a sweet boy."

Rick stiffened. He didn't want to hear about Jill's boyfriend. Just then Jill looked over and waved. Her hair was tied back in a ponytail. She had on a pair of jeans that flattered her long slender legs. A blue sweater picked up the color of her eyes.

"Hello, Jill," Mrs. Kerrigan called.

Jill stopped and came up the walk. "Hello, Mrs. Kerrigan," she said, then looked at Rick. "Rick."

Her voice sent a tremor through him. "Jill."

"Isn't everything beautiful?" Mrs. Kerrigan asked. The woman took Jill over to the side porch, showing her the new trim. "Rick did this himself."

Jill glanced over her shoulder at him. "You did a wonderful job."

"Thank you."

"I'd better go," Jill said. "I promised Karyn I wouldn't be gone long."

"You're such a busy girl." Mrs. Kerrigan shook her head. "Going to school, working all night, taking care of Lucas. You never have time for fun."

That damn Lucas again, Rick thought. Where the hell was this man? And why did he need so much taking care of?

Two nights later the last employees had gone home and Jill locked the front door of the restaurant. She'd promised Maria she'd close up tonight. With Lucas being sick, she'd missed a lot of work lately.

Now he seemed to be on the mend, so he was staying with Karyn and Bob tonight. Jill was lucky to have friends like the Ashmores. She didn't know if she could have handled raising her son and going back to school without Karyn's help. Now Jill couldn't imagine her life without Lucas. He was the man in her life, the only man she needed.

She walked into the kitchen, giving things a last once-over before heading home. Maria was adamant about a spotless work area, and Jill didn't want her employer to come back in the morning and find anything amiss. She was about to hit the lights when she heard a noise under the sink. She crossed the room and opened the cabinet door. Water gushed out and she screamed as she slipped and fell on the floor. Fighting off the spraying water, Jill struggled to her feet. She had almost made it, but the force of the water caused her to slip again.

She had to get to the shutoff valve. She began to reach under the cabinet when she looked up and saw Rick Covelli rush into the room.

"What are you doing here?" she gasped, expecting to be alone.

"Saving you," he said as he crossed the wet floor and helped her up. "You're drenched. Get out of the way. I'll shut off the water."

Within a minute or so the spray of water died and she pushed her wet hair out of her eyes. "Oh, no, the kitchen is a mess." Wading through the small lake on the floor, she went to the cupboard and grabbed a mop.

Rick nodded. "Looks like we've got a big job on our hands."

Jill was suddenly aware of how he was dressed. Or, rather, undressed. The man didn't have a shirt on. His chest was bare. His faded jeans rode low on his hips, the top button unbuttoned and a trail of dark hair arrowing from his navel to below… Heat suffused her face, but she managed to find her voice, "Where did you come from?"

"I'm staying upstairs."

She smiled. "Well, thanks for coming to my rescue and turning off the water."

Rick walked to the sink and examined the pipe. "I think Mom needs some new plumbing."

Jill shivered in her wet clothes and through clenched teeth she explained, "She…has a plumber coming in next week."

"Looks like he better come first thing in the morning, if she wants to be open tomorrow night."

"Should I call her?"

"I will," he said. "I'll do it upstairs, and I'll bring you back something dry to put on."

Before Jill could protest, he was gone. She picked up a towel and began drying her hair. Why did this man always have to be around? Why couldn't one of the other Covellis show up and rescue her? Rick had her off balance and it scared her. It had scared her two years ago when he'd been so kind to her. Keith had been the only other man who had gotten to her. And look what happened. She couldn't afford to make that mistake again. Her heart might not survive. "Here."

Jill jumped and turned around to find Rick holding a black sweat suit.

"It's all I have that will come close to fitting you. Mom said to clean up the best we can and leave the rest until morning."

"Go back to bed, Rick. You have to get up early in the morning."

"I'll be fine. Change into these dry clothes, Jill."

"But—"

He sighed. "No buts." He grabbed her mop and pushed the sweats into her hands. "Listen, it's late. It only makes sense if we both clean up. Then we can get it done in half the time."

It did make sense, darn it. She turned and headed for the

rest room. A few minutes later she came out to find that Rick had opened the floor drain and was mopping in its direction.

Jill allowed herself a minute to watch as his powerful arms worked the mop. The muscles in his back flexed with each movement. Her gaze came to rest on the long scar displayed on his biceps. She couldn't help but wonder how he'd gotten it, and the pain the wound must have caused.

"It looks worse than it is."

Jill blinked. "What are you talking about?"

"My scar. The way you were staring at it, I thought you might be curious about it. I got caught on some barbed wire when I was in the Marines."

"It must have hurt," she found herself saying.

He grinned. "Hurt like hell at the time. Now, it's just ugly as can be."

"It's hardly noticeable," she said, but the scar was the only mark on his bare skin. She raised her gaze to his and discovered he was looking at her. Embarrassed, she grabbed a mop and began pushing the water toward the open drain.

The cleanup job took thirty minutes.

"I think we can finally call it a night," Rick said. "And you should be getting home."

"You're right about that." In more ways than one, Jill thought as she went to retrieve her purse. She needed to get away from Rick. She rechecked the locks, then grabbed her things and went out the back door. Even though it was a cool April night, a bare-chested Rick followed her.

"Thanks again for all your help," she said as she walked to her car.

"Sure. But next time let's do it without the water."

He grinned and Jill's stomach did somersaults. She quickly climbed into her car and put the key in the ignition, but when she tried to start it, nothing happened.

"Why now?" she groaned. This old car often gave her trouble, but it was all she could afford.

She looked up to discover Rick walking toward the car. Without a word he popped the hood and after a few minutes said, "Try it again."

She turned the key. Nothing.

He poked his head out and slammed the hood. "Your battery's dead."

She groaned and got out of the car, slung her purse over her shoulder and started walking across the lot.

"Where are you going?"

"I've got to get home."

He grabbed her arm and swung her around to face him. "Not walking, you're not. Give me a minute and I'll drive you."

"I can't ask you to do that."

"You're not asking. I'm offering." He escorted her back into the restaurant. "It'll just take me a few minutes to get some clothes on." He went up the steps two at a time. Jill wanted to run away before he could return. When he touched her she couldn't seem to think straight. And around Rick Covelli she definitely needed to be able to think straight. But more than that, she worried about the undeniable fact that she was attracted to him.

After pulling on his boots, Rick grabbed his leather jacket and helmet. He couldn't believe how his heart rate had accelerated at the mere thought of taking a woman home. He'd done it many times, and usually with a promise of more than a polite thank-you when they arrived.

He took a steadying breath and went down the stairs, a little surprised Jill was still waiting for him.

She pointed to his helmet. "What's that for?"

"So I can drive you home." He walked out the door.

Jill rushed to keep up. "Wait! You expect me to ride on your motorcycle?"

"That's what I planned." Rick continued in the direction of his bike.

"But I can't." He'd stopped and she nearly ran into him. "I've never done that before."

Seeing her fear, he wanted to wrap her in his arms. "It's easy. All you have to do is hang on—to me." He pressed his hand against the small of her back and guided her to his bike.

Rick took off his jacket and put it over Jill's shoulders and zipped it up. She poked her arms through the sleeves, but still the coat nearly swallowed her. Then he handed her the helmet.

"What about you? Won't you get cold?"

He wanted to laugh. Just the thought of Jill Morgan straddling the bike behind him was enough to keep him warm.

"All of us Covellis are hot-blooded."

"But what about your helmet?"

"In Indiana it isn't a law, so I'll manage a few blocks."

She finally slipped the helmet on her head as he swung his leg over the seat and released the kickstand. He turned the key and hit the starter, and the Harley's engine roared to life.

"Climb on."

She hesitated, then did as he told her.

"Put your arms around my waist and hang on."

The moment she did, Rick took off down the alley. Once on the surface street, he tried to settle back and enjoy the feeling of Jill's body against his. Impossible. She was reeking havoc with his nervous system. When he turned the corner her grip tightened, and her full breasts pressed into his back. He bit back a groan and hoped she didn't sense his tension. He could have driven this way forever....

Jill couldn't believe how good the cool air felt blowing in her face. A thrill shot through her as they drove down the dark streets. It was exhilarating. Almost if she was doing something she shouldn't and was on the verge of getting caught. She wanted to laugh, or cry out into the night.

All too soon they made it to her street, and Rick pulled up in the driveway by the steps to her apartment. He cut the engine. Jill let go and climbed off the bike, then removed the helmet.

"Wasn't as bad as you thought, huh?" Rick said.

She shook her head and offered him a smile. "No, it wasn't."

He set his kickstand and swung his leg over. Then he stood up and took the helmet from her. "Maybe we can go for a ride in the daytime. You can see a lot of pretty countryside when you're on a bike."

"Maybe," she said breathlessly.

Rick came toward her and unzipped the jacket she wore. Jill froze as his head lowered to hers. His midnight eyes held hers captive. She couldn't breathe, couldn't move. *Please, let him kiss me.*

Then suddenly she felt the jacket slide off her shoulders. She swallowed her disappointment and looked into his eyes.

"Good night, *cara.*"

Rick walked back to his bike, fighting the urge not to turn around, pull Jill Morgan into his arms and kiss her senseless. Instead he started to put on his helmet when suddenly he heard a noise coming from the upstairs apartment. It sounded something like a...

"What the hell...?" he murmured as Jill took off for the stairs. He quickly followed, wondering if someone was hurt. By the time he got through the door, he found Jill cradling a golden-haired child in her arms. The boy was dressed in pajamas and big tears were running down his red cheeks. Standing beside Jill was another woman. She was a little older than Jill and obviously pregnant.

"I tried everything," the woman explained. "I just couldn't get him to sleep. Bob carried him up here before he went on duty." The woman's hand combed back the baby's blond curls. "I think his ears are really bothering him."

"It's okay," Jill said. "Karyn, I'm sorry I was late getting home. I'll take over now and talk to you tomorrow."

"Sure," Karyn said, then grabbed her jacket. She smiled at Rick before walking out the door.

Rick's gaze went to Jill, then to the child she held in her arms. The resemblance was remarkable. So this was the man in her life.

"I take it this little guy is Lucas," he said.

Jill's chin raised as she rocked the baby in her arms. "Yes, this is my son."

Chapter Three

Rick spotted the covered wishbone hanging upside down over the doorway of his mom's kitchen, and memories came flooding back. Since childhood he remembered seeing chicken wishbones wrapped in red ribbon in the Covelli home. It was for good luck, Nonna Vittoria had told him, something she'd brought from her heritage.

Rick shook his head. He never thought he was much on superstition, but his *nonna* did. She had sent him the red horn, La Corna Rossa, to hang on every oil well he and Leo had ever drilled.

He glanced around the huge kitchen. The light wood-grained cupboards were as perfect as the day Rafaele Covelli, Sr., had crafted them. White-tiled counters gleamed, as did the copper-bottomed pots and pans that hung over the island in the middle of the room. The morning sun came through the windows, inviting Rick in, as it had in his youth. The kitchen was the heart of the home, Maria Covelli had always said. Every major family decision, announcement and punishment had been decided on in this room—at the big rectangular oak table his father had built before any of the Covelli children were born.

Rick pulled out a high-back chair and sat down. He ran a hand over the scarred surface. The deep grooves and scratches seemed to only add to the character of the wood. Chuckling to himself, Rick found he could put names and dates to a lot of the marks. He almost could hear the voices of the brothers arguing, his baby sister crying. A tightness gripped his heart as he recalled how long ago that had been. How long since he'd felt like a part of the family.

He glanced up as Nonna Vittoria entered the room. The tiny, seventy-three-year-old woman shuffled along in her black slipper shoes, wearing a dark print housedress that seemed to hang on her fragile body. She wore her snowy white hair in a bun. Her skin was wrinkled with age, but when she smiled her bright brown eyes lit up the place. But today the family matriarch was not smiling. Today her eyes flamed as she turned and glared at her granddaughter.

Rick's sister, Angelina, had followed the old woman into the kitchen. She was petite and had black hair and stunning blue-green eyes. She was as independent as they came, and she let everyone know it. Right now Angelina was talking angrily to her grandmother. They both stopped when they saw him.

"*Buon giorno,* Enrico." Nonna made her way across the room.

"Good morning, Nonna." He went to her and kissed both her cheeks. Then he turned to his sister. "Lina. How are you?"

"A lot you care," she muttered.

Rick frowned. "You wound me. I care."

"If you cared, you would have come home. Instead, you hide out in the apartment I was planning on moving into."

"*Ma che!* Nonsense!" Nonna said. "A good girl does not leave her parents' home before marriage."

Angelina looked at Rick. "See how it is? All I want to do is be on my own. Nonna thinks I'm going to be living a life of sin. Explain to her, Rick," she pleaded.

Rick put his arm around his sister, having trouble himself thinking of her as a grown-up. He leaned closer. "Just cut her some slack, Lina. Where she grew up young girls didn't—"

"This isn't Italy," Angelina interrupted. "And I refuse to be treated like a child."

"Then stop acting like one."

For that he got a glare that made him wince. "Look who's talking. You come home on a Harley-Davidson without a care in the world. You know nothing about what it's like around here."

"Please!" Nonna shouted, then clutched her hands to her heart. "Can't we have peace in this house? We have Enrico home. Now we can concentrate on finding a husband for Angelina."

"Nonna, I don't want a husband. I haven't even had a chance to live."

"Enrico," she pleaded as she raised her hands. He leaned over so she could touch his face. "You talk to your sister. Tell her what a man wants in a wife. I will go pray to St. Antonio to find her a suitable husband." With a final glare at her wayward granddaughter, the older woman marched out.

Rick shook his head at his sister. "Why can't you two get along?"

"Because Nonna picks on me all the time. My skirts are too short. I have on too much makeup. I'll never get a husband if I can't cook." She placed her hands on her hips. "I'm sorry, Rick, but I don't like to cook. I want a career."

Rick leaned back against the table. "Then go for it."

"Easy for you to say. You've been gone all these years. You have no idea what it's like to live here, especially being the only girl. I'm expected to get married and have a family. Why?"

"She wants you to be happy. And I think she blames herself for the curse."

Angelina's expression softened. "But she didn't do anything but fall in love. I know she still goes to church every day and prays in hope to bring back the bride's ring. She said it belongs to me. Rick, I don't need a man to be happy."

"That's good. But do you have a problem with marriage *and* a career?"

"No, but thanks to Rafe, most of the guys I try to date have been scared off."

Rick threw back his head and laughed. "Big brother has been a little heavy-handed, huh?"

She nodded. "There aren't many men in Haven Springs in the first place."

"You're only twenty-three, Lina." He placed his hands on her shoulders and looked into her eyes. She had grown into a beautiful woman. No wonder Rafe and cousin Tony had to watch her so closely. "The right man will come along."

"But, Rick, I haven't experienced anything of life. I thought if I went away to school I'd get a little taste of…freedom."

"Whoa, hang on a bit, little one." He called her by her old nickname. "If we're talking about sex…"

Angelina rolled her eyes and blushed. "You can stop worrying. Justin and I wanted to wait…."

Rick blew out a long breath. "That was a good idea."

"Oh, right." She brushed away a tear. "I bet you weren't a virgin at twenty-four."

Rick didn't want to have this conversation with his sister. "What kind of talk is that?"

"It's called honesty. Why is it great for a man to experience sex, but for a woman it ruins her reputation?"

"I don't know." He hugged her, wanting the questions to stop. "But please, Lina, just promise me you'll wait until you are in love. It's too dangerous out there just to experiment."

Rick's thoughts turned to Jill. She had to have been pregnant the first time they met after the funeral. Had her baby's father deserted her? His anger stirred along with his protective instincts as he remembered how lost and alone she'd looked that night. If she'd been his would he have been able to walk away?

Whoa. He'd never been much good at hanging around...but with a child on the line? How could a man walk away from his son? Or a woman like Jill Morgan? Rick thought back to last night. It had taken all his will-power not to detour to the first motel and carry her to bed.

Rick shivered.

Angelina pulled back. "You okay?"

He was embarrassed at how he'd let the woman get to him. He stepped away. "Just working too many hours."

"I guess we have to be grateful. The work these days has been hard to come by."

"It's going to pick up, you'll see. Rafe will bring in more business."

Angelina shrugged. "As you well know, we're barely surviving." She nibbled on her lower lip. "If only the new owner of Grand Haven Hotel would give Covelli and Sons a chance to bid on the renovations. There're even rumors of a convention center in the future."

Rick had heard a lot of talk since being back, but that was all it had been so far—talk. "So nobody knows who took over the old building?"

Angelina shook her head. "All we can find out is that it's a company based in New York, Rossi International." Her eyes twinkled mischievously. "I could fly there and introduce myself to my fellow Italians."

"No wonder Nonna is in church every day praying for you." Rick gave her hair a good yank.

"I never go anywhere." She smacked his hand away. "Maybe when you go back to Texas I can come, too."

"And have Mom and Nonna skin me alive? No thanks. You can come for a visit, but that's all."

Angelina started to argue when the phone rang. Rick went to answer it. "Hello?"

"Rafe?"

He recognized Jill's voice. "No, Jill, it's Rick."

There was a silence, then, "Oh, Rick. Is your mother there?"

"Just a minute." Rick put his hand over the mouthpiece. "Lina, where's Mom?"

"She had a doctor's appointment."

"Sorry, Jill, she's at the doctor's. Is there anything I can do?" His thoughts turned to last night and the feel of her against him.

"Please tell her that Lucas is still sick and I got Irene to fill in for me. Tell her I'm sorry."

Rick heard the panic in her voice. "Don't worry about Mom, she can take care of things here. Your concern is Lucas. You sure you don't need any help?"

"No, I'm fine," she said, but he could hear the panic in her voice, also Lucas crying in the background. "I just wanted to let Maria know. I've got to go. 'Bye." There was a click in his ear.

He hung up and looked at his sister.

"Lucas is still sick," he said. "Is Jill raising the boy on her own, or is the father involved?"

"Lucas's father has never been part of his son's life."

"Well, surely he helps support his kid."

Angelina shook her head. "From everything I've heard, Keith Dillon never wanted the baby. Jill left him. Not knowing where to go, she just started driving and ended up here." Angelina smiled. "Mom hired her right away. Jill worked during her pregnancy up until a week before she delivered. Right after Lucas's birth, she thought Keith needed to know that he was a father. That's when she discovered he'd been killed in an accident."

Rick felt a tightness in his chest. Jill had handled a lot for someone so young. Now she had a sick kid. He remembered how it was being sick as a child. And how rough it must have been on his mother, but at least Nonna and his father were around to help. Jill was all alone. He headed for the door.

"Where are you going?"

"I got an errand to run."

Angelina smiled. "If you say so. Just be careful—that little Lucas will steal your heart."

"I'm not going to be around long enough for that to happen."

Rick drove the old Chevy truck with the Covelli and Sons logo to the Ashmore home. After parking on the street, he got out and headed up the driveway along the side of the house to the garage apartment. Taking the steps two at a time, he made it to the small porch and knocked on the door.

He paced the limited area until finally the door opened and Jill appeared with a crying child in her arms.

She looked shocked to see him and nervously brushed at her mussed hair. "Rick, what are you doing here?"

Without answering, he pushed his way inside. "Looks like I'm here just in time."

Rick took her son from her and hoisted him high in his

arms as he began pacing the small area in the living room. After a few minutes Lucas's cries turned into soft hiccups. He dropped his head on Rick's shoulder. "Hey, little guy, you need to give your mother here a break," Rick crooned, then turned to her, seeing her messy hair and jeans and old sweatshirt. She looked tired but beautiful. "Seems you two have had a rough morning."

Jill stood there in amazement. Where had he come from? By the time she found her voice, there was a knock at the door. It was the delivery boy from the pharmacy with Lucas's medicine.

Jill hurried into the kitchen and put some of the antibiotics in the baby medicine dispenser. "This should help, honey." Lucas opened his mouth without a fuss. He appeared content resting against Rick's broad chest. And why wouldn't he be? To have those strong arms holding you, letting you know you were safe and secure. How long had it been since Jill had felt that way?

Rick continued to walk her child until the boy finally fell asleep. "Looks like the little guy finally gave in."

"Yeah, he's had so much pain in his ears he hasn't been able to sleep." Jill pushed her hair away and stared at Rick. Why did it look so natural for him to be holding Lucas?

"I'd better put him down," she managed to say.

"You tell me where, and I'll do it."

"In here." Embarrassed at the condition of her apartment, she led Rick to the crib in the bedroom. She watched as the man lifted her son and easily placed him in bed. Jill covered Lucas with his blanket, then Rick followed her out of the room.

"I bet he's a sweet kid when he's feeling okay."

"The best. But this ear infection is really doing him in. I wish I could do more. The doctor said he might need tubes put in. But he's still a baby. I don't want him to have surgery.'' She felt the tears well in her eyes. No, she wasn't going to let herself fall apart.

Rick reached out and drew her into his arms. She didn't have the strength to fight him. Her head rested against his chest. His arms felt so good around her back.

''Shh, Jill. You're not alone,'' his husky voice rumbled in his chest. ''Watching a child suffer through illness is one of the downsides of being a mom. Somehow the kids survive.''

He managed to get her to the sofa and seated. Jill didn't want to let go, but she was embarrassed that she'd let herself break down. She grabbed a tissue from the box on the table and wiped her eyes. ''Sorry I fell apart on you.''

He smiled. ''Lack of sleep will do that to you. Besides, having a sick child is frightening. And it's no fun for the kid, either. When I was young I had asthma. I spent a lot of time in bed. I know my condition scared my mom. Every time I had an attack, all the times my medication didn't work and I ended up in the hospital, I could see the fear in her eyes.''

Jill was shocked. A big strong man like Rick Covelli had asthma? ''But you look so healthy.''

He leaned forward and rested his elbows on his thighs. ''I was a pretty puny kid, believe me. But I was fortunate and outgrew the disease by the time I hit puberty. Just the same as Lucas will stop getting these ear infections.'' He stood. ''Now why don't you lie down and try to get some sleep?''

''Oh, but I can't. Lucas will wake up.''

''And I'll be here to listen for him.'' He pulled the blanket from the back of the sofa and covered her. ''You need rest.'' His hands touched her back, and warmth shot through her. It felt so good....

''Just for a little while.'' Jill burrowed her head into the pillow. This chance to rest was heaven. She began to drift off to sleep.

The dream began. It was nighttime and Jill was standing on her tiny porch. Suddenly the stillness was shattered by the sound of an engine, and she glanced over to see a big, black-and-chrome motorcycle pull into the driveway. The rider stopped, then straddled the bike and took off his helmet. It was Rick.

He looked up at her and she met his dark gaze. His eyes told her he wanted her. Somehow her fear turned into exhilaration as he dismounted the bike and headed for her apartment. He marched up the steps determinedly. The closer he came, the faster her heart raced. Finally he was standing in front of her. Without a word, he reached out to her, cupping the back of her neck, and drew her closer as his mouth lowered to hers. She closed her eyes in anticipation of the kiss.

"Jill…Jill."

She rolled onto her back, blinked and opened her eyes. Rick was squatting beside the sofa, smiling at her.

"Hello, *cara*. Did you sleep well?"

She jerked upright. Oh, gosh, she'd fallen asleep. She looked back at Rick to discover that Lucas was with him.

"Mommy!" Lucas cried.

Jill pushed back the blanket and sat up. She reached for her son. "Mommy's here." She touched his forehead to discover that his fever was gone. "You feel better, sweetheart?"

Lucas shook his head. "No hurt."

Jill smiled and looked at Rick. "How long have I been asleep?"

"A few hours."

Jill glanced at her watch. It was almost five o'clock. "I've been asleep for three hours."

"You needed it," Rick said. "And Squirt and I were able to keep busy. I even managed to change his diaper."

Jill tried to tidy hair that hadn't seen a brush all day. "You could have woken me up. You shouldn't have to care for Lucas."

He reached out and touched her hand. "I wanted to do it. We had a good time."

Lucas raised his chubby hand. "Ree...Ree..."

"Yes, we read." He turned back to her. "I've gone through his library of favorite books."

Jill glanced down at her barefoot son, dressed in a disposable diaper and clean T-shirt. "I limit Lucas's stories to two books, or I can never get him to bed."

"I'll remember that next time. Right now I think the little guy is hungry. I wasn't sure what to feed him." He stood up, and smiled. "I was going to run out and get some hamburgers."

Jill's heart pounded in her chest as she studied this good-looking man who had forced his way into her life. She wasn't sure whether or not she was happy about it.

She put her son down and got to her feet. "Hamburgers would be nice. But Lucas is limited to just fries until he gets a few more teeth."

Rick reached out and stroked his finger down her cheek. Jill felt the heat all the way to her toes. "What about you? What do you like, Jill?"

Jill could conjure up all sorts of wicked thoughts. She swallowed and managed to say, "I'd like a hamburger."

"Then I'll pick some up from the Pixie Diner?" He tossed her a sexy grin. "I'll be back in thirty minutes." He tickled Lucas and walked out the door.

Jill stood at the door and knew it wasn't wise to be excited about his return. But that didn't stop her.

Minutes later Rick pulled up the truck in front of the Carlton house. He jumped out and hurried toward the crew working on the porch. Charlie spotted him and directed him to his brother in the back.

Rick rounded the huge, old Victorian home and found Rafe talking with one of the workers.

"You'll need to pull off two rows of shiplap along the eaves and put up new shiplap before the roofers come tomorrow morning," he was saying. Then he noticed Rick. "Where have you been all day?"

Rick waited until the worker walked away, then grabbed his brother by the shirt and shoved him up against the house. "You having a good laugh? All this time you knew Lucas was Jill's son, but you let me believe…otherwise."

Rafe grinned. "He's a cute kid, isn't he?"

It had been a long time since Rafe had gotten the best of him. Rick released his brother. "He's a sick kid right now. Where the hell is her family?"

Rafe shrugged. "From what little I know of the situation, her mother has visited a few times. Jill's father's is still disappointed in his daughter. And Lucas's father is dead."

Rick clenched his fist, realizing how great his own family had been. They'd never turned their backs on him, no matter what. He thought of his father. Not even Rafe, Sr.

"The Ashmores are Jill's family now," Rafe continued, "and of course, she has us. Mom's pretty flexible on her work hours. But Jill has a lot of pride. She won't take charity."

Hell. The last thing on Rick's mind was giving her charity. She had him half-crazy from wanting her. But damn. A kid. That changed the rules. Drawn to her or not, he couldn't see her anymore. Jill Morgan needed a man who was going to stay. And that wasn't him. He started to walk away.

"Hey, you coming to work tomorrow?" Rafe asked. "Mrs. Kerrigan says her front door is sticking."

"Tell her I'll be there first thing in the morning," Rick called over his shoulder.

"So I win the bet?" Rafe called back.

Rick stopped in his tracks. He always hated losing anything, even a stupid bet. But he didn't want hurt Jill. Jill had been jerked around too much already. Besides, as much as he was drawn to her, he knew before long he had to go back to Texas. He couldn't do that to her.

He swung around. "As much as I'd love to see that tattoo on your backside, all bets are off."

Chapter Four

In the kitchen of the Ashmore house, Jill poured herself a cup of tea, along with one for Karyn. She spooned in a little sugar, then went back into the dining room, walked around the long oak trestle table with its eight matching Windsor chairs and found Karyn huddled on the oak window seat, peering out through the sheer Priscilla curtains.

Karyn waved Jill over. "Rick's out there."

"Of course he's out there. Covelli and Sons started working this morning." Jill sat down at the table and took a sip of her tea. She didn't want to give her friend any idea that she was attracted to Rick. "You should be happy. You've been waiting for months to redo the outside."

"I'm happy. I was just hoping you'd be a little more excited about having such a good-looking man only a few feet away."

Jill squinted into the April sunlight at the group of construction workers taking a break. She refused to admit her pulse quickened as Rick leaned against the porch post and drank from his water bottle. She watched as drops of water ran down his jaw, over his neck and then were absorbed by his faded T-shirt. Her gaze went to his mouth. She closed her eyes, but it didn't stop her from wondering what his lips would feel like against hers. A stirring began in her stomach and slowly dipped lower, causing the same deep ache that had kept her awake nights, dreaming impossible dreams. Jill released the curtain as if she'd been burned. Just two nights ago he'd come by again, feeding her and Lucas hamburgers and fries and reading her son bedtime stories. When he left, Jill had already been wishing she could call him back.

"Must be nice to have a man like that coming to your rescue," Karyn said.

Jill studied her friend's face and wondered where all this was leading. "It's safer if I just depend on myself."

"But not as much fun."

Jill sighed and glanced at her friend's rounded belly. She was due in a few months—wasn't that enough to occupy Karyn's thoughts? Jill wondered. "Is this leading somewhere?"

The petite brunette crossed her arms. "Maybe you should pay attention to Rick's interest."

Jill had a soft spot for both Karyn and her husband, Bob. If knights in shining armor existed, Bob was one of them. "Why? I'm not in the market for a man. I need to finish college."

"That doesn't mean you can't find a nice man."

Jill wasn't sure she was brave enough to try love again.

"Not all men are jerks like Keith," Karyn added.

Jill tensed at the mention of Lucas's father. The man she'd loved enough to give up everything. All too soon she'd discovered that Keith's love for music and playing with his band were all that mattered to him. When she'd told him she was pregnant, instead of declaring his love for her and the child she was carrying, he'd told her to get rid of the kid. Then he died before he had a chance to meet his son.

She trembled at the painful memory.

"Not all love stories turn out as tragically as yours did." Karyn's voice broke into Jill's thoughts. "Don't let one bad experience keep you from happiness."

"The only happiness I need is to rebuild a relationship with my parents. My son may not have a father, but I want Lucas to know his grandparents. So I have to finish college."

"And if you're the perfect daughter, they'll allow you into their lives." Karyn clenched her hands into fists. "I'm sorry, Jill. I know how important this is for you, but it still doesn't make it right. Parents aren't supposed to abandon their kids when they're in trouble. When they've been hurt."

There was a knock on the door and both Karyn and Jill went to answer it. When the big oak door swung open, they found Rick standing on the porch. Dressed in his usual work clothes of T-shirt and jeans, a carpenter's tool belt hanging around his waist, he smiled at them and said, "Good morning, Karyn. Jill."

"Good morning, Rick." Karyn stepped aside to allow him across the threshold.

He shook his head. "I'd hate to mess up your clean floors." He nodded at the glossy hardwood. "I just wanted to let you know we'll be pulling up the rotted porch floor, so you'll have to use the back door for the next few days."

"No problem." Karyn said. "Bob and I usually use the back door, anyway."

"Good." Rick flashed that killer smile again, showing off an innocent-looking dimple in his cheek that masked his rough-around-the-edges image. Then his dark eyes turned to Jill, and she felt heat surge through her. "How's Lucas doing?"

"He's fine." She gestured toward the back of the house. A room off the kitchen where there was a crib. "He's down for a nap right now."

Rick nodded. "I missed you at the restaurant last night."

"I switched shifts so I could study for a test."

Karyn jumped in. "Jill's graduating in June."

"I know," he said. "Mom sings her praises all the time." Rick's gaze returned to Jill. "Pretty impressive."

Jill shrugged. "A lot of people do it."

Rick was staring at her again, making her self-conscious. She could feel her cheeks reddening.

"Rick?" Karyn said, drawing his attention away. "Bob and I are having a few of the neighbors over this Sunday afternoon for a barbecue. We'd sure like you and your family to come. You could reacquaint yourself with some of the people in Haven Springs."

Rick smiled at Karyn. "Thank you, I'd like to come. I'll pass the invitation on to my mother." Then he glanced over his shoulder at the two workers busy removing the spindle post from the porch. "I'll get started on the porch. 'Bye, Karyn. Jill."

Karyn closed the door.

"Why did you do that?" Jill asked.

"Do what?"

"Don't play dumb with me, Karyn. You just now decided to have a barbecue."

"You may be foolish enough to let an opportunity pass you by, Jill, but I'm not. You need someone like Rick in your life."

Three hours later Rick walked through the back door of the restaurant. He started up the stairs to the apartment, needing a shower and a cold beer, when he caught sight of his cousin.

"Hey, Tony. How's it going?"

The fair-haired Tony smiled. "Great." His lighter colored hair and brown eyes were a contrast to the rest of the family's dark coloring, but his features had a definite Covelli stamp. "You got a minute?"

"Sure, grab a couple of beers and come upstairs."

Rick climbed the steps two at a time, taking off his shirt as he went. Ripping apart a hundred-year-old porch had been a messy job. He opened the door to the small apartment and tossed the T-shirt on the pile of dirty clothes in the back of the closet. Next he yanked off his waffle-soled work boots.

Tony showed up and handed him a beer.

"Thanks." Rick wrapped his hand around the bottle and took a hearty pull. "Ah, you can't beat a cold beer after a long day."

Tony took a long swallow of his own. "Just don't let Aunt Maria hear you say that."

"And feel her wrath? No way. I consider myself blessed she's welcomed me back into the fold."

Tony grew serious. "You were never out of the fold, Rick. I hope you know that home was always here for you. We were all here for you."

"Thanks, cuz. I guess I knew that, but sometimes it takes a while for things to get through my thick skull." Rick didn't want to talk about the past. "What's up?" he asked.

"I wanted to thank you for giving us the money. It'll be a while before…ah… The company funds are pretty low, so we can't pay you back for—"

"You think I'm worried about getting paid back? I couldn't care less. I just want to help keep Covelli and Sons in business. Rafe should have called me sooner." Maybe he should explain to Tony that this loan was just a drop in the bucket to him. He didn't want his cousin to feel guilty accepting it. But Tony raced on.

"He's having trouble with what's been happening. But we're going to turn this around. All we need is to get a few bids."

"Rafe told me about the hotel and the possibility of a convention center."

Tony's eyes lit up. "It's going to be months before we know, but we're going to do everything in our power to get that bid. The convention center is still up in the air, but I'm going to do my damnedest to win the carpentry bid for Covelli and Sons. In the meantime we're keeping things moving with the renovations. We just found out from the Community Redevelopment Commission that we've been awarded the job of restoring the section of storefront on north Main Street. We're expanding a little to see where that leads. We can't just stay strictly carpenters. We hired more crew today."

"Great." Rick wanted more than anything to get the business back on its feet. Then he'd be able to head back to Texas without any guilt.

"Rick, there's something else. Remember the old movie theater and post office farther down the block?"

"Yeah, they been boarded up for years."

Tony nodded. "But we could change that. We could buy up the block at a steal, then renovate the buildings and make them appealing for future retailers." He shrugged. "Who knows, maybe even enhance the idea for building that convention center if the town has more to offer."

Rick liked his cousin's idea. This should keep the family business going for a long while.

"Look, Rick. These are all relatively inexpensive ventures. We could put in low-income apartments upstairs and get a tax break. Since it's inner-city property we qualify for a grant and only have to put up thirty percent of the money. And think what this will do for Haven Springs. This could bring the town back to life.''

Rick was interested. Very interested. But that would tie him down. He'd have to stay in town, at least for a while. His thoughts went to Jill. Yes, that would keep him in town—and around Jill. She was tempting. But so young and innocent in more ways than he could count. She should find someone else.

The idea didn't sit well with him.

How was she supposed to work if Rick was staring at her the entire evening? Jill wondered. She carried two bowls of minestrone to the corner table, filled the couple's wineglasses and smiled before heading back to the kitchen.

Once there she stood aside and took a long drink of water. Didn't the man have anything else to do but hang around and watch her?

''Jill—'' Maria came up to her ''—are you feeling okay?''

The older woman looked worried, and Jill appreciated her concern.

''You look flushed. Do you have a fever?'' Maria touched her forehead.

''No, Maria. I'm fine. I need to get back to work.''

''You need more than work and school. You need some fun in your life.''

''Maybe one day,'' Jill said with a smile. Excusing herself, she hurried back into the dining room and made a trip to the bar again to clear away some dishes. Then it happened. She looked up to catch Rick's sexy grin, and the plates slipped from her hands. Wanting to die from embarrassment, Jill bent down to clean up the mess.

Rick came around the corner of the bar and grabbed her hand. ''Be careful not to cut yourself,'' he warned, and helped her pick up the broken plates.

She nodded, feeling the heat from his touch. Darn, the man was making her so nervous she couldn't do her job. "Don't you have something better to do than hang around and watch me break dishes?" she asked.

He grinned. "Are you saying I've been distracting you?"

"No, of course not." The last thing she wanted to admit was the fact he made her nervous.

"Well, I'll be leaving shortly. I have to meet someone." Suddenly Jill didn't want him to go. And who was he meeting? An old girlfriend?

As promised, Rick left ten minutes later, and Jill managed to work the rest of her shift without breaking another dish. But her gaze kept going to the corner of the bar, hoping to see Rick sitting there again. Finally she realized he wasn't going to be back tonight.

At ten o'clock, Jill locked the front door and put the Closed sign in the window. The other waitress finished up her duties, waved goodbye and walked out the back. Maria had gone home at nine. So there was just her and the seventeen-year-old busboy, Mike Parson.

Jill walked into the kitchen to make sure everything was ready for tomorrow. Mike turned off the outside lights and was heading for the back door when Jill went to get her purse. Beside it lay the sweatshirt and pants Rick had lent her the other night. She'd planned to give them back to him. She looked toward the staircase off the kitchen. The staircase that led to Rick's apartment. Was he up there now?

She told Mike to go on, she'd be a few minutes, then she headed for the steps. By the time she reached the second floor, her heart was pounding so loudly she couldn't hear anything else.

Jill started to knock on Rick's apartment door, but hesitated, then turned to walk away. She stopped herself at the stairs. What was wrong with her? All she wanted to do was return his clothes. Clutching the garments, she moved back to the door and knocked firmly.

The door swung open and Jill was met by a half naked man. She had to resist the urge to back up as her gaze washed over his wide shoulders and muscular chest, which was covered with a swirl of black hair that disappeared into faded jeans. Her breath caught and she raised her eyes to his face, seeing his black hair mussed and his eyes heavy from sleep.

Oh, Lord. She'd been crazy to come up here. And from the look on Rick's face, he thought so, too.

"I…I'm sorry I woke you," Jill said. "I just wanted to return these." She held out the clothes with a trembling hand.

That slow, sexy smile appeared on his face, and Jill nearly melted on the spot. As he reached for the clothes, their hands brushed and the sweatshirt fell to the floor. They both bent to retrieve it, and their heads collided.

"Ouch!" Jill cried as she pulled back and rubbed the sore spot on her forehead.

"Sorry." Rick took hold of her arms and helped her stand up. The warmth of his hand burned through the light sweater she wore, causing feelings she knew she had to resist. But for some reason she couldn't pull away.

Rick's voice was husky and soft. "You know it's dangerous for you to come up here."

Jill's gaze locked with his and she nodded.

A slight tug was enough to draw her into his apartment. He caressed her arms, then moved up to her shoulders, wrapping her in his warmth.

"The first night I saw you, I thought you were an angel."

She looked away, but he put his fingers on her chin and turned her head back. "I wanted to kiss you so badly that night. But not nearly as much as I want to kiss you now."

She closed her eyes and concentrated on steadying her breathing. "I want you to kiss me, too," she said bravely.

"Open your eyes, Jill," he breathed as his hands cupped her face. His mouth touched hers and pulled back, causing her to whimper. "Easy. I'll give you more. I just want to savor this."

Soon his lips were on hers, moving slowly, devouring her, making her forget the hunger, the loneliness. He deepened the kiss and his tongue pushed past her lips to find hers. He drew a sob of pleasure from her throat, and Jill's arms went up to his chest, then encircled his neck. She wanted him, no matter how dangerous it was.

Rick pulled back and smiled. They were both breathing hard. "Damn, lady. You make it hard for me to keep thinking angelic thoughts."

"I'm not an angel."

"You are to me, *cara*." He took her mouth in another onslaught of searing kisses. Jill's hands fluttered over his chest again, causing him to groan with pleasure.

"I want to touch you, kiss you everywhere," he whispered as he kissed his way down her neck. Jill bit her lip and raked her fingers through his hair.

"Hey, Jill," a voice called.

She jumped back. "Oh, no, it's Mike." Quickly pulling herself together as best she could, she went out into the tiny landing and leaned over the railing. "Mike, I thought you'd gone home."

The blond teenager smiled shyly. "Mrs. Covelli said I should never leave without walking all the ladies out. I was waiting outside."

"I'll be right down."

After hearing the door click shut, Jill turned around to find Rick leaning against the doorjamb, smiling. "Looks like you got your own knight," he said. His smile faded as he came closer and touched the curls that had fallen from her ponytail. "And you needed one. I was having some pretty wicked thoughts a few minutes ago."

She picked up her purse and smiled. "So was I." She took off and hurried down the stairs.

Two hours later Rick sat on the sofa, flipping TV channels with the remote. Hell, he never watched television. He had a dozen other things to do besides stay awake all night, thinking about a woman who frustrated the hell out of him. Not to mention the kisses that about put him over the edge. He groaned and changed the channel once again.

She was the last woman he should get mixed up with. She came with emotional baggage and a kid. Although Lucas was a wonderful child, he was more responsibility than Rick wanted.

Hell, he was thirty, too set in his ways to settle down. Too old for her, and more than just in chronological years. In experience. Besides, he had a life in west Texas. Midland was the closest he'd come to settling down. But restlessness still plagued him. His dad had been right when he'd said Rick couldn't handle responsibility. And the last thing Jill Morgan needed was another man running out on her.

Rick closed his eyes and Jill's face appeared. The way she'd smiled at him tonight. Hell, he could still remember how she'd looked that night in the garden. A picture he hadn't been able to get out of his head the past two years. Just one touch of her hand, and something had happened to him.

Now, she wasn't just a dream. She was real. And too close.

Chapter Five

You look like an angel.

Rick's words echoed in Jill's mind throughout her long, sleepless night. She touched her fingers to her lips and closed her eyes, remembering the kiss. Her body began to stir and she groaned.

Going to his apartment had not been a wise move, but she hadn't been able to stop herself. Well, she'd better learn to stop herself or she'd end up in big trouble. Trouble she didn't know how to handle.

A quick glance at the clock told her it was nearly time to begin her day, anyway. Grabbing her robe, she made her way out of the bedroom, careful not to wake Lucas. In the kitchen she switched on the light and then the coffeemaker.

She ran a hand through her mussed hair as she looked around for a stray rubber band to pull the heavy strands away from her face. She gave up the search when there was a soft knock on the door. It was probably Bob. He'd promised to fix her leaky bathroom faucet before he went to work this morning.

Jill opened the door and was shocked to find Rick, not her landlord, on the stoop. He wore a pair of faded jeans, work boots and a black T-shirt that hugged his broad chest. She felt her fingers tingle as she remembered caressing those hard muscles and quickly shook away the wayward thought.

"Rick, what are you doing here?"

He grinned and held up a brown paper bag. "I brought some of Nonna's *berlingaccio.* I love this orange sweet bread." He stepped into the apartment. "Hope you made coffee."

Jill closed the door and followed him, pushing her hair out of her face. "Well, yes, but…isn't it awfully early?"

His dark gaze traveled over the length of her. "It's never too early."

She tugged the lapels of her robe together. "But what if I was still in bed?"

He grinned again. "I waited in the car until your light came on. I like your hair down and your eyes hooded with sleep. You look sexy…and touchable."

Jill felt her face warm. She glanced down at her old flannel robe. No way.

"C'mon," he coaxed. "Sit down and I'll fix breakfast." He guided Jill to a chair at the table. Then he went to the cupboard and pulled out a couple of glasses, mugs and plates. After pouring some orange juice, he brought everything over, then sat down across from her.

"Dig in," he said as he picked up a roll and took a big bite. "It's good. Nonna makes the best. That's something I really missed being away. Was your mother a good baker?"

Jill nearly laughed, thinking of Claudia Morgan, Ph.D., baking. "No, my mother isn't domestic." Jill finally gave in to the mouthwatering roll and began eating. "Oh, this is good." She munched away, then asked, "Aren't you supposed to go to work?"

He shrugged. "Can't start until after seven. The neighbors get cranky when you start pounding and sawing too early."

"Imagine that," she said, hiding her smile.

Rick's dark eyes met hers. "I also couldn't sleep. It seems this angel appeared at my door last night, then suddenly disappeared. I couldn't get her out of my head."

Jill's tongue refused to work.

"I lay awake most of the night remembering how good she felt in my arms. How her lips felt against mine." He popped the rest of his roll into his mouth.

"You couldn't sleep?" she asked, aware of her racing pulse and the panic in her voice.

He nodded. "Your kiss sure packs a wallop. Do you know what it does to a man?"

With her heart pounding in her ears, Jill got up and started to walk away.

Rick stood up, too, and grabbed her arm. "It makes a man dream, Jill. He begins to think about warm nights on cool sheets, about a beautiful blonde with her hair spread across his pillow." He touched Jill's hair. "Her calling out his name..."

Jill shut her eyes, but it didn't erase the picture Rick was painting. She swayed, feeling his breath on her cheek. Shivers of awareness rippled up her spine. She knew she should stop him, but by then his mouth was on hers and she was already moving into his arms. She moaned as his lips began to work their special magic, coaxing hers to part. Then his tongue dipped inside to mate with hers.

She was drowning in the feelings he stirred in her, and it scared her. Using all her strength, she pushed him away, breaking off the kiss, breathing hard.

He raised his hands in surrender. "I apologize. You're just too hard to resist, *cara.*"

"I can't do this, Rick. It's happening too fast. I'm not ready."

He reached out to stroke her cheek. "You can't deny the attraction between us."

Jill blushed as she stared at Rick. His dark gaze glowed with fire, and she, too, knew they were close to being out of control. Suddenly Lucas cried out, saving her any more embarrassment. She hurried into the bedroom and shut the door.

She dragged in a few uneven breaths, then lifted her son out of his crib and changed his diaper. Maybe if she waited long enough, Rick would be gone. Finally she couldn't hold off Lucas's breakfast any longer. She let Lucas toddle into the other room, and she followed him—only to see him head straight to Rick, who soon had the boy giggling with excitement.

"Looks like his ears aren't giving him any more trouble."

"The doctor said the infection is clearing up."

"So you got a reprieve, huh, little guy?" He touched Lucas's nose. "I know how that can be. I'd rush right out and play like crazy before my next attack had me back in bed."

"You must have been lonely," Jill said, watching how easily Rick played with her son.

"My *nonna* was always there. Playing games or telling me stories about growing up in Italy. I liked the attention I got, but I would much rather have been outside with the other kids."

A tightness gripped Jill's chest as she pictured a little dark-haired boy sitting in a room by himself staring out the window.

Just then, another knock sounded at the door, and before

she could stop him, Rick went and answered it. Bob Ashmore stood on the other side, wearing a T-shirt and old jeans, carrying his trusty toolbox. Her landlord looked uncomfortable as his gaze shot to Rick and then her.

With Lucas on his left hip, Rick stuck out his hand. "Hi, Bob."

"Good morning, Rick. Morning, Jill." He stepped inside. "I hope it isn't too early."

Could she just die of embarrassment and get it over with? Jill thought. "No, it's not too early, Bob. As you can see, you aren't my first visitor. Rick brought some of Nonna Vittoria's sweet bread. Want some?"

"Uh, no thanks. Speaking of visitors, Rick, your crew pulled in just as I was coming up here."

"Guess that's my cue to get to work." Rick handed Lucas over to his mother. "I'll see you later."

"Thanks for the rolls," Jill said, holding tightly onto Lucas.

Rick smiled. "And thank you for bringing back my sweats last night," he said with a wink.

Jill blushed, knowing how close she'd come to letting things get out of hand.

Bob broke the tension when he announced, "I'll just go ahead and look at the faucet." He disappeared into the bathroom.

Jill watched as Rick started out the door. He stopped suddenly and pulled her close and gave her a quick, hard kiss.

He grinned. "I need that to get me through the day." She could only stand there, aching for more.

"Gotta go. 'Bye, little guy." He walked out the door.

"Bye-bye...Ree" Lucas jerked his small hand up and down.

Bob reappeared. "Sorry about earlier," he apologized. "I mean about interrupting you and—"

''There's nothing to be sorry about. Rick showed up ten minutes before you did. I had no idea he was even coming here.''

Bob smiled and glanced at the table set for two.

''He brought breakfast over,'' Jill explained. Even to her it didn't sound innocent.

''Is the guy giving you trouble?'' Bob asked suddenly, slipping into his authoritative police officer's voice.

Jill shook her head. ''No,'' she said, and sank onto the sofa as Bob returned to his chore. She looked at her son. What a liar she was. Rick Covelli was giving her all kinds of trouble. He was stealing her heart.

Rick met Charlie on the Ashmores' porch. Today they were going to lay new three-quarter-inch flooring, then he had to mount the lacelike brackets along the top of the posts. He'd spent all day yesterday in the shop routing out the replacements. Charlie had to finish the window sashes. Soon the porch would be finished. He glanced behind the Ashmores' house at the apartment over the garage and thought about the woman who lived there.

He smiled. Her kisses were unbelievable. So unbelievable he'd been awake all night, then waiting on her doorstep at dawn for more.

Damn. He didn't need this. He couldn't let these feelings for Jill interfere with what he needed to do. He had to focus on helping his family and finding the people responsible for his father's death. When that was finished, he'd be gone. In the meantime it would be wise to stay away from any temptations.

''Hey, Rick, how's your little girlfriend?''

Rick glanced up and saw Charlie coming down the ladder. ''She's not my girlfriend.''

''Saw you coming from her place this morning.''

''Just took her some of Nonna Vittoria's bread.''

Charlie nodded knowingly. "Rafe told me all about the bet."

Rick stiffened. "There isn't any bet, Charlie. Rafe and I called it off."

"In my day a man didn't call off a bet."

Rick started to argue but became distracted by a truck that pulled up in front of the house. He squinted into the bright sunlight and watched as a tall sandy-haired man climbed out of the cab.

Rick grinned as Leo Tucker placed the familiar gray cowboy hat on his head and with his slow, deliberate gait made his way up the walk.

"Hey, Tuck, you old cuss," Rick called as he jogged across the lawn to greet his friend and business partner with a bear hug. "What the hell you doin' out of Texas?"

"I just got dang tired of waiting for you to come back," Tuck said. "After the well hit, I decided I deserved a few weeks off. After talking with your pretty mama, she convinced me that Indiana was an interesting place to visit." He frowned. "I also thought you might be in need of my help."

"Who's handling things at the well?"

"Don't worry, Hal Johnston's wrapping things up. You know he's more than capable, and he's been chomping at the bit for this chance."

Rick smiled. "Maybe you're right. But it's hard to give up running the show."

Leo Tucker nodded. Not quite thirty-five, he had a few gray streaks in his brown hair, and his sun-weathered face showed he'd lived every one of those years to the fullest. They'd hooked up about six years ago when Rick had taken a job on an oil rig. He'd known nothing about oil drilling. It had been Tuck who'd shown him the ropes and taught him about the business. The two men had become best friends.

A year later they'd pooled their savings and invested in a lease on an existing well. After months of drilling and nearly living on the rig, they had finally hit oil. Not enough to make them rich but enough payout so they were able to drill another well. Then another. One thing for sure, the Covelli curse had never interfered with Rick's ability to make money.

"Have you heard anything from Billy Jacobs?" Tuck asked, referring to the private investigator he'd hired for Rick.

"He called and introduced himself and said he'd be heading down to Louisville this week. He asked to speak to Tony to get more info on the other workers and suppliers. Think he'll find anything?"

"I know Billy is the best at what he does. If there's any info in Louisville, he'll dig it out. Just give him time."

Rick didn't have a lot of that. The longer he stayed in Haven Springs, the harder it was going to be to leave. He turned and saw Jill walking down the drive. She was dressed in a long crinkly print skirt and a pink T-shirt. Her hair was pulled back in a clip and she carried a backpack over one shoulder. His heart sped up as their eyes connected and held. It was only seconds, but long enough to ignite sparks between them. Finally she nodded to acknowledge his presence, then continued on toward her car, parked on the street.

"Lordy, lordy." A slow whistle slid through Tuck's lips. "Now there goes a real pretty filly." He looked at his friend. "I can see why you don't mind hanging around here. Who is she?"

Rick shrugged. "Jill Morgan. She works evenings for Mom at the restaurant and goes to school during the day."

"You interested?"

"She's a little young for my taste."

"Never heard you say that before."

"Let's just say she's off-limits." Rick didn't want to talk about Jill. He and Tuck had other things to talk about. "How 'bout we get you settled in at my apartment and let the family know what's going on with the investigation?"

"I'm for that. Since I left Texas, my mouth has been waterin' for some of your mama's cookin'. Think she'll mind havin' another mouth to feed?"

"She'll love it. And I guarantee you'll put on ten pounds before you leave here. Of course for you that's good. You need to fill in those ugly bowed legs of yours."

"You're just jealous of my trim physique."

"Hell, that'll be the day." Rick grinned. "It sure is good to have you here."

Tuck gripped his friend's shoulders. "I figured you needed a little help on this one."

"You got that right." Rick's thoughts went to his family and the problems with Covelli and Sons. He wanted desperately to help. So he needed to concentrate on that and cool things with Jill. If he let himself get close to her, he wouldn't be able to walk away, and for all their sakes, he couldn't let that happen.

That evening, after one of Maria's famous lasagna dinners, Rick remained at the kitchen table, along with the rest of his family and Tuck. In five minutes he'd used his southern charm to win over Maria and Nonna Vittoria. Angelina hadn't been excluded, either. She'd been hanging on his every word since they'd sat down to eat.

A bottle of wine was passed around the table, then Tony stood and raised his glass. "First of all we want to say welcome to Tuck." The rest of the family joined in. "We're happy to share our home with you."

Smiling, Tuck stood. *"Grazie."* He looked to the women at the table as he raised his glass. "To the *bella signoras* and *signorina* for the *magnifico* supper. And that's about all the Italian this old Texas boy knows.'' He winked at Angelina and added, ''Is anyone willing to teach me?''

The baby of the Covelli family blushed as she took razzing from everyone. Rick noticed the concerned look on his brother's face and murmured to Tuck, ''Be careful, my friend. Your flirting has alerted the troops.'' Rick lifted an eyebrow toward Tony and Rafe.

Tony got everyone's attention again. This time he turned serious. ''As everyone knows, there's been a lot of things going on around town during the past few months. First, the federal money for historical preservation allowed us to renovate the eight old Victorian homes. If that project hadn't been awarded to Covelli and Sons, we'd be out of business. That, and the money Maria and Rick lent us has kept us going.

''But it's evident we can't rely totally on the carpentry business anymore. We need to look for other avenues of income.''

Rick sat back and listened to members of the family throw out ideas on how to keep the business from going bankrupt. Tony began laying out his idea for the downtown property. He passed out cost sheets that itemized his plan, from expenses to a projected profit.

''With these empty storefronts available at such a low cost it seems crazy not to buy them up.''

''But what if we spend the money and put the time into renovation,'' Rafe said, ''and it doesn't bring business back into town?''

''It's all a gamble, Rafe. The Grand Haven Hotel has been sold. Word is out that the owner will be remodeling and opening it for business within the next two years. Even if we don't win the bid on the hotel renovation, why can't we make a profit in other ways? When the hotel opens up, guests will come here because of what the area has to offer—Patoka Lake in the summer, Paoli ski resort in the winter. There's also the fall foliage and the mineral springs. People will spend money. So why wouldn't they spend it at specialty shops here in Haven Springs?

"Mom's restaurant and a few other small business are already downtown. If we buy up and remodel a section of storefronts close to the hotel, we could lease them out. To antique dealers, other restaurants or an ice-cream parlor. A souvenir shop."

"You have plans for the old theater?" Rafe asked.

"Why not show movies?" Angelina suggested. "The kids in town have no place to go unless they drive to Bedford."

Suddenly everyone started talking at once, each with different ideas. It was obvious everyone in the family was excited about purchasing the buildings.

Then Maria stood and motioned for quiet. "I think this is all splendid. Your father would be so proud of his family." She clasped her hands. "I will help in any way possible. I vote we go with Antonio's plan."

"Do you think the bank will lend us the money?" Rafe asked. "They haven't been real receptive lately. Since Dad's accident, rumors have been circulating about the reliability of Covelli and Sons."

"Let me worry about the money," Tony said. "I'm looking into some federal grants. Now I'll let Rick tell you about the other problem."

Rick stood up and all eyes turned to him. It had been a long time since he'd been to a family gathering, but he remembered that they discussed all kind of things. It was something their father had started when they were young.

"Tuck didn't just come to visit me," Rick began. "He came all the way from Texas, first because he's my good friend and partner, and second because I asked for his help." Rick took a deep breath. "I need him to help us clear Dad's name. We can't let it continue to be tarnished with lies. Tomorrow Tuck and I are going to Louisville to meet with a private investigator to see if we can get to the bottom of this mess.''

Tears came to Maria's eyes. Nonna Vittoria blessed herself. Rafe raised his glass to Rick. ''Good luck, my brother.''

Chapter Six

A perfect day for a barbecue.

It was warm and sunny, just a few billowy clouds floating lazily in the blue April sky. The Ashmores' house buzzed with activity. Bob was hard at work setting a table on the freshly mowed back lawn. Neighbors were carrying over card tables and chairs to accommodate the crowd expected about noon.

Standing in the Ashmores' kitchen, Jill turned to Karyn. "You know, this has gotten out of hand."

"I think it's going to be great," Karyn answered, eyeing the pies and cakes lining her counter. "I love baking."

"I'm not talking about the food, Karyn. I'm talking about the hundred people who are going to invade your backyard in about an hour."

Karyn waved her hand. "There isn't going to be a hundred. Just sixty-seven."

"Sixty-seven!" Jill gasped. "I was kidding. But you're serious. How did you happen to ask all those people?"

"Well, I didn't exactly. Word just seemed to get around. I thought this was going to be just a block party, but then everybody started asking if they could bring someone. Bob asked people from the department." She shrugged. "I guess people just like to party."

"Karyn, you're eight months pregnant and in no condition to handle a party this size."

"It's not so hard. Everyone is helping. I'm thinking about making this an annual event."

Jill shook her head. All week Karyn had been excited, but Jill knew she needed help to pull this off.

Just then they heard voices on the back porch. The screen door opened and Rick sauntered into the kitchen. He smiled. "Morning, ladies."

Jill drew in a deep breath, trying to control her runaway pulse. She hadn't seen him since the morning he'd come to her apartment carrying his nonna's sweet bread.

"Good morning, Rick," Karyn greeted him. "Isn't it a gorgeous day?"

"A perfect day for a barbecue," he agreed, then turned to Jill. She could feel the heat of his gaze. "Don't you think so, Jill?"

She managed to nod as she studied his attire. He had on a burgundy-colored polo shirt, khaki walking shorts and a pair of beatup tennis shoes. She tried to tell herself that he looked just like any other man going to a neighborhood barbecue, but she sure didn't react to him the same way. Her gaze rose to meet his smoldering one.

"Bob told me I was to ask you where you needed me."

A forbidden thrill ran through Jill and she felt her face redden as her mind suggested torrid ideas of how to use Rick's services. Dear Lord, what was happening to her?

Karyn spoke up. "Oh, I don't know. Those legs of yours are pretty distracting," she teased. "You've rendered my help speechless."

"Karyn…" Jill said warningly, ready to strangle her friend.

Rick smiled as he swept an appreciative glance over Jill's shorts and shirt. "I'd say you're going to do a little distracting yourself. Looks like you're ready to play… volleyball, too."

"I don't—"

"Oh, that reminds me!" Karyn cried. "Rick, can you set up the volleyball net between the two oak trees in the back of the yard? I want to make sure it's ready when the kids get here."

Rick saluted. "No problem." He ran his gaze over Jill one more time, started to leave, then stopped. "Karyn, thanks for inviting Tuck."

"You extended the invitation to your family, didn't you?"

He nodded. "Mom says thank-you. They may stop by later."

Karyn smiled. "Good."

Rick turned to Jill. "I forgot to ask—where's Lucas?"

"He's taking a nap so he'll be ready for the party."

"Well, I brought him a little something." His eyes never left hers as he cocked a thumb over his shoulder. "It's in the truck. I'll bring it to you later. Right now we need to get ready for this barbecue." He went out the door.

Karyn sighed. "My, my. That man's eyes would melt me on the spot if he looked at me the way he looked at you."

"What way?" Jill said, feigning ignorance but unable to stop the racing of her heart. "All he said was he had something for Lucas."

"My God, Jill. Has it been so long since a guy paid you attention that you can't recognize hunger when you see it? Rick couldn't take his eyes off you."

Blushing, Jill glanced down at her white T-shirt and pink shorts. "Just stop playing matchmaker."

"I don't need to play anything, Jill. The man is *interested*." Karyn put her hands on her friend's shoulders, turned her around and gave her a gentle push toward the door. "Now forget about school and work for a while, and go outside and have some fun."

"I can't forget about school. Lucas's future, and mine, depends on me getting a teaching job. This financial struggle has been tough—pinching every penny, living in close quarters. A good job for me would mean the world to us."

"I know, friend. That's why I watched your son last fall while you did student-teaching." Tears welled in Karyn's eyes. "I care so about you both. I just want you happy."

Jill sighed, her own emotions surfacing. "I'm happy now. I have Lucas…" She paused and swallowed. "If I hope for too much…I'll only get hurt."

"But don't turn your back on finding love, Jill. It's so wonderful to have someone to share your life with. You got a bad deal with Keith, but not everyone is like him. And you're a very lovable person." She gave Jill a hug, then stepped back and rested her hands on her hips. "Now fess up, friend, you wouldn't be protesting so much if you didn't already have feelings for that gorgeous Italian who was just standing in here grinning at you."

Jill started to argue, but what was the use? She nodded. "That's what I'm afraid of."

Rick watched Jill as she helped the kids with their lunch. She was making sure they each had a hot dog and something to drink, while managing to handle Lucas in the high chair.

But it wasn't her mothering skills he was interested in. Acutely aware of how she looked in her shorts and T-shirt, he had trouble keeping his concentration on the volleyball game. He'd missed two easy shots already.

Tuck walked over. "Hey, you playin' or watchin' the scenery?"

"I think I've had enough of a workout for a while," Rick said. "Maybe I'll go and grab something to eat."

Tuck glanced around the yard. "Not a bad idea. Tons of good food, and a passel of pretty ladies to choose from."

"Just be careful that the lady isn't spoken for," Rick warned. "I'd hate to see you run out of town."

A slow smile appeared on Tuck's face as he pushed his cowboy hat back off his forehead. "Wouldn't be the first time I've had to make a quick getaway."

Rick grinned as he started across the thick green lawn. There were colorful bedding plants lining the edge, and every bush had been neatly pruned. Big oak trees protected the back of the house from the hot sun.

Covelli and Sons had completed all the work on the Ashmores' home Friday. The only thing left to do was to paint the three-story structure. Karyn and Bob had spent two years putting all their extra money and a lot of hard work into restoring the inside of their dream house. Now that everything was nearly completed, they acted as though their life was perfect.

Well, if you loved living in an old house with a wife you adored and your first child was on the way, maybe it was. But there were people who envied Rick his lifestyle, his freedom, being his own boss. And the money he earned was phenomenal. Even though he felt he couldn't be totally up-front about his wealth, he still wished to share it with his family. There were times, though, he was lonely.

Rick looked at Jill and felt a tug at his heart. The one thing he'd never had was someone to share his life with. He never let anyone get close enough. It could be blamed on the Covelli curse, but Rick knew he had been the one who kept his distance. He thought about his dad and recalled their last argument. It was when he'd dropped out of college. Rafaele, Sr., had told him that he needed to act like an adult, handle responsibility and plan for the future. The next day, Rick had joined the Marines.

Was it because of his troubled relationship with his father that he'd pushed everyone else away? Or maybe he just hadn't found the right person. He recalled his grandparents' famous love story. Secretly that was what he wanted, too.

Rick thought back to the night in the garden when he'd first seen Jill. It was like a dream, her standing amongst his grandmother's roses. He couldn't take his eyes off her. When she'd agreed to sit with him, he could feel her warmth and understanding as they shared memories of his father, good and bad. Maybe the wine helped loosen his tongue, but he had a feeling it was Jill. She had soothed his aching heart. He had no idea that she, too, was going through turmoil. Although not showing, she'd been pregnant with Lucas. He regretted not knowing about her pregnancy then. Maybe he could have helped her somehow. There was still now—if she would let him.

He went to his truck and lifted a cardboard box from the back. He walked to the table where Jill sat with the excited kids. "Looks like you've been busy. Maybe I can help you out." He set down the box and dumped out the contents. A whole bunch of wooden blocks of different sizes tumbled out onto the patio.

The toddlers cheered and began to play. Rick had held on to a small wooden wagon. He placed it on the ground next to Lucas.

"Here, little guy. This is for you." He held out the ball on the end of a knotted string that was attached to the pull toy. The flat wagon, with the name "Lucas" carved on the side, held an assortment of blocks.

"Oh, Rick, it's beautiful!" Jill exclaimed. "Did you make it?"

He shrugged. "I used some extra wood from the shop. I didn't paint it because I didn't want him to swallow any chips if he puts the blocks in his mouth."

Lucas took hold of the string and began tugging his little wagon across the grass.

"What do you say, Lucas?" Jill called after him.

The boy smiled, showing off four tiny teeth. "Tank... Ree..."

"You're welcome, Lucas."

Jill looked up at Rick and smiled. A guy could get lost in their sapphire depths, he thought.

She broke the connection and glanced at her son. "That was a nice thing you did. Thank you."

"What can I say, I'm a nice guy." He stepped in front of her. "Think you can get someone to relieve you so you can play volleyball?"

Jill shied away a bit. "I'm not good at sports. My parents wanted me to concentrate on academics."

"Such a shame," he said softly. "I bet you'd be a natural."

Karyn arrived at the table. "Oh, go on and play. I'll keep an eye on Lucas."

"But...but..." Jill stammered, then glanced at her son who was busy playing and obviously wouldn't miss her. She couldn't use him as an excuse. "Okay, maybe for a little while."

Rick placed his hand on the small of her back and felt her warmth, her softness, making him realize how delicate she was. He walked her toward the back of the yard. He stood by her side as they watched the others play. He explained some of the rules, showing her how to use her hands to hit the ball. When two players decided to leave the game to eat, Jill and Rick took their places.

He watched Jill protectively as the other team served and the ball came at her. To his surprise, she reached up and tapped the ball upward in the air. It was high enough that he managed to hit it sharply over the net to score. Their team cheered. They got the serve and shifted positions.

Rick leaned over to Jill and whispered, "We make a pretty good team."

She blushed.

They continued to play for the next thirty minutes. Jill even managed to score once, too. Rick smiled as she jumped up and down with excitement. She was really getting into it. He noticed tiny beads of perspiration along her upper lip. He wondered if her flushed skin would taste salty. He forced himself to concentrate. When the game ended, their team had won.

Euphoric, Rick lifted Jill in his arms and swung her around. Featherlight, she was heavenly to hold. His fingers nearly spanned her tiny waist. Their eyes locked in a heated gaze. Knowing he had to release her soon, he brought her against him and savored the feel of her luscious curves sliding down the front of his hard and aching body. She drew in a sharp breath and closed her eyes.

He was pretty far gone himself. He wanted to carry her off somewhere...

She blinked and pulled away.

"Have you eaten?" he asked.

She shook her head. "I was waiting for the kids to finish."

"Good, then we can eat together." But instead of heading to the tables, he pulled her off into the side yard, out of earshot, but where they could still see Lucas playing with his new toy. "How would you like to go to dinner with me tomorrow night?"

By the look on her face, he'd caught her off guard. "Oh, Rick, I can't."

"Why?"

Her gaze darted away. "I don't date."

"Well, don't you think it's time you did?" He smiled, but she didn't return it. He leaned closer and inhaled her peach scent. He was light-headed and dying to pull her into his arms. Hell, she looked so young, so innocent. He had to be crazy to get mixed up with her. But he couldn't seem to help himself.

"Look, Rick, I'm just a short time from finishing school, and Lucas takes up all my free time."

"Just a few hours, Jill. A fun evening with no strings."

She remained silent for a long time and he could tell she was mulling it over. "It would have to be after eight o'clock so Lucas will be asleep. I don't want to deprive him of any more of my time than necessary."

"I understand. How about I make late dinner reservations at a place over by Patoka Lake? And I'll bring you home right after."

"That sounds nice," she said almost shyly.

He wondered how long it had been since Jill Morgan had gone out on a date. How long it had been since someone treated her as if she was special. Rick wanted to be that man.

"Wait, you aren't going to make me ride on your motorcycle, are you?"

He laughed. "No, not this time. We'll be going in a car. But I haven't given up on your learning to love my bike." He escorted her toward the food line.

"Don't hold your breath." Jill smiled mischievously and hurried on ahead.

Rick watched as she picked up her son and swung him around. They both giggled and her face lit up, her blue eyes sparkling. He groaned, knowing he was headed for trouble. But he was used to that.

With Rick close at her side, Jill filled her plate with a

wonderful assortment of food, then they went to a picnic table and sat with Bob and Karyn. Jill was happy that Lucas stayed busy playing with the other toddlers, giving her a chance to eat.

Jill had to admit she enjoyed Rick's attention. She also enjoyed the conversation with her friends. For the first time in a long time she felt as if she was part of a couple.

Then Lucas started demanding attention. Stilling Jill with a hand on her arm, Rick got up from the table. He reminded her he'd be back. Soon. Then he shocked her by planting a soft kiss on her mouth.

Jill sat at the table with Karyn as Rick and Bob and some of the other men played with the kids. She watched Rick play with her son. He would toss Lucas a ball and encourage him to throw it back. Jill smiled when Rick cheered Lucas for his efforts. She'd been lucky. Even though her child didn't have a father, he'd been blessed with a lot of loving father figures, thanks to Bob and the Covellis.

Jill had to keep focused on safety in numbers. Don't single out any one man for the role of Lucas's father. That way she wouldn't get emotionally involved with a man.

And no one was going to hurt her again the way Keith had. She'd made a promise to herself that she was going to concentrate on finishing school and get back on track with her parents. When she'd ended up pregnant, her father had stopped speaking to her. Her mother had only visited her grandson twice. Of course she'd sent gifts and money periodically, but Jill knew there were still wounds that needed healing.

Her thoughts turned to Rick and how he'd spent the day with her, practically glued to her side. Was he staking a claim? His plans were to help out his family, then eventually go back to Texas—to his oil wells. Was his business there so profitable he'd never leave it behind? She wondered if anything—or anyone—could tempt him to stay.

A deep longing settled in her stomach as she realized she didn't want him to leave Haven Springs. Now her problem was how to protect her heart.

The party broke up at about nine, and Rick took the next hour to help with the cleanup. After the chairs and tables had been stacked, he went inside to dry the dishes Bob had been washing so his pregnant wife could get off her feet.

It was nearly ten by the time Rick was set to leave. Tuck had already hitched a ride with a cute brunette divorcee. Rick thanked Karyn and Bob for the nice time, then asked where Jill had gone. His hostess informed him that she had taken Lucas home to bed.

A little hurt that she hadn't said goodbye, Rick walked out the back door and up the steps to Jill's apartment. He knocked softly, knowing that Lucas was probably asleep.

After a long wait Jill finally answered. "Oh, Rick."

"I missed you when you left," he said. "I was hoping for at least a good-night."

"I needed to get Lucas home," she said. "I looked around for you but…"

Rick reached for her and pulled her into his arms. "I was helping Bob with the dishes."

She stiffened in his arms. "I guess I didn't look inside."

"What's wrong, Jill?"

The porch was dim, but when she looked him in the eyes, he could see her nervousness. "Just a little tired."

"It's been a long day." He frowned. "You sure it's nothing more?"

She sighed and pulled out of his embrace. "I'm not very experienced with dating. Lucas's father was the only man… I've ever gone out with."

"What are you worried about, Jill?"

She shrugged.

"It's a date, Jill. Two people getting to know each other,

sharing a meal. Just like we did today." He couldn't believe how hard he was working to ease her mind. "The only difference is that we'll be alone."

Her gaze shot up to meet his, her eyes wide.

"You aren't afraid of being alone with me, are you?"

She shook her head and her soft, touchable curls danced against her shoulders. He ached to run his fingers through the silken strands. That wasn't all he wanted to do. He couldn't resist and drew her into his arms. "Good. I want to treat you special. Like a woman should be treated."

Her eyes drifted shut and Rick touched his mouth to hers. He moved slowly, wanting to drink in her honeyed taste bit by delicious bit. Finally he released her. She looked a little breathless, her lips swollen from his kiss. He ran his finger across their moist surface. "That's something else I prefer to do when we're alone." He smiled. "I'll pick you up at eight tomorrow night." He planted another soft kiss against her incredibly tempting mouth. "That's so you won't forget me."

As he took off down the steps, he heard her say, "Not much chance of that."

Jill ran around her bedroom, searching for her other shoe.

"Lucas, you better not have put my shoe in your toy box," she mumbled. Her son was perfectly content on the floor, playing with the blocks Rick had given him. She was touched by Rick's kindness. No one had ever given such a special gift to her son. She examined one of the blocks and imagined him running his roughened hands over the bare wood. She couldn't get over the fact of the big, sexy man who had lovingly taken the time to shape each block. All the sure, firm strokes it had taken to smooth the surface. How would those hands feel on her?

Suddenly her body warmed. Oh, God! What was she thinking?

She pulled the comforter up and looked under the bed, finally locating her shoe. She slipped her foot into the heeled sandal and buckled the strap.

With a groan, she looked in the mirror. The mauve-and-blue-print skirt hung to midcalf, and her pink T-shirt and denim vest placed her outfit somewhere in between dressy and casual. She had no idea what Rick wanted her to wear, but things were pretty informal at the lake.

Darn, this was exactly what she didn't want to do. She was absolutely not going to rearrange her life for a man again.

Brushing her hair, she left the curls loose against her shoulders. She heard a knock on the door. "Oh, my gosh." She grabbed her watch and slipped it on her wrist. She picked up Lucas from the floor and rushed to answer the door. She found both Bob and Rick standing outside.

Seeing Rick, her breath caught. He was dressed in a wine-colored shirt that accented his dark hair and eyes. His slate-gray trousers were pleated but didn't hide the muscular build underneath.

Quite a contrast to Bob who was in old jeans and a sweatshirt.

"I'm here to pick up Lucas," her neighbor said. "C'mon, kid. You're spending the night with your uncle Bob and aunt Karyn." That seemed to make her son happy until he spotted Rick. "Ree…" he called as he opened his little arms wide.

Rick didn't hesitate and reached for the boy. "Hey, little guy, you gonna be good tonight, so I can take your mother out to dinner?"

"Ma…ma…" Lucas began to cry.

What was she doing? Jill wondered as her son fussed. But standing firm, she handed the diaper bag to Bob. "I think this has everything Lucas needs. You sure you don't want me to collect him when I get home?"

Bob shook his head. "No. I'm off tomorrow, so don't worry about it. We'll have a great time." Bob smiled as he took the child from Rick. "You two have fun. Karyn and I will let you repay us when our baby comes."

"It's a deal," Jill said, then kissed Lucas goodbye and watched Bob walk down the stairs.

Rick and Jill were alone.

Rick picked up a single perfect pink rose from the railing and handed it to her. "You look beautiful," he said.

"Grazie." Excited, she took the flower and inhaled the sweet fragrance. She'd never gotten flowers before, except when Karyn and Bob brought her a bouquet when she was in the hospital after giving birth to Lucas. This was only one rose, but it was a first—from a man. She didn't even have a vase. She went to the cupboard and pulled down a tall glass, all the time conscious of Rick watching her. She looked at him. "Is there something wrong?"

Smiling, he shook his head. "No, everything's…perfect. You ready to go?"

Barely able to speak, she nodded and walked across the room. She picked up her purse and the jacket Karyn had lent her, and allowed Rick to hold open the door. Once downstairs, she stopped when she saw a new Dodge Durango in the driveway. The sport utility vehicle was a gleaming, wicked black. "Who does this belong to?"

"It's mine," Rick said proudly. "I picked it up when I was in Louisville last week. Since I'm going to be around longer than planned, I thought I might need something more practical than my Harley."

She guessed his oil business was doing pretty well. "It's very nice." Rick opened the door for her and she sat down on the leather seat, breathing in the wonderful new-car aroma. "Maybe someday I'll be able to afford a new car," she murmured softly.

He climbed in beside her. "Maybe someday what?"

"Oh, just promising myself a better life. Hopefully after I graduate and get a job, I can afford a few luxuries."

"I'm sure that will happen, Jill. What will that job be?"

"Teaching school, I hope. Then I'd have the same schedule as Lucas. I hate the thought of putting him in day care for eight hours every day."

Rick backed out of the drive and headed down the street. "I bet it's hard not being home to watch him grow up."

She gave him a sideways glance. He looked comfortable behind the wheel. "I have no choice."

"What if you get married?"

"Right now, a husband is not at the top of my list of priorities." As if, she mused, there were dozens of men out there who wanted to marry a woman with a eighteen-month-old child. "What about you, Rick? You're what…thirty?"

"Just turned," he said.

"Why haven't you gotten yourself a wife and a few kids?" she asked.

He glanced at her. "You haven't heard?"

"Heard what?"

"About the Covelli curse."

"Some. Will you tell me?"

Rick grinned. "Someday. But not tonight. I want to concentrate on you, *cara*."

They arrived at the Lakeside Inn restaurant on the shore of Lake Patoka and were seated in front of a window that looked out over the moonlit water.

Jill ordered steak and glanced up to see Rick smiling at her.

"It's nice to see a woman with a good appetite," he said after sending the waiter off for a bottle of burgundy.

She blushed. She rarely ate steak. "I burn a lot of energy."

"I'm not complaining. Order whatever you want."

The waiter appeared and poured some wine into Rick's glass. Jill watched as he raised the glass to sample it. She couldn't take her eyes off his broad hands, workingman's hands. Hands able to handle fine crystal without looking out of place. But that's how she felt—out of place.

Rick nodded his approval and the waiter filled both glasses. When they were alone, Rick raised his drink. "To more times together."

"I don't think..." Jill paused. "I'm not very good at this. I never dated much." She put down her wine and clutched her hands in her lap.

"This isn't a contest, Jill. We're spending time together...as friends." He raised his glass again. "To friendship."

"To friendship," she agreed, picking up her wine and touching her glass to his.

Soon Jill began to relax and Rick got her talking. When she finally smiled, a warm feeling poured through him. Suddenly he wanted to know everything about her. "Tell me about Lucas's father."

Jill gasped at the direct question. "What?"

"I didn't mean to startle you, but I thought we should stop tiptoeing around the issue. I already know you're a single mother, never married," he prompted her.

"What if I don't want to talk about him?"

He shrugged. "That's okay, too. But, Jill, I'm not going to judge you."

She stared at him a moment. "Keith Dillon was a musician," she said. Her voice contained no emotion, as if she didn't dare let herself feel or remember the pain. "We met when I was a junior in college. He was the lead guitarist in a band that played the campuses in the area. My roommate was the one who talked me into going to one of the dances. We met Keith at an after-hours party. I ditched class the next day to be with him before he left to go on the road again. I was naive—and a fool.''

Rick bit back a smile. He'd done worse. Much worse.

''The next weekend, Keith returned. He called and asked me out. We saw each other every weekend for the next few months. When my parents found out, they came to school to meet him. They hated his long hair and the fact that he wasn't in school. My dad and I argued and he forbade me to see Keith.'' She played with her wineglass. ''Well, how could I do that? I was in love with him. My life had been filled with academics up to that point. I thought that love was the only thing I needed, and so I ignored my father's orders.''

''You never dated in high school?''

She shook her head, and he watched as her gorgeous golden curls moved against her shoulders.

''I was a real geek. A brain. Boys didn't give me the time of day.''

''I can't imagine that.''

''I had braces and wild curly hair I didn't know what to do with. And talk about flat-chested...'' She stopped, then said, ''I mean I was skinny.''

He raised his glass. ''You filled out nicely.''

''Thank you.'' She smothered a grin. ''Having a baby will do that.''

''So I take it, this guy—Keith—didn't want to be a father.''

Jill nodded, pain etched on her face. ''When I told Keith about the baby, he told me to get rid of it. After Lucas was born I tried to locate him. That's when I found out that his bus had crashed and he was killed. In my heart I hoped that Keith would change his mind after he saw his son.'' She shrugged. ''I guess it doesn't matter now.''

Rick wanted to take her into his arms. ''The night of Dad's funeral—were you pregnant then?''

She nodded. "I was three months along, so I barely showed." Her voice faltered as tears filled her eyes. "I had finally realized where I stood with Keith, so I packed up my things and left. Just started driving. I didn't know where I was headed, but ended up just outside Haven Springs when the car engine overheated. That's when Bob Ashmore found me. I was crying hysterically. He brought me into town so I could phone someone to come and get me. But I couldn't call my parents." Jill's eyes connected with Rick's and he could imagine her panic.

"Bob must have felt sorry for me. He took me to his house and I met Karyn. They offered me a place to stay the night. The next day I poured out my troubles to Karyn. That evening she and Bob offered to rent me the apartment over the garage. I thanked them, but said I didn't have any money. Karyn suggested I interview for a waitress job at Maria's Ristorante." Jill smiled. "Your mother was wonderful. Not only did she hire me when I was pregnant, your family has practically adopted me and Lucas. I can never repay their kindness."

"Mom has an unlimited capacity for love," Rick said. And for forgiveness, he added silently.

"That's what I want for my baby. I never want Lucas to feel unloved. From the minute I discovered I was pregnant, I wanted him. Loved him."

There was silence for long moments, then Jill spoke again. "I never wanted anything bad to happen to Keith. It's terrible that Lucas will never know his father. Who knows—Keith might have changed his mind and become a real father to his son."

"But your son has you. He's a lucky little boy."

"Thank you."

Jill's eyes glowed as she talked. Rick picked up her hand and saw that her nails were clipped short and neat and void of polish, honest and unpretentious like her. He rubbed his fingers over her knuckles. He felt her shiver. Then all too quickly the waiter came with their food and the moment faded.

For the next hour the conversation centered on his family and the efforts to clear his father's name. She listened to every word as he explained about the private investigator. Rick lingered over his coffee, not wanting the night to end. He wanted more time with Jill.

Finally the check came. He paid with his credit card, then stood up and reached for her hand again. "C'mon, there's time to take a short walk by the lake."

She started to argue, but finally nodded. "That sounds nice."

They went outside and silently walked down the pathway to the wooden pier. A few other couples were around, but soon Rick and Jill found themselves alone. Rick plucked some rocks from a flower box along the walkway's edge and began to skip them across the water.

"We used to come here years ago," he said. "Dad and Mom loved the water. So did we."

"I can't wait to get Lucas into swimming lessons." Jill looked at him. "I bet you were a good swimmer."

He tossed another stone. "Not really. Back then I spent a lot of time on the shore. With the asthma, I couldn't handle much physical activity."

"Oh, Rick, that had to be rough on you." Her face mirrored her concern.

"Yeah, but by thirteen I'd outgrown it. But if you want to talk about being skinny, you should have seen me. When I went into high school at fourteen, I was the proverbial ninety-eight-pound weakling.

"My height reached six-one over the next four years, but I was still thin. I didn't add any muscle until I joined the Marines." He cocked an eyebrow. "So don't tell me about boys not paying attention to you. The girls in junior high wouldn't even give me the time of day. And I was picked on all the time. If it hadn't been for Rafe, I would have been beaten to a pulp.''

She shook her head. "You Covellis are so handsome I just figured that the girls were all over you.''

That had come later, but he didn't think it wise to discuss the subject with Jill. He smiled and leaned back against the edge of the pier railing. He tugged on her arms until she stepped between his open legs. "I wish I'd known you in school, Jill Morgan. You'd have been great for my ego. Truth is, I never felt like I fit in. Sometimes not even with my own family.''

Jill could see the sadness in his eyes. "Is that the reason you left and stayed away so long?''

She saw his jaw tense.

"I'm sorry, that's none of my business.'' She started to move away.

His grip tightened on her hand, stopping her from leaving. "Look, Jill, I think between tonight and two years ago in the garden we've told each other enough personal things to know we can trust each other.'' His voice lowered. "Do you trust me, *cara?*''

Jill found herself nodding.

"Good.'' He smiled. "My father was obsessive about his kids getting an education. That's one of the reasons he took in my cousin Tony when his parents couldn't afford the tuition. When my asthma subsided, I guess I went a little crazy with my newfound freedom. I discovered I liked fast cars, motorcycles, anything that gave me a rush.

"That didn't make Dad happy. My new hobbies were a little too wild for his taste. He believed in hard work. He wanted all his sons to learn carpentry. When he was finally able to expand his construction business, he wanted his sons alongside him. I was seventeen and wanted to play.'' Rick sighed. "So he clamped down on me. Thought if he sent me away to college I'd straighten out. But I was never a good student. I don't know if it was because I had to stay quiet all the years while I was sick or if I liked to rebel, but I flunked out of college. Dad ordered me home to work in the business. I joined the Marines, instead.''

''What did your father do?''

Rick looked up into the night sky. ''He didn't speak to me for two years. I tried to call him, but the man was stubborn. It had to be his way or no way. After my four-year hitch was up, I came home, but I still couldn't be what Dad wanted. I took off for Texas, got a job in the oil fields and met Tuck.'' He shrugged. ''We got to be friends and decided to pool our money and invest in an oil well. The six years passed so fast. I kept in touch with Mom, but I couldn't seem to get my father's attention. Then I was too late. I only made it home to see them put my dad in the ground.'' How Rick had wanted his father to see his success. But all his money—all the money in the world—couldn't buy that now.

The lake water lapping on the shore under the pier was the only thing that broke the night's silence. Jill remembered how Rick's father's death had affected him. She'd seen firsthand a man whose world had been devastated. That was the reason she'd stayed with him that night. He'd needed to know someone was there for him.

Jill stepped into Rick's arms, embracing him. She felt the steady beat of his heart and understood the guilt he'd carried inside for so many years.

''Your mother is happy you're home,'' she whispered. ''Your family really loves you. They've missed you.''

His dark eyes held hers and she had trouble breathing. He bent down and his lips grazed her cheek. ''Still playing my guardian angel?'' He hugged her. ''*Grazie,* Jill. You've made me feel better.''

She swallowed hard. ''You're welcome.''

His gaze moved over her face, almost as if he was contemplating kissing her again. "I'd better get you home before I break my promise and keep you out too late." At that moment she wished he would.

The drive home was comfortable with soft music playing on the radio. Rick reached across the seat and took her hand, lacing his fingers with hers. They stayed that way until he pulled into the driveway. He got out, came around and opened her door. Together they walked up the steps.

"I want to thank you for a wonderful evening," she said as she pulled out her key.

"You're welcome. But it was your company that made the evening perfect."

After unlocking the door, she turned around to find him close behind her. They didn't say a word as his head lowered. Jill closed her eyes anticipating a kiss, but when it didn't come she blinked and discovered him looking down at her.

"As much as I want to kiss you, Jill, I don't want to do anything to upset you. So if this goes any further, you're going to have to be the one who initiates it."

Jill's heart pounded in her chest. What was he asking? She couldn't just grab him and kiss him. Maybe she should run for cover, but the truth was, she didn't want to. She wanted to be in his arms, to have his mouth on hers.

He groaned. "Damn, woman. Are you going to put me out of my misery or not?"

Jill raised up on her toes, gripped his shirt and kissed him. That was all she had to do. Rick took over and pulled her against him as his mouth slanted over hers. The kiss was demanding, and she answered it with equal ardor, casting aside common sense. Her heart leaped with pleasure as his hands roamed from her waist to the inside of her vest, then cupped her breasts through her T-shirt. She released a soft moan when his fingers stroked the hard peaks of her nipples.

At last he dragged her mouth from hers and mumbled something in Italian. She gasped for air and discovered she was having trouble standing on her own. Leaning against his body, she felt tremors ripple along the muscles of his arms.

An unbearable ache swept through her as he placed more kisses along her neck, then went for her mouth again. He gave a rough groan, and she pressed closer to his body, wanting his warmth, his touch.

Rick broke off the kiss and captured her face between his hands. His eyes were dark and searching. "I want you, *cara,* more than you can imagine, but I'm going to walk away before you start hating me." He touched her lips tenderly with his, then released her. "Sleep well, Jill."

Unable to move, Jill watched him leave. Her lips felt bruised from his kisses. She tasted him on her tongue and wondered if this wonderful evening had been a terrible mistake.

Chapter Seven

The next afternoon Rick pulled his car into the Ashmores' driveway. He'd been working all morning over at the Johnson house replacing the gable dormers on the second story. He'd found he liked being just a few feet away from Jill, but now the work on the Ashmore house was completed. And Covelli and Sons had to speed up the progress on the renovations so they could start on the downtown project. Rafe had told the crew this morning to plan on working overtime for the next few weeks.

Rick climbed out of the truck carrying a white paper bag. He headed for the stairs, then took them two at a time, anxious to see Jill.

It had been nearly twelve hours since he'd dropped her off after their date. He smiled. Twelve hours since she'd kissed him. And what a kiss. Just the thought of her sweet, tempting mouth under his had him hard and awake most of the night. Damn, he was in trouble.

Even knowing that, he knocked on the door.

Within seconds Jill appeared.

"Rick."

He smiled. "I thought I'd bring you some lunch."

She was dressed in jeans and a blue blouse. Her long hair was pulled up in a disheveled, but enticing ponytail. When she realized she had on glasses, she pulled them off. "But I wasn't expecting... I need to study...."

"And I have to get back to work." He checked his watch. "In about thirty minutes. I thought we both could use a food break." Holding up the bag of hamburgers and fries, he stepped inside and gave her a quick kiss on the mouth. "But if you want me to leave..."

Jill smiled. "Well, maybe you could stay a little while."

"I thought the food might persuade you." He felt a tug on his leg and looked down to see Lucas. Rick picked him up. "Hello, little guy. You letting your mommy study?"

Lucas nodded and said, "Good boy."

"I bet you are. And I brought a hamburger just for you." Soon they were seated at the table, with Lucas in his high chair, eating hamburgers.

"Don't tell Mom I'm feeding you fast food."

"Your secret is safe with me," Jill promised.

Seated across from her, Rick watched Jill eat. He'd never thought before that he could enjoy such a simple pleasure. A little voice in his head began sending him a message. *Keep it light*. He ought to listen to the warning, but all his good sense seemed to disappear when he was with Jill.

Without a speck of makeup on her face, tiny freckles showed across the bridge of her nose, and her long dark lashes contrasted with her rich blue eyes. And what she did to a pair of jeans was sinful, the fabric stretched taut over legs that went on forever, that could wrap around his waist. Desire shot through him.

Damn. What the hell was he thinking? It was the middle

of the day, a small child was sitting at the table with them, and all he could think about was sex. He darted a look at Lucas.

The boy laughed and offered Rick a french fry.

"Thank you," Rick said, and took the soggy potato.

"It's a whole different experience eating with an eighteen-month-old," Jill said.

Lucas began kicking his feet and yelling for attention.

"Stop making so much noise," she said, then looked at Rick. "He's showing off for you."

Rick hadn't been around many kids, except his sister, and he'd been six years old when she'd been born. Before Jill, if he found out a woman he was dating had kids, he usually made himself scarce. That was what he should do now—just get up and walk out the door. But after last night, he didn't think he could. Something about Jill drew him.

"Ree…ree…" Lucas whined. "Ree…"

"What's the matter?"

"He's just tired." Jill wiped Lucas's face and hands, then lifted him from the high chair. The child twisted and turned in her arms, so Rick took him from her. Lucas immediately stopped fussing.

Jill looked embarrassed. "He needs to be changed and go down for a nap."

"Come on, squirt, it's nap time." Rick followed Jill into the bedroom and set Lucas on the changing table. He stood back and kept the boy entertained while Jill put on a clean diaper.

Once again, Lucas fussed when she put him in bed. Firmly Jill told her son to go to sleep. Rick knew he would have caved in by now and picked up the little guy.

As if sensing Rick's weakness, Jill shoved him out into the other room. After about thirty seconds Lucas gave up and stopped crying. Jill put her finger to her lips as they moved away from the door.

Once they were out of earshot, Rick said, "I'm sorry. I didn't realize I would disturb things by coming here."

She shook her head. "Lucas is just tired. I suspect he and Bob were up late last night. I had trouble getting Lucas going this morning."

Rick could see Jill was tired, too. Although she looked beautiful, fatigue was etched around her eyes.

"It's rough on you, too, isn't it?" he said.

"What—raising a child?" Jill shrugged. "Sometimes. But worth it."

Rick knew her parents hadn't given her much support. Maybe not any. So except for help from friends like the Ashmores, she'd pretty much handled everything on her own.

How ironic. While Jill Morgan had faced up to her responsibilities, he'd spent years running away from his. Rick's thoughts turned to his dad, and sadness and shame engulfed him. While he'd been off chasing the next well, his family had been trying to hold things together without him. Would they resent him if they knew the extent of his wealth, considering how they'd struggled?

"Rick, are you okay?"

He glanced at Jill. She looked at him, her expression so sweet...so innocent. She deserved much better than someone like him. She deserved a man who was going to stick by her. One in it for the long haul. Rick doubted he was capable of that. "Yeah, I'm fine, but I need to get back to work."

She followed him to the door.

"Thanks for lunch, Rick. I didn't realize how much I needed a break."

"You're welcome." When he turned, she was close. Close enough to touch, to kiss. But he couldn't, because once he started he wouldn't stop. "Goodbye, Jill."

Before he lost his nerve, he hurried through the door and

down the steps, knowing he left a confused woman standing at the door. But for once he'd done what was best. For her.

Damn, being a good guy hurt like hell.

Two days had passed since Rick stopped by the apartment with lunch. Jill had seen him at the restaurant, but she'd always been too busy to stop and talk to him. And Rick had always disappeared by the time she could take a break. She tried not to make anything of it, but Jill knew that something was wrong.

She waited until her shift was over at ten and then quickly climbed the stairs to Rick's apartment before good judgment could call her back.

There wasn't a light on under the door, but she could hear the sultry voice of Trisha Yearwood singing "How Do I Live Without You" coming from the apartment. Jill raised her hand and knocked. Her heart drummed in her chest as she waited... and waited. Suddenly the door jerked open.

Rick stood there in a pair of shorts and tank top with Dallas Cowboys across the front. She couldn't breathe. Her gaze shot to the dark stubble on his jaw to his black hair hanging in waves across his forehead.

Oh, my. He was beautiful. So beautiful.

"Jill, what are you doing here?"

She shrugged, trying to read his expression. "I haven't seen you around much."

"I've been downtown working on the storefronts." His voice held no welcome.

She nodded, trembling. "I understand."

Jill stood there for what seemed like an eternity, her heart aching for what she couldn't have, wanting to die because she'd let herself hope again. *The man doesn't want any part of you. Just leave.* "Well, I'd better go." Tears began to well in her eyes. God, she had to get away. ''See you...around.''

''Jill...''

She heard him call, but if she turned around, he'd see how upset she was. But before she could get to the stairs, Rick gripped her arm and swung her around to face him.

She kept her head lowered as she fought to free herself. ''Please, let me go.''

Ignoring her resistance, Rick pulled her into an embrace. ''I can't,'' he whispered. ''God, I wish I could.''

She pushed away and met his gaze. Confusion swept through her when she saw desire flare in his ebony eyes. Then relief quickly came when he bent his head and kissed her. A moan escaped her as his mouth moved over hers, tasting her, his tongue relaying his need.

He finally dragged his lips from hers. She gasped for air, clinging to him. She had promised herself she wouldn't let this happen again, but she couldn't seem to walk away. Her legs were too weak to hold her up.

As if he'd read her mind, Rick picked her up and carried her into his apartment. He sat down on the sofa, cradling her against him, bending his head to taste and tease her lips again and again, making her hungry for more. She reveled in the feel of his firm mouth on hers as the soft music continued to play in the background. His hands roamed over her, causing her whole body to clench with desire.

Rick knew this was leading to trouble, but damn, she felt so good. ''We should stop,'' he murmured against her mouth.

''I'd better go.'' She started to get up off his lap.

''No, Jill.'' He stopped her, then gently took her face between his hands. ''I just meant that if we keep going we're both going to end up in trouble.''

She looked startled.

''Dammit, Jill, don't you see? I'm trying to do the honorable thing here. I want you so badly I'm going crazy.'' He cupped her head against his chest. Her silky hair teased his skin. Why did she have to feel so good? ''I'm trying to keep my hands off you.''

She looked up at him, her eyes searching. ''You want me?''

He shifted her on his lap to prove his point. She gasped and his mouth covered hers once again. His tongue parted her lips and stroked her hungrily, emulating what he wanted to do to her.

Finally he released her and, breathing hard, said, ''This isn't working, Jill. I can't keep stopping. I can't keep walking away.''

''What if I don't want you to?''

Another wave of desire soared through him. ''You want a man to make love to you…without a commitment?''

She flinched, and he wanted to take back the cruel words, but he couldn't. Somehow he had to make her understand. ''I don't want anything permanent. I'm headed back to Texas in a few weeks.''

Jill nodded and moved off his lap. He had to fight himself not to stop her from leaving.

She straightened her hair and tucked in the white uniform blouse. ''I appreciate your honesty.'' Her voice cracked. ''I should get home, and don't worry, I won't bother you again.''

Rick stood. ''I never meant you were a bother, Jill.'' He saw the pain etched on her face and knew she didn't believe a word he said. ''I'll walk you to your car.''

Not bothering with shoes or shirt, he led her downstairs and out the back of the restaurant to the parking lot. Jill remained silent as she unlocked her car and climbed in. Rick saw the tears on her cheeks and hated himself for causing them, hated the look of loneliness and despair he'd seen in her eyes. He knew what loneliness was and he sure as hell would know it better in the days to come.

Once she was settled, he closed her door. Their gazes connected one last searing time and it was all he could do not to yank her out of the car and into his arms.

With the last of his strength, he took a step back.

She turned the key in the ignition and drove away.

"I'm sorry, *cara*," he whispered into the night. "I never meant to hurt you."

The following Sunday was Maria Covelli's fifty-third birthday, and Jill and Lucas had been invited to the family party.

How was she going to spend the afternoon with Rick and pretend that nothing had happened between them? But then, what had happened? Nothing. They'd gone out on *one* date and shared a few kisses.

No. It had been more. She had shared her heart, had dared to dream again.

Jill and Lucas walked up the steps of the beautiful two-story brick home on Sycamore Street. The Covelli home was like a lot of houses that had been built around the turn of the century when Haven Springs had become wealthy from the influx of tourists there to enjoy the healing powers of the mineral springs.

At the time the Covellis bought the house, the old place had been neglected for years. She'd heard stories from Maria about how her husband got the house for next to nothing and lovingly redid every room.

At the double oak doors, she was greeted by Angelina. "Oh, Jill, you came." The pretty brunette scooped up Lucas in her arms, then waved Jill inside.

The living-room walls were painted a soft wheat color. The huge fireplace was brick, with an carved oak mantel lined with dozens of pictures of the Covelli kids and a picture of handsome Rafaele and beautiful Maria on their wedding day.

A long sofa of hunter-green velvet was adorned with crocheted lace doilies, as were the gold-hued wing chairs positioned on either side of the mahogany coffee table. Her attention was drawn to the picture of Saint Anthony hanging above the antique desk that had belonged to Rafaele.

The love that radiated from the room was incredible, making Jill envious of those who'd had the wonderful experience of growing up here.

Suddenly she heard voices and turned to see Maria Covelli come into the room, followed by Nonna Vittoria. The two women gave Jill a hug.

"Thank you, Jill," Marie said, "for coming on your day off."

"I wanted to be here." As much as Jill loved Maria and would do almost anything for her, the thought of having to face Rick had nearly kept her away. The way she'd acted last week, throwing herself at him...

Thank God, the family had no idea she and Rick had gone out together.

Maria smiled, her brown eyes warm. "I've been blessed this birthday. All my children are home."

Jill glanced around nervously. That meant Rick was here. "Well, thank you for including me." She handed Maria a gift.

"Oh, thank you," Maria said. "I feel as if you and Lucas are my family, too."

Jill was always amazed at the love this woman showered on her. Maria had never once lectured her on being a single mother.

Rafe walked into the room, carrying a glass of wine. He hugged Jill. Moments later Tony arrived. Soon after, Rick walked in with his friend, Tuck.

She froze, struck again by his good looks. Dressed in

new-looking black jeans and a tan long-sleeved shirt, he looked better than her fantasies. A pair of shiny black cowboy boots made him seem even taller. Her heart pounded when he turned on his dazzling smile. She couldn't do this.

Rick came across the room. "Hello, Jill. How have you been?"

Darn it, she was trembling. "I...I've been fine," she said.

"How is the studying going?"

"Finals are in a few weeks."

Silence reigned and she wished someone else would join in the conversation. She glanced away and saw that Lucas was garnering everyone's attention. He was no help. She bravely turned back to Rick. "How are things going downtown?"

"Good. We hired high-school kids to help gut the insides of the building." He smiled. "Even got Tuck working."

They stared at each other for a long time. The air filled with tension and an all-too-familiar awareness.

Sex—it's all he wanted from you, she reminded herself. Oh, how desperately she wanted it, too! But not without love, commitment...

Rick's eyes widened as if he'd read her mind.

Jill wanted to disappear.

Finally Lucas came through for her and began to fuss. He made his way over to her. But when she bent to pick her son up, he didn't want her—he raised his arms to Rick.

"Hey, what's the problem, little guy?" Rick picked the boy up. "Bet you're getting hungry."

To everyone's surprise, Lucas stopped crying and nodded. "Eat...Ree."

The room broke into laughter and so did Lucas.

"Aren't you something, big brother?" Angelina said. "You even manage to charm babies." She looked at Jill and smiled.

Jill's face flamed as she glanced away and caught Rafe's knowing look. Had they guessed about her and Rick going out?

Finally Nonna saved the day by calling the family to the dining table. Rafe took his mother by the arm, Tony escorted Angelina and that left Rick carrying Lucas.

Tuck offered Jill his arm. "May I have the honor?" he asked.

Jill nodded, her heart aching as she allowed him to escort her to the table.

With his eye on Jill, Rick escorted Nonna Vittoria to the head of the table as Rafe assisted their mother to the other end. Tuck was the one who sat down beside Jill with Lucas on her other side on a booster seat. Rick walked around and occupied the seat next to the little guy. At least Lucas was giving him some attention, Rick thought, even though Lucas's mother was directing her conversations toward Tuck. And his friend didn't seem to mind at all that he was monopolizing Jill. Not to mention the fact that Tuck was sitting too close and had that annoying habit of touching her hand when he was telling her something funny. Well, none of it was making Rick laugh. What the hell was a Texan doing showing her the correct way to eat pasta?

Worse, Jill didn't seemed to mind. So why should he?

After everyone had consumed enough of Nonna Vittoria's veal scallopini, Rafe stood and Tony refilled the wineglasses.

"This is a day to celebrate," Rafe said. "Our mother's birthday. We already know how old she is, so we'll dispense with elaborating on the number." He grinned charmingly at his mother. "Besides Maria Covelli's youthful spirit and beauty is ageless." He raised his glass. "Like fine wine, Mom, you only get better with the years. *Salute.*"

Everyone followed the eldest Covelli son in lifting their glass. *"Salute."*

Rick sat silently as Maria opened her gifts. He took another drink of his Chianti and tried not to think about Jill being so close.

He heard a gasp from his mother and glanced up to see that she'd opened his present. A delicate gold-filigree watch.

"Oh, Rick. You shouldn't have."

Rick felt himself blush when all the siblings looked his way. "I thought it was about time to replace the one I broke."

Maria looked confused for a moment, then began to laugh. "Oh, the one you took apart to see what made the hands move. Then you couldn't get all the parts back inside."

"I remember that," Angelina asked. "I think you took apart a few of my toys, too."

Maria stood and came around the table to Rick. "When your brother was little, he was very sick. Much of the time he had to stay quiet." She cupped Rick's cheeks and kissed him, then said, "I would have bought a thousand watches to give you a healthy childhood."

Rick hugged his mother back. How he'd missed her all these years. "I know, Mom, I know. But you gave me what was important. Love."

"You will always have that from me, son."

Rick watched his mother as she went back to her chair and opened another present. He had to force himself to stay put in his seat.

It had been so long since he'd spent time with his family that he didn't know how to handle the open emotions. He looked around the table. Rafe had resented having to ask Rick for the business loan. Did Tony and Angelina feel the same way? Did they want him to stick around? Whoa. What was he thinking? He couldn't stick around.

He glanced at Jill. Her eyes met his and he suddenly wished that wasn't true.

Thirty minutes later, the Covelli men convinced the women to go sit in the living room while they did the dishes. Nonna warned them to not break her china. With a solemn promise, Tony managed to steer her out of the kitchen.

Jill went into the living room and watched as Maria sat in an old rocker and began to rock a tired Lucas. Finally the child stopped fighting sleep and closed his eyes. Jill knew she should say her thanks and head home. Then she wouldn't have to worry about spending any more time with Rick.

Angelina sat on the carpeted floor in front of her grandmother. "Nonna, tell us the story about you and Nonno Enrico falling in love."

Nonna Vittoria smiled. "Again?"

"Please, I want Jill to hear the story. It's so romantic."

Jill glanced at Vittoria Covelli and could see the joy and pain in the older woman's dark eyes.

Vittoria nodded and began the story of her family in Italy during the Second World War. Although it had been more than fifty years ago, Nonna told the story in vivid detail, as if it were only yesterday.

The love of Vittoria's beloved Enrico was expressed so wonderfully it brought tears to Jill's eyes. To find such a perfect love with a man. Jill thought about Rick and wished things could be different.

Angelina sighed dreamily. "Oh, Nonna. It's such a wonderful story."

Maria continued to rock a sleeping Lucas. "Don't forget, Mama, you and Papa still had to tell Giovanni."

Vittoria sobered and went back to the story. "We both went to see the Valentes. To say the least, Giovanni was furious when I said I couldn't marry him. He refused to release me from my promise. Enrico argued that I'd already been promised to him. Giovanni ignored him and took the bride's ring and slipped it onto his little finger. He said he'd wear it as a symbol of his stolen bride. Then Mama Valente place a curse on the rings, stating that until they were joined again, it would be a rough road to love for the Covelli family."

There was silence in the room as Nonna Vittoria got up, went to the desk and took out a velvet box. She came back to her chair and sat down. She opened the case and turned it toward Jill, showing her a beautiful ring, a circle of small diamonds and a bloodred ruby. "I had the groom's ring to give to my husband, but it doesn't matter. We need both rings together to erase the curse."

"Do you ever have regrets about what happened?" Jill asked.

Vittoria smiled. "I regret the curse. I pray every day that something will happen to erase it. It hasn't been an easy road. I wanted *bambinos,* but it took many years to have my sons." She looked at Angelina. "Then your mama and papa nearly didn't make it to the altar because of a silly argument."

"At the time, I didn't think it was silly," Maria argued, then went on to explain. "Your father got jealous because I was working a lot of overtime at my job. He thought my boss just wanted to be with me."

"Was he right?" Jill asked.

Maria smiled. "Yes, and I quit my job, but I never told Rafaele."

"See, the curse," Vittoria said. "So many things have happened over the years. We lost your *Nonno* and your papa at such an early age. Young Rico stayed away so many years…'' Tears came to the old woman's eyes. Suddenly the decades of pain showed in every line. ''But my love for Enrico was so strong and our time together so special. Nearly forty years and I would never change anything. I married the only man I loved. Love is the only thing that matters. Sharing your life with the man you love is wonderful, and I wish that for each and every one of you.''

''I'll never find another man who will love me like Justin did,'' Angelina said with a heavy sigh.

Vittoria leaned forward and stroked her granddaughter's raven hair. ''Someday you will find that special man who loves you above all else, and you'll know he's the one.''

''But, Nonna, I'm twenty-four. Besides, any guys who come around are scared off by Rafe and Tony.''

''You are so beautiful, my Angelina. One day, when that man comes into your life, there will be nothing your brothers can do to stop it.'' Vittoria smiled at Jill. ''Same for you, Jill. You, too, will find your special man.''

Jill swallowed hard. She wished she could believe Vittoria's words. But Vittoria didn't know that Jill had already given her heart away.

It had been a long time since Rick had spent time with his brother and Tony, and some things hadn't changed. They still argued about who had to wash and who had to dry the dishes. At this rate they would be stuck in the kitchen until midnight.

''Hey,'' Rick complained, ''I have better things to do than hang around here all night.''

They ignored him and Tony turned to Tuck. ''Rick said you're going back to Texas.''

''Just for a week,'' Tuck verified. ''I need to take care of some business. There's a new well being drilled. I need to be there to supervise.''

"Tuck is a little superstitious," Rick said as he picked up another plate and began to dry it. "He thinks it's bad luck if he isn't on site when they put the drill in the ground."

Rafe rinsed off another dish. "Hey, if you've made so much money, why do you have to go back?"

Tuck grinned.

"To protect our interests. And your brother wants to hang around here to help get your papa's accident straightened out."

Tony stacked the clean dishes on the table and looked at Rick. "Wish we could talk you into staying for good. I'm kind of getting used to seeing your ugly mug around here. I know your mom would like it, too."

"Hey, but if you stay, bro," Rafe added, "you'll need a haircut."

"You're just jealous." Rick smiled. "Women love my hair." He wound his towel into a tight rope then flipped it at his brother's hip, hitting his target.

"Jealous, right." Rafe retaliated by cupping soapy dish water in his hands and whipping it at Rick, soaking the front of his shirt.

"I'm more attractive to women than…that out-of-date buzz cut of yours," Rick responded.

Tony ran a hand through his own neatly trimmed hair. "Hey, maybe I should let mine grow long, too, if I could get someone like Jill to go out with me. Hell, Rick, it worked for you."

Rafe's head swung around. "No way, Rick. Tell me that Jill Morgan didn't go out with you."

Rick felt like he was in a police lineup as his brother stared at him. "Hey, lighten up. I'm not that ugly."

"But Jill?" Rafe darted a look at Tony. "You sure?"

Tony nodded. "Mike Harper saw them at the Lakeside Inn. He's been trying to date Jill all this past year. She's always told him no. Rick's only been in town a few weeks and he's already taken her out.''

Rick remembered Harper from school, and he was glad Jill had never gone out with him.

Rafe smiled. ''It's a good thing we called off the bet.''

''What bet?'' Tony asked.

''It's nothing.'' Rick glared at Rafe.

Tony laughed. ''That's a first. Rafe never calls off anything, especially if he thinks he can win. Spill it.''

Rafe scowled. ''Okay, when Rick first came home, I saw that he was interested in Jill. I made a bet that he couldn't get her to go out with him. I thought it was a sure thing, because Jill had never gone out with anyone. I can't believe she fell for your line of bull...'' Rafe's voice died out slowly as his gaze swung to the doorway.

Rick looked over his shoulder to find Jill standing there, her face etched with pain. She'd obviously heard every word. ''Jill...'' He started toward her, but she stopped him with her hand.

''Uh... I came to see if the coffee's ready,'' she said, avoiding everyone's eyes.

''Sure, Jill.'' Tony grabbed the pot. Rafe took the cups. Tuck found something he needed to do in the next room.

''Jill, just let me explain,'' Rick said as he stood in front of her.

''Explain what? You took me out and won the bet. Congratulations. You don't need to say any more.''

He saw the tears in her eyes. ''Jill, it wasn't like that. Maybe at first, but later I just wanted to be with you.''

''Like you wanted to be with me the other night?'' She started past him. ''Excuse me, I've got to take Lucas home.''

He reached for her, but she pulled away, angry tears threatening. ''Please. Leave me with a little dignity.''

He finally released her. ''I'm sorry, Jill.''

She turned away, so much hurt in her expression that pain tore through him.

A little while later he heard a commotion in the living room, and the front door opened, then closed. Damn. What had he done?

Suddenly his brother, cousin, sister, mother and Nonna burst into the kitchen.

"What happened?" Rafe asked.

"What do you think happened? She's angry. And can you blame her?"

Rafe looked abashed as he combed his hand through his hair. "Didn't you tell her you called off the bet a long time ago?"

"What bet?" Mom demanded to know.

Ashamed, Rick said, "When I first arrived home, Rafe and I were kidding around and I bet that I could get Jill to go out with me."

"It's not all his fault, Mom," Rafe argued. "I egged him on to get him to stay. I thought Jill wouldn't give him the time of day." Rafe shot a warning glare at Rick. "What did you do to her?"

"I didn't do anything," he said. "In fact, I walked away so I wouldn't hurt her."

"La maledizione!" Nonna Vittoria cried.

Rick wished he could blame this mess on the Covelli curse, but he'd messed this one up all on his own.

Chapter Eight

Holding back her tears, Jill lifted her sleeping son out of his car seat and carried him up the stairs to her apartment. Despite fumbling with the lock on the door, she managed to get inside without disturbing him. Once in the bedroom, she took off his clothes, but when she was changing his diaper he began to whimper. She placed him in his crib and spoke to him softly, rubbing his back until he went back to sleep. Then she brushed his cheek with a kiss and went into the other room. Although tired herself, she was too keyed up to go to bed and decided to straighten the apartment.

Jill tossed Lucas's blocks into the toy box in the corner of the room. She needed to occupy her mind so she wouldn't have to think about what happened at the Covellis' house.

She grabbed the wagon Rick had made for Lucas and a pain hit her. She sank to the sofa as an unbearable ache gripped her stomach.

She knew she was naive. Before Keith, her life had been sheltered. Was that why men like Rick were attracted to her? Was that the reason they used her?

Suddenly she heard the rough engine sound of a motorcycle. She went to the door and looked out to see a black Harley pull into the driveway. Rick. Panic raced through her. She didn't want him here. She hurried down to the bottom of the stairs as he climbed off the bike.

"Turn around and leave," she said quietly, hoping Bob and Karyn wouldn't come outside.

Ignoring her request, Rick pulled off his helmet. "I'm not going anywhere until we talk." His sure, determined gait brought him close.

"We've said everything we needed to say back at your house. Now leave."

He stood there with his feet braced apart. "I called off the bet a long time ago, Jill." His dark eyes searched her face. "The first time I kissed you, I knew this wasn't a game anymore."

She remembered that kiss. Both the power and the gentleness of his touch had made her feel incredibly special.

No! She couldn't let herself think about that. "It's been a game all along, Rick," she said. "But it doesn't matter. You let me know I wasn't your type. At least the other night you were honest enough to tell me that the only thing you were interested in from me was…sex."

He glanced away, then back. "I didn't know what else to do. You scared the hell out of me."

He walked to the base of the steps and she had to fight the urge to run. "Dammit, Jill, I thought I could handle us being together. I was wrong." His voice lowered. "But no matter what I still can't stay away from you."

His words were like an aphrodisiac, yet she refused to let them move her. "Then just tell yourself you're not welcome here. I don't need or want you in my life." She started to make her grand exit when he reached out and grasped her hand.

"Don't, Jill. What I did was wrong, I admit that." He drew her hand to his chest and placed it over his heart. "I've never been able to talk to anyone the way I talk to you." He came closer, and she could feel his breath on her face. "I want you in my life."

Her fingers tingled against his warm skin, and her heart was pounding as hard as his. She began to sway toward him. "Why me, Rick? There are plenty of women that you can take out."

"But they aren't you, *cara*," he said as his heated gaze burned away her resolve. He reached out and cupped her face in his palms. "They don't turn me inside out with just one look."

Every argument seemed to fade as his head lowered to hers, but before the kiss took place, the phone in her apartment rang. "Oh, no." She dashed up the steps, hoping to catch it before the noise woke Lucas.

She ran into the kitchen and grabbed the receiver before the third ring.

"Hello," she said a little breathlessly.

"Jillian?"

Jill closed her eyes at the sound of Claudia Morgan's voice. "Hello, Mother."

"Where have you been? I've been calling all day."

"Sorry, Lucas and I went to a birthday party for Maria Covelli."

"That's the woman you work for, isn't it?"

"Yes, but Maria is also a friend."

"Good, I'm glad you have someone to spend time with."

"Maria has been wonderful to me, allowing me to work around my college classes."

"I know, Jillian," she said, but there was sadness in her

voice. "I'm proud of what you've accomplished. I just wish I could have been there with you."

Tears welled in Jill's eyes. "I wish so, too, Mother. But we don't always get what we want." Jill's thoughts went to Rick, knowing she couldn't have the man she wanted.

"I wish things were different, but you know your father."

"And I let him down," Jill said, wondering if her father was ever going to forgive her for her past indiscretion.

"Forgiveness takes time. Maybe after you graduate," Claudia said.

"Are you and Dad coming to graduation?" They'd waited a long time for a daughter they could be proud of. And Jill was trying her best to erase the tension of the past.

There was a long silence, and Jill already knew the answer. "He's not coming, is he, Mother?"

"You know how stubborn he can be. But I'm working on him, dear. I think he'll come around in the end."

Jill feared she would always be a disappointment to Jackson Morgan. "I hope so. Well, Mother, I'd better be going. I need to get in some studying tonight." Jill scrubbed the tears from her cheeks, then looked up and saw Rick standing in her living room.

Oh, God. She didn't want him seeing her like this.

Jill turned around again, blinking back the fresh tears that threatened to fall. "Mother, I have to go. I'll talk to you later. Please give Father my love."

"I will, Jillian, and give little Lucas a kiss for me. Goodbye."

The line went dead, but Jill continued to hang on to the receiver, trying to get a grip on herself. She finally let go and hung up.

"Rick, will you please leave," she said.

He nodded to the phone. "Was that your mother making you cry?"

"Please go."

"I will in a bit. When I know you're okay." He closed the short distance between them. "It's been a rough day, and I'm responsible for most of it. I can't leave you here alone when you're hurting like this."

"Having you here hurts." He stood there, looking at her. Jill wanted to deny everything, but she couldn't. Her heart was breaking into a thousand pieces. "Life isn't fair."

"No," Rick said softly. "It's a real bitch sometimes."

A tear rolled down her face. "Why? Why did you…hurt me? Why couldn't you just have left me alone when I asked?"

"God, I'm sorry, *cara.*" He reached out and pulled her into his embrace.

Jill let him. For just this once, she wanted someone to hold her and take care of her, because it would be a long time before she'd let anyone get close again.

Rick got home after four in the morning. He didn't want to leave Jill, but when she fell asleep he knew he'd better go. She'd throw a fit if he stayed the night. If he ever did stay, he'd make damn sure she wouldn't regret it the next morning.

Besides, he needed to talk with Tuck before he took off. Rick walked into the small apartment and found his friend seated at the table writing something on a pad of paper.

"I was wonderin' if you were going to make it in. So you get everything straightened out with Jill?"

"Not really. But she's not throwing things at me." Rick glanced away. "I've hurt her, Tuck."

His friend watched him quietly. "Never known you to worry so much about a woman before."

"Jill's different," Rick said. "She doesn't know how to play the game." Yet, it was her very innocence he found appealing, he realised.

"Then why aren't you running the other way?"

"I've been trying."

Tuck stood. "Then the only advice I have to give you is take it slow and easy. At least while I'm gone." He went to the sofa and grabbed his duffel bag. "You've got my cell-phone number. Call if you need me and I'll give you a ring when I get things going at the drilling site." He paused and looked Rick directly in the eye. "Your family has no idea what you're really worth, do they?"

Rick shook his head.

"That would be between you and your family, then."

"Thanks, buddy, I appreciate everything you're doing."

"I'm doing exactly what I love to do," Tuck said, "and that's making money. In fact, I'm thinking I might branch out and look into other business ventures, like Covelli Enterprises. Might be a place to sink some of *your* money."

"Covelli Enterprises?"

"I guess you missed that discussion. Last night after you left, Tony, Rafe and Angelina were sitting up talking about forming another corporation. Covelli Enterprises was the name they picked and Tony is heading it."

Rick was a little hurt that he wasn't around for this latest discussion. But why should his family wait for him? He hadn't been there for any other planning sessions, so why should it matter now? He looked at his friend. "So you're going to invest in this town?"

"Maybe. Tony's gonna send me more info after he talks to a couple of banks. I'll only be gone a few weeks, maybe a little longer. Think you can stay out of trouble until I return?"

"I'm going to try. All I've been doing is work."

Tuck slapped Rick on the back. "Look, you and Jill will straighten things out. And if it's meant to be between you two, it'll happen."

"Nothing is going to happen, Tuck. In a few more

weeks, after this mess with Papa is straightened out, I'll be heading back to Texas. There can't be anything long-term between Jill and me.''

''If you say so.'' Tuck headed for the door, then stopped and walked back to the small table in the kitchen. ''I nearly forgot this.'' He picked up the *corna rossa,* the red-ribbon wrapped wishbone. ''Can't leave Nonna's good-luck charm behind.'' Tuck paused and turned to Rick. ''You know buddy, your family would love to have you hanging around permanently. Being an orphan myself, that kind of feeling wouldn't be too hard for me to handle. In fact, if I had what you have here, I don't think I'd ever leave.''

Rick's chest ached. ''I already tried it once. I don't fit in.''

Tuck shrugged. ''Maybe it's because you haven't given yourself the chance.''

On Monday morning Rick pulled his new Dodge into the parking lot of Hardin and Son Building Supply Company. He got out of the truck and spotted Billy Jacobs walking across the asphalt to greet him.

''Hi, Rick,'' the private investigator said.

''Good to see you, Billy.'' They shook hands.

About forty, the investigator was tall with a husky build. He was dressed in dark pants, a plaid shirt and a pair of ostrich-skin cowboy boots. He was a good old Texas boy.

''What did you come up with?'' Rick asked.

''Well, y'all wanted me to talk to the supply company. That was easy.'' He took a notepad from his pocket. ''The company has been around for nearly thirty years and has a spotless reputation. They only sell top-grade materials. They aren't a big operation, but they do well for themselves. Now, here's the funny part. The invoice your brother gave me says that Hardin's was the place your daddy got the materials from. Like he'd been doing for years." The PI shook his head. "Their records here don't show any shipments of lumber to Covelli and Sons."

"You're saying that the lumber for the strip mall that killed my dad didn't come from here?"

Billy shook his head. "All I'm sayin' is that Hardin has no record of the sale of those materials for that date or any time near it."

"But we have proof," Rick countered. "There are invoices that say differently."

Billy held up the yellow receipt with the Hardin logo across the top. "The guy behind the order desk said they haven't used that type of invoice in maybe five, six years."

"He's lying," Rick said, his anger building inside, ready to explode. "I saw the work sheets myself. The materials came from Hardin's. Have you talked with Pete Hardin? He'll remember."

Billy nodded. "I did. But he wasn't around two years ago last spring. He'd had a heart attack and was away from the lumberyard for about six months. His son, Peter Jr., was running things during that time." Billy scratched his head and glanced around the large parking lot as several trucks, loaded down with lumber, pulled out. "Something's staring us in the face, Rick, and we're too blind to see it. But we will. I need to find this guy—" he checked his notes again "—Adam Kirby. He was working the order desk back then."

"He doesn't work for Hardin anymore?"

Billy shook his head. "No. He up and quit about a month after the accident. Something about that smells as bad as two-day-old roadkill."

"Yeah," Rick agreed, determined they were going to solve this mystery. And the guy who caused his father's death was going to pay. Rick would see to it personally.

"It gets even stranger. This guy Kirby doesn't seem to want to be found. No one knows where he's gone."

Rick tensed and nodded toward the lumberyard office. "You think they're trying to protect him?"

"It's always been my practice to ask questions before start pointing the finger. Right now I'm still gathering a lot of puzzle pieces. If we're lucky, they'll start fittin' together soon."

"So what are you going to do first?"

"Find Kirby."

"You need more men on the case. I have the money—"

"No thanks, Rick. I work better alone." Billy smiled. "Or maybe with one partner. Too many people asking questions scares folks off. Want to come inside with me while I talk with Pete Hardin again? I'm a little curious about how well his son handled the business in his absence."

Rick nodded in agreement. Why not? He had nothing else to do today, unfortunately. His thoughts turned to Jill. It had been two days since he'd spoken with her. He'd figured distance was the best thing right now since she'd probably been thinking he was the biggest jerk around. He couldn't blame her, either.

It was best to concentrate on what brought him back home to Haven Springs in the first place. He wanted to clear his dad's name and help put the family business back on track. Then get the hell out of town before he wasn't able to leave.

Jill finished classes early on Tuesdays. Today she went into the restaurant to work the earlier shift while Maria went to her dentist. The afternoon seemed quiet as she and Lisa prepared for the dinner rush.

The phone rang and Jill answered. "Maria's Ristorante. May I help you?"

"Jill, it's Rick," he said. "Is Mom around?"

Jill felt her heart race. "No, she went into Bedford for the afternoon."

"Oh."

There was a long pause. "Can I help you?" she asked.

"Do you know where Angelina is?"

"She drove your mother to the dentist."

She heard him grumble something incoherent.

"Rick what's going on?"

Another long pause. "I'm at the Mayfair Clinic."

Her heart thudded against her ribs. "Oh, God, what happened?"

"I didn't duck fast enough. I was working at the old storefront and I was hit by a falling beam. Got a couple stitches in my head. Charlie dropped me off, but he can't leave the site unsupervised for long. Rafe seems to have disappeared, and the doctor won't release me unless someone drives me home. Do you think you could come and get me?"

"I'll be there in five minutes." She hung up and yelled for Lisa. "I have an errand to run. Finish putting the tablecloths on the tables and do the napkins. I'll be back in twenty minutes." The young waitress nodded as Jill ran out the door.

She was still running when she entered the clinic doors and went to the desk. "I'm here for Rick Covelli," she said breathlessly.

The nurse behind the desk gave her a once-over. "I offered to take him home with me, but he said he already had someone. Lucky girl."

Jill followed the nurse down the hall and past one empty stall, then, behind a curtain, she found Rick sitting on the edge of the bed talking to the doctor. One arm was in a sling and he had a bruise under his right eye and several scratches on his face. A white bandage adorned his forehead; no doubt the stitches were underneath.

She glanced down at his faded denim shirt, spotted generously with blood, and her stomach clenched even before she finished tallying the rest of his injuries. Oh, God. He could have been killed.

Taking a deep breath, Jill managed to get her panic under control and walked into the room. "Rick," she said softly.

He looked up with a grimace. "Jill." He stood up too quickly and began to sway.

She hurried to his side, careful of the arm in the sling. "Are you sure you should go home? Do you have a concussion?"

"I've got a hard head."

"And stitches," she answered, studying him. "What happened to your arm?"

"He sprained his shoulder," the doctor said. "Along with a mild concussion and numerous cuts and bruises, Mr. Covelli will need to be monitored for the next twenty-four hours. Are you the one who's going stay with him?"

Jill nodded without thinking, then listened as the doctor gave her some instructions. A male nurse brought a wheelchair and helped Rick into it while Jill went out and wheeled her car to the clinic entrance.

The short drive back to the restaurant was a quiet one. Once they arrived, Jill parked in back and helped Rick out of her small car. He leaned against her as they made their way through the back door and upstairs to his apartment.

"Thanks," he rasped. The springs squeaked as he sat down on the metal-framed bed. "I'll just lie down for a while."

"No! You can't go to sleep."

He looked at her and his mouth formed a crooked smile. "With this mother of a headache, I doubt that'll be a problem."

"I'll get your pills," Jill said as she backed out of the room. She went to the sink and poured water into a glass, then opened her purse and took out the bottle of painkillers the doctor had given her. She returned and found Rick stretched out on the mattress. He had unbuttoned his shirt, but left it on. The same with his dirty work boots.

She went to his side and handed him two tablets, then held up his head as he swallowed them with some water. He winced when he lay back down on the pillow.

"Does your shoulder hurt?" she asked, knowing it was a stupid question.

"Everything hurts."

She went to the end of the bed and began undoing the laces of his boots. She pulled off the crepe-soled shoes and dropped them on the floor, leaving him in white socks.

"Thank you," he murmured.

Her gaze roamed over his bare chest, noting the bruises on his ribs. "How did this happen?"

"A beam collapsed on us."

"What do you mean, *us?*"

"The Lafferty kid was with me."

"Josh Lafferty?" She knew the family. They often ate at the restaurant. "Was he hurt?"

"No. He ended up underneath me. Somehow I managed to get my sorry ass between him and the beam."

Jill realized that Rick might have saved Josh's life. She leaned nearer. His eyes were closed, but there was pain etched on his face. "Is there anything else I can do before I leave?" she whispered.

"Not unless you can get rid of this headache," he groaned.

Jill couldn't stand seeing him hurting. Hopefully the medicine would take effect soon. Just the thought of what could have happened caused a flood of emotions. The urge to touch him was overwhelming. She needed to feel his warmth, his strength, so she would know he was all right.

Jill reached out and placed her hands on Rick's temples.

He sighed and she could feel him begin to relax as she moved her fingers in slow, easy circles. She sat down on the edge of the bed, careful not to jar him as she continued the soothing motion. Soon she could see some of the tension ease from his body.

Jill wished she could do the same. Night after night, she'd tried to push this man from her thoughts and somehow he kept pushing his way back in. Oh, God. How was she going to keep him from finding his way into her heart?

"I'll pay you whatever you want not to ever stop," he murmured as his eyes remained closed.

"Sorry, my hands aren't for sale. They're reserved for special people."

Rick opened his eyes. The dark depths seemed to hold her captive. She couldn't move. "You seem to have come to my rescue again."

"I don't remember any other time," she said, but she knew he was talking about the night at the Covelli house after his dad's funeral.

He continued to hold her gaze. "Jill, I never meant to hurt you."

She placed her finger against his lips. "Don't say anything, Rick. It doesn't matter anymore."

Their eyes met and he swallowed. "Think we can try and be friends again?"

"I'd like that." Jill picked up his water and helped him take another drink. She knew she was flirting with danger, but she couldn't seem to stop herself.

"You smell good," he whispered.

She smiled, embarrassed. "I probably smell like garlic."

"No, like…peaches."

"Oh, that's my shampoo." Jill reached up to discover that most of her hair had come loose from her ponytail. She must look a mess. "I'd better get back to the restaurant." She stood up, but Rick put a hand on her arm.

"Will you come back?"

She nodded. "Yes, I'll check on you in an hour. Just don't go to sleep."

"My own special angel," he murmured. "I like the thought of you waking me up."

"Believe me, you won't like it if I find you asleep. The doctor said it can be dangerous. Just holler if you need anything. It's the slow time of the day. Your mother should be back soon, unless you want me to call her at the dentist?"

"No," he groaned. "I just need some quiet. Thanks, Jill. Thanks for taking such good care of me." He raised her hand and brought it to his lips. He placed a kiss on the inside of her wrist and whispered some words in Italian.

She shivered, feeling his warm breath dance across her skin.

"Do you want to know what I said?" he asked.

She shook her head ardently, swallowed back the dryness in her throat and backed away from the bed. "I've got to get downstairs." She turned and nearly collided with Maria Covelli.

The older woman was pale as she rushed to Rick's bedside. Jill watched as she gently kissed her son's face, then proceeded to question him about every cut and scrape on his body. Jill didn't want to interrupt and started to leave.

"Just a moment, Jill," Maria called. "Could you stay late this evening?"

"Sure. I'll just need to call Karyn and tell her I'm working the supper shift."

"No, I need you to stay with Rick. I have the Reynolds party in the private dining room tonight. I have to prepare the menu."

Jill swallowed as she caught Rick's knowing look. "What about Angelina?"

"Angelina dropped me off, then went to visit her friend at the university."

"I'll stay with him," Jill said. "Just let me call about Lucas." She went into the other room and phoned Karyn.

"Jill, what's up?" her friend asked.

"I'm sorry I'm not home yet, but there was an accident and Rick was hurt at the construction site."

"Oh, no. Is it serious?"

"He has a mild concussion and some stitches. Maria asked if I could stay awhile longer because he needs to be monitored every hour. I hate to ask, but could you watch Lucas tonight?"

"I'd love to, but it's Tuesday. Bob and I go to our childbirth class tonight."

Jill groaned. "Oh, I forgot." What was she going to do now? Looks like it was going to be her and Lucas babysitting Rick. "Well, do you think you could drop Lucas by here on your way?"

Within the hour, Jill had two to care for, her son and Rick. She couldn't help but wonder who was going to give her the most trouble.

Chapter Nine

About nine that evening Rick had had his fill of resting and got out of bed. With the help of the medication, his headache had dulled to a slow pounding. He'd probably be worthless tomorrow with the pain in his shoulder. The one bright spot in all this was the fact Jill had stayed with him. An hour ago, however, she'd taken Lucas and disappeared into the other room.

Rick smiled, recalling how the little guy had come in earlier, plopped down next to him on the bed and played quietly with his blocks for a time. But soon, the boy had corralled Rick's help to put together a wooden puzzle. Then they moved on to the coloring book. It was amazing what the kid could do. Of course, Jill was his mother.

Rick took off his sling and carefully removed his shirt. He wrinkled his nose when he got a whiff of himself. "Definitely time for a shower."

He tossed the shirt in the corner of the closet, then

grabbed some clean underwear and a pair of jeans from the bureau. When he walked into the other room, he found Jill sound asleep on the sofa.

She looked so peaceful lying there with her golden hair spread out on the pillow. She'd changed from her uniform into an oversize white T-shirt and faded jeans that nicely fit her soft curves. His gaze wandered down her long legs until he spotted her bare feet and the hot-pink nail polish on all ten of her delicate toes.

His body tensed. Looked like his shower was going to be a cold one. He went to Lucas's playpen and made sure he was asleep, too. Dressed in blue sleepers with feet and clutching an old teddy bear, the kid was oblivious to everything. Rick wasn't, feeling the slow tugging on his heart.

He turned his attention back to Jill. He liked having her here with him. But he wanted to do more than look at her. He wanted to lie down next to her and make love to her until they were both so exhausted all they could do was fall back to sleep in each other's arms.

Just the thought made him hard—and frustrated that he wasn't able to resist her. He didn't need any entanglements, especially not with a sensitive woman like Jill. He was leaving soon. Nothing permanent for him. Just as his dad had said. Rick Covelli wasn't a dependable type of guy.

He walked into the small bathroom and shut the door. If he was such a wanderer, why did his insides ache just at the thought of leaving Haven Springs? Leaving Jill? He turned on the faucet and stripped off his jeans. Without waiting for the water to heat up, he stepped into the tiny stall, allowing the cold spray to drive the raging need from his body.

A few minutes later there was a knock on the door. "Rick," Jill called softly, "what are you doing in there?"

Rick grabbed a towel and wrapped it around his waist.

He opened the door to find a sexy, sleepy-eyed Jill standing there. The cold water had been useless.

"What do you think? I'm taking a shower."

"But what if you got dizzy and fell?" Her gaze went to his chest. "Oh, Rick. Look at all your bruises." She reached out and touched the marks on his ribs. "You could have really been hurt today."

He shrugged. "It's just a few cuts and bumps. Nothin' to worry about."

"But if something happened…"

"It didn't, and I'm fine."

She nodded, her eyes luminous with raw feeling. The sight sent a jolt of awareness through him. He was in trouble.

"I think maybe you should take Lucas and go home," he suggested, knowing he wouldn't be able to keep his distance for long. "Mom will be up in a little while."

"I can't leave. You might need me."

He stepped closer, dangerously closer. "Jill, I already need you so badly that I wish you'd do something to put me out of my misery."

She glanced away, but Rick cupped her chin and made her look at him. "Don't go shy on me, *cara*. When you showed up at my door the other night, you wanted me as much as I wanted you. Question is, what are we going to do about it now?"

He watched as her blue eyes widened.

"I don't want…" she whispered.

He shook his head. "You're lying." He reached out and jerked her against him, letting her feel his desire through the thin towel. She gasped, but didn't back away. That was when he lowered his head and kissed her. Their passion sizzled as his tongue parted her lips and swept inside to taste her. She moaned and opened wider to give him access as her hands slid up his chest and circled his neck. He nearly exploded when her tongue darted out and danced with his.

With the last of his willpower, he tore his mouth away, leaving her clinging to him. His mouth went to her ear and he whispered, "Do you have any idea how badly I need to be inside you?"

She made a purring sound as his hands smoothed down her back to her shapely bottom, drawing her against him. He'd started on her sweet mouth again when he heard someone coming up the stairs. He released her, almost causing her to lose her balance.

There was a knock on the apartment door. "Hey, bro. I'm here to baby-sit you," Rafe said as he swung open the door, then froze seeing the two of them standing there in the bathroom doorway. "Oh, sorry," he said when he noticed Rick's towel and Jill's thoroughly kissed mouth. There was little doubt what they'd been doing. "I'll leave you two alone."

Jill was the first to recover. "No, Rafe. I'm glad you're here. I…I have to get Lucas home." She dashed around the apartment gathering her things, not looking at anyone. She had the diaper bag filled and ready to go in less than a minute.

"Here, let me help," Rafe volunteered as he picked up Lucas, careful not to wake him. "I'll bring the playpen by tomorrow."

Rick wanted to stop Jill's departure, but realized this wasn't the time to discuss what had almost happened between them. "Thanks for staying," he said as she maneuvered past him.

Jill flicked her eyes in his direction. "I'm glad you're feeling better. 'Bye, Rick."

He watched her walk out the door, aching to call her back. "I'll be seeing you, Jill," he said. "We have unfinished business."

* * *

Three days later Rick returned to work. The doctor had wanted him to take more time off, but Rick knew that Rafe was shorthanded. They needed to finish gutting the two buildings downtown.

But after ten hours of tearing out woodwork, Rick wished he'd taken the doctor's advice and let his sore muscles heal a little longer. He rotated his shoulder to try to relieve some of the stiffness. He'd felt worse, he knew, remembering days on the oil rigs.

What the hell would he be doing if he wasn't working? Lying around thinking about how badly he wanted Jill? He'd done that already. And all it had gotten him were long sleepless nights and an ache in his gut only she could ease.

The hell with it. He had to get back to work. He took the crowbar and wedged it behind the rotted baseboard and pulled until sweat beaded on his forehead.

Too bad he couldn't block out the memories of how good Jill felt in his arms or how sweet her kisses tasted. It was even worse now that she'd been in his room, sitting on his bed.

Damn, he couldn't even sleep there anymore. Every time he shut his eyes, he smelled her fragrance. He gripped the crowbar and went after another strip of baseboard.

"Hey, Rick," Charlie called, "you think you can come up here?"

Rick removed his hard hat and wiped the dirt and sweat from his forehead, careful of his bandage. He walked to the staircase. "What do you need?"

"Just come up here."

Rick climbed the rickety steps and followed the foreman into the second room. Charlie went to the closet.

"What you got?"

"There's lots of junk in here," Charlie said as he moved some of the boxes that looked as if they'd been around since the fifties.

"I'll get a couple of the boys up here and have them carry everything out to the Dumpster," Rick said as he started to leave.

"Wait. I spotted something you might be interested in."

Charlie dragged a filthy rocking horse from the closet. "I found this old guy. One of the rockers is missing and the paint's a little faded, but this was hand-carved."

Rick came close and knelt down to examine the horse more closely. He ran a hand over the carved wooden mane and tail. Unbelievable craftsmanship, every detail top rate.

Rick was intrigued. "I could run off two new rockers easily enough."

"It would be about perfect for little Lucas," Charlie said. "You'd have a friend for life. Bet it would make some points with his mother, too."

Rick studied the foreman for a moment. "What are you up to, Charlie?"

"Just thought it might be a good way to get on Jill Morgan's good side again. Maybe if you fill your other hand with some flowers she wouldn't be feelin' left out and all."

Rick's pulse raced at the thought of seeing Jill again.

"Maybe flowers would be a good idea." Rick picked up the damaged horse and started out the door, knowing he had some work to do before it was fit for Lucas to ride. Suddenly he was excited just thinking about seeing the boy's eyes light up—and wondering if Jill's eyes would light up when she saw him again.

Jill hadn't had a decent night's sleep for the past five nights. Her dream had been keeping her awake. The same dream over and over again.

She was on the back of Rick's motorcycle, riding down the highway. It was nighttime, with only moonlight to guide them to a side road, where they parked in a grove of trees. Then he took her in his arms and kissed her, telling her how much he wanted her. Jill didn't deny she wanted him, too. He spread a blanket on the cool grass and they lay down on the soft bed as Rick began to take off her clothes. Naked under the stars, he began to run his roughened hands over her skin—

Then she would wake up, frustrated, unable to go back to sleep. Jill glanced at the clock. Nine o'clock. Enough studying. She closed her books, got up from the table and paced the quiet apartment. Lucas was sound asleep. It was too quiet. A familiar restlessness took over. What was wrong with her? She'd never felt like this before. She had finals coming up. She couldn't let herself get distracted, but that was exactly what she was. Distracted in the extreme. And the cause was Rick Covelli.

Dear Lord, the man had driven her crazy every day since he'd arrived in town. Now he was keeping her awake nights, too.

Jill plopped down on the sofa and rested her head against the pillow. She was almost afraid to close her eyes. The man had invaded her privacy, her thoughts. No matter how often she told herself she didn't want Rick in her life, the lonely ache in her chest indicated something different.

A soft knock at the door drew her attention. Who was it? She glanced at her watch and stood up. Nine-fifteen. Other than Bob and Karyn, no one came by this late, unless it was… Her heart pounded with hope as she opened the door.

"Rick."

"Hi, Jill." He smiled and she had trouble breathing. He looked so handsome standing there dressed in a dark T-shirt and jeans. There was still a small bandage on his forehead.

She was flustered and unsure what to do next. All she knew was she was happy to see him. She'd been so worried when he had the accident. She knew then she couldn't deny her feelings for him anymore. "How's your head?" she asked.

"Fine. I had my stitches out today."

"Good." She sounded breathless. Why was it every time she was around him, he had her off balance?

"But I've been miserable," he said. "I've missed you. I can't stop thinking about you. The way you look at me, the way you smell, the feel of your skin…"

She wanted to shout for joy. She wasn't going to drive herself crazy anymore about him not hanging around or making a commitment.

Still, every time she saw him with Lucas, she dreamed about a future. And she knew deep down, Rick wanted the same.

"I couldn't stay away any longer." He looked as vulnerable as she felt when he walked inside and pulled her into his arms. "I ache for you." He covered her face with kisses, then finding her mouth, began taking teasing nibbles.

The time for hesitation, for subtlety, had passed. Jill took his face between her hands and held him still as she captured his mouth and took control, changing the intensity of the kiss.

Then he pulled back. "Is Lucas asleep?"

She managed a smile. "Yes, and has been for hours."

Rick reached back and shut the door. Leaning against it, he drew her between his legs and she released a soft moan.

"I want you, *cara*. If you don't feel the same, you better throw me out—now." He kissed her again, pushing his tongue into her mouth, letting her know his intentions.

Jill answered with fervor and Rick responded with a strangled groan. He lifted her in his arms, carried her to the sofa and followed her down to the cushions without giving her a chance to change her mind.

Jill knew she couldn't deny either of them. Not when he

spoke her name over and over again, sending shivers through her body. She was falling in love with him. She believed she had been since their night together in the garden.

Somehow the buttons of her shirt came undone. Then her bra was swept aside. His hand covered her breast. Blood pounded through her as she sought the fiery heat of passion in Rick's arms.

"You're so beautiful," he whispered, then his mouth took her nipple, first bathing her flesh with his tongue, then sucking until the bud grew hard.

Jill cried out and tugged at his shirt, wanting to touch and stroke him. Finally Rick sat back, pulled it off over his head, exposing his beautiful chest. Jill reached up and combed her hands through his hair, loving the feel of the wavy strands.

"You're the one who's beautiful," Jill said, and pressed her mouth to his jaw. Then she trailed kisses down his neck to his chest. Under a swirl of dark hair she found his flat nipple and, with her tongue, traced a circle until the nub hardened.

"Oh, *cara,* I can't stand it anymore," he said, and began to remove the rest of her clothing.

Once he had her naked, he knelt beside the sofa and looked at her. Although the light was dim, Jill was self-conscious. She went to cover herself.

He stopped her and took her hand in his, kissing her palm. "Don't hide from me. You're beautiful."

"I've had a baby," she stammered. "I have stretch marks, and my breasts are—"

"I see no flaws, *cara.*" He kissed her again, quickly driving her insane.

"Oh, Rick, please…"

"Please what?"

"Make love to me."

He reached behind her and tossed some pillows off the sofa, giving them more room, then stood and kicked off his boots. She watched intently as he popped the buttons of his jeans and removed his pants.

Jill's gaze went to Rick's face, then traveled down over his powerful body. Her blood surged. She needed this man as much as she needed air. She raised her arms in welcome and he lay down beside her.

He pulled her into an embrace. Jill didn't want to think anymore. She wanted to close out the world. This time and place was just for her and Rick.

Smiling seductively, he raised both her hands over her head and started to tease and torment her body. His skilled fingers toyed with her breasts, then his lips followed suit. He sucked and nuzzled one nipple, then the other, while his hand moved over her damp skin, stealing her sanity. She began to sob with need.

Jill ran her hand over Rick's damp skin, the hard muscles of his arms and back, until he, too, was groaning with desire.

"Jill, I can't wait any longer," he whispered as he reached down beside the sofa for his jeans and dug into the pocket.

Wide-eyed, Jill waited as Rick prepared himself for their lovemaking. He returned to her, parting her legs and stroking her.

Jill gasped as her hips came off the sofa. "Rick, please."

"Hold on, *cara*," he said as his fingers worked their magic. He quickly had her writhing under him.

Finally he was poised over her. "Open your eyes and look at me."

Jill did as he asked. He pushed inside her and she whimpered in pleasure. Instinctively her legs closed around him and he began to move. His pace increased as she grabbed handfuls of his hair, then raised herself to give him a long, searing kiss. She slid her hands along his solid shoulders, not wanting to let go of him or the wondrous feeling he created in her.

But their climax wasn't to be denied. Rick whispered soft, cherishing words, even as he increased the rhythm, and finally drove them both to the edge and over…into paradise.

Jill cried out and clung to Rick as everything became a swirl of brilliant colors. He, too, groaned out her name, and then collapsed against her. He rolled over, pulling her into the circle of his arms.

Jill's eyes misted. This moment had been like nothing she'd ever known. She wished the feeling could go on forever.

Silently Rick pressed Jill against his side, his emotions too raw to speak. He'd never felt like this with anyone. Finally he whispered, "Jill, you okay?"

When she didn't answer, he raised himself and looked at her. He saw the tears and his gut tightened. "Oh, *cara*, what's wrong?"

She tried to laugh. "I guess I'm just a little emotional," she said, and brushed at another tear. Then she glanced away. "It's been a long time since…I made love."

Rick was touched: she'd given him a precious gift. "I know. I was afraid I'd…been too rough."

"Oh, Rick, you didn't hurt me. It was wonderful."

He grinned and touched her cheek. "You were wonderful, too. I've never felt so…" He paused, careful to choose his words. "Let's just say you made me crazy." Rick lowered his head and kissed her. His eyes locked with hers, catching her mischievous gleam. "Jill, I can't tell you how much I missed you."

He kissed her again, then his gaze traveled down to her breasts. "Did I mention you're beautiful, too?"

''I like that you think so. You must have been with a lot of women.''

His gaze went back to hers. ''Not as many as everyone seems to think. If you're worried, I've always used protection. I would never risk something happening to you.''

''Thank you,'' she said.

Rick reached for the blanket on the back of the small sofa, covered them both, then tucked Jill's head on his shoulder. He knew he should get up and leave.

Soon, he thought. There would be too many complications, too many expectations if he stayed. He didn't need that. But he needed Jill. He needed her warmth, her sweetness, to hold him together. Just for now. He'd get up in a little while, he promised himself as his closed his eyes. Just for tonight, he'd pretend he was the kind of man who could stay, the kind who deserved the love of the woman in his arms.

A man she could rely on.

Chapter Ten

The next morning, Jill rolled over and stretched, unable to ignore the tenderness in certain parts of her body. A smile appeared when she recalled the reason.

Rick.

Her eyes shot open as she pushed herself from the sofa and glanced around her living room. Disappointment engulfed her when she discovered she was alone. Rick was gone.

Well, what did she expect? She dropped back against the pillow. He'd told her enough times he wasn't the type to hang around. So of course he'd steal away in the night.

Hurt, Jill pulled the blanket around her nakedness and brushed the hair from her face. Just forget about last night, she told herself. But flashbacks of Rick's tender lovemaking played vividly in her head, their entwined bodies hot and needy. They hadn't been able to get enough of each other.

Twice he'd taken her to a place she'd never known existed. She'd never experienced the heights she shared with Rick; never before had she'd been so open or so vulnerable with a man.

She sat on the edge of the sofa. Maybe it was just as well he was gone. What could she say to him after last night? What must he think of her? She started for the kitchen when she saw a rocking horse next to the table.

She walked over and knelt next to the antique hand-carved horse. The rockers looked new, but closely matched the rest of the toy animal. There was a note taped to the saddle:

Jill—

It was rough leaving you last night. But I didn't want the neighbors to wake up and see my truck parked outside your apartment. I hope you don't mind if I stop by for breakfast.

Rick.

P.S. Found this pony on the job site. I think he needs a home and a little boy's love. What do you think?

"I think Lucas is going to love it," she murmured. "You're a fraud, Mr. Bad Boy Covelli."

She went into the bedroom and found her son still sound asleep. Good, she had time for a shower. Gathering her clothes, she went into the bathroom. When she stepped under the warm spray, her thoughts immediately turned to Rick and how his skilled hands had caressed and teased her flesh. How his mouth had driven her to ecstasy.

She closed her eyes, wishing he was with her now. To have the water pulsating over their naked bodies, his hands roaming over her skin, searching for her secret pleasure spots. Her breathing grew labored as she recalled his mouth on her breasts.

Jill's eyes shot open. Oh, God! What was she thinking? She quickly finished her shower, then hurried into a pair of navy cotton shorts and a white polo shirt. After pulling her hair into a ponytail, she spent a little time putting on some makeup.

She returned to the kitchen and made coffee. She'd barely gotten the first swallow down when there was a knock at the door. Excitement raced through her as she placed her cup on the sink and hurried to answer the door. Jill swung it open and found Rick standing there.

His midnight eyes sparkled as he grinned at her. "Good morning," he said in a husky murmur. He handed her a small bouquet of yellow daisies along with an aromatic paper bag as he came through the door.

"Good morning." Suddenly shy, Jill gazed at the flowers.

"How did you sleep?" he asked.

She shrugged and answered honestly, "I missed you when I woke up."

He closed the door and drew her into his arms. "You have no idea how hard it was for me to walk out that door last night. But I'd never do anything to embarrass you."

She nodded, loving the feel of his chest. She looked up. "Thank you."

"How about I show you how much I missed you?"

Jill's heart drummed against her ribs as Rick reached up and cupped her face in his palms. Then he bent down and his mouth closed over hers in a tender kiss. He drew back slightly, his ebony eyes gazing into hers, and she saw the heat burning in their depths.

A feeling stirred deep in her stomach. She dropped the sack and flowers to the sofa and became the aggressor. She slid her hands up his chest, circling his neck as she pressed herself against his aroused body. This time when her mouth touched his there was a sense of urgency that automatically deepened the kiss, causing a hunger within her even stronger than last night. Their tongues stroked as their bodies struggled to get closer.

Finally Rick pulled back and let out a low whistle. "You pack quite a wallop. If it wasn't for your son in the other room, I'd strip off those cute little shorts and shirt and make love to you right now."

Jill shivered. "Lucas is still asleep," she whispered.

Rick cocked an eyebrow and his hands moved down her back to her hips, crushing her against him. "But for how long?"

"Probably not long enough," she breathed, feeling her own frustration.

Rick placed random kisses along her jaw. "So maybe we should cool things?"

"We should." Jill turned her mouth in his direction and he captured her lips again.

Then came Lucas's familiar cry from the bedroom. They broke off with a groan.

"I better go get him before he tries to climb out of the crib." She went into the bedroom and Rick followed her.

"Good morning," she said to her son, who was already standing up in the crib.

"Mommy," he cried, and raised his hands. "Out!"

She lifted her son out, carried him to the changing table and took off his diaper as Rick kept Lucas entertained. Then she went to work putting on her son's clothes for the day. Lucas fought her all the way.

"Whoa, little guy. Give your mama a break." Rick held the boy in his lap while Jill finished tying his tennis shoes.

Lucas looked at Rick. "Block."

"I brought you something else today. You want to see it?"

Lucas nodded and smiled.

"You have to be a good boy for your mother."

"Good boy," Lucas echoed.

"All right." Rick swung Lucas up in his arms and carried him into the other room. He set him down next to the horse.

Lucas pointed his finger. "Horsey!" he cried, his eyes wide with excitement.

Rick helped the boy up onto the rocking horse, showing him how to hold on and to rock back and forth. Soon her son was riding like a pro. Jill leaned against the doorjamb and watched as Rick cheered him on. Her heart leaped hearing Lucas's laughter. This was a family scene. This was how it was supposed to be.

The sound of Rick's pager drew her attention. He stood and pulled the small black box off his belt. He frowned when he checked the number. "It's Tuck. Jill, can I use your phone?"

She nodded and pointed toward the kitchen. She busied herself with rocking Lucas, but couldn't help but hear part of the conversation. She knew Tuck was in Midland. There was some sort of problem. After ten minutes Rick hung up and came into the living room.

"I've got to go," he said.

Again she nodded. "Is there a problem in Texas?"

"An explosion on the rig." He combed his hand through his hair. "Tuck needs me to help out. Damn. It's all a big mess."

Jill's heart raced. "Was anyone hurt?"

"No, but the whole operation had to be shut down." He came closer. "I hate to leave you, but…"

"I understand, Rick. You have to go."

Together they walked to the door. He pulled her into his arms. When their lips met, Jill clung to him, taking everything he had to give. With a groan he tore his mouth from hers. "God, what you do to me. I'll call you, *cara*." He said a quick goodbye to Lucas and was gone.

She stood and watched until his truck pulled out of the drive, then came back inside and closed the door. Lucas was busy on his new horse, and suddenly she was miserable. She had opened herself up to Rick last night, allowed him to tear down all her barriers, making her vulnerable again. But she couldn't stop the love she felt for the man. Then all too soon the outside world intruded on their peace and tranquillity, letting her know he had other commitments. He had a life and business in Texas. Would he come back to her? Her mind told her that Rick would come back. But her heart wasn't so sure.

Three days later Rick picked up the phone and punched out Jill's number. Surprisingly this had been the first chance he'd had, the first time he'd been able to get off the rig. This morning had been the first shower he'd taken since he'd left Haven Springs. He and Tuck had been staying at the well around the clock, helping assess the damage, then pushing to have the inspection so they could start drilling again. Every day the well was shut down was a day they lost money. A lot of money.

Not that he and Tuck hadn't lost before, but they had an especially steep investment in these three wells. Suddenly he cared about his future. And maybe that future could also include Jill and Lucas. Since leaving her days ago, he had trouble concentrating on anything but hurrying up and getting home to her.

Tuck strode into the office trailer, still carrying the dirt and grime from working on the rig. "Did you get hold of her?"

Rick hung up the ringing phone and dropped his booted feet off his desk. "No, and the first thing I'm going to do when I get back is buy Jill an answering machine."

"Doesn't she have finals this week?"

"Not sure," Rick said, pushing aside his concern. "I'll be heading back tomorrow, anyway." He thought about the first thing he planned to do when he saw her. His body warmed and he shook away the thought of kissing every part of her naked body until she cried out in pleasure. Whoa, he corralled his wayward thoughts. He still had business to handle here.

"Sound like you're a little anxious."

"There's a lot I left unfinished. I'm supposed to meet with Billy again about the investigation." He caught Tuck's knowing smile. Hell, who was he trying to kid? "Okay, so I want to get back to Jill. Is that a crime?"

His partner sat down on the edge of the desk. "So the love 'em and leave 'em guy has fallen hard. You plannin' on stayin' in Indiana permanently?"

"I can't think of anything permanent until I clear up a few things. My dad's name, for one. I might not have been the best son when he was alive, but I need to prove to myself I'm worthy of carrying the Covelli name."

Tuck nodded. "You know what I think?"

Rick shook his head. "But I know you're going to tell me."

"I think your daddy would be very proud of you."

It had been four days and no phone calls. Not a word. Jill had to face it—Rick wasn't coming back. She always knew he'd be going back to Texas, but she never realized it would be so soon. If he'd just called her, let her know he'd decided to stay in Midland…

Noises from clanging dishes and people chatting vibrated in her head, but all she could feel was her heart breaking. Tears welled in her eyes and she bit her lip, praying she could make it through the shift, thirty minutes, before she fell apart.

By now she should be used to being left. Her father had turned his back on her, Keith had abandoned her, along with their child, and now Rick. What was it about her that made her so easy to leave? Angry, Jill decided she wasn't going to give Rick Covelli the satisfaction of knowing he'd hurt her.

There was a sudden commotion and Jill turned around to see Maria and Nonna standing by the kitchen with Rick. Oh, God. He'd come back. Her breathing stopped and her gaze combed him. In jeans and a white shirt, he looked tanned and handsome. Suddenly he glanced up and smiled at her. What could she do? She smiled back.

He started toward her and her panic surged. What was she going to do? She couldn't talk to him here.

"Jill," he said.

"Hi, Rick." She stood back so he couldn't touch her. If he touched her she was a goner. "How was your trip?" she asked politely.

"Hell, I missed you."

"Maybe you should have called," she said, unable to stop herself from letting him know he had hurt her.

"I tried, but I was on the rig most of the time."

She glanced around the nearly deserted restaurant. "Look, Rick, I can't talk now. I've got to get back to work."

He took hold of her hand before she could escape. "Jill, later, can't we go some place and talk? I want to be with you."

"I can't. I'm working late."

He glanced around the empty restaurant. "Afterward, come upstairs."

"I can't."

"Then I'll follow you home. Jill we need to talk."

"Okay, I'll come up for a few minutes."

* * *

Rick climbed the stairs to his apartment shortly after ten. He'd spent the past ten minutes talking with his mother, getting filled in on what had been happening while he'd been gone. He didn't actually hear much of what she'd said. He couldn't take his eyes off Jill.

He stripped off his shirt and pants and went to take a quick shower. After five minutes under the cool spray, he put on clean jeans and pulled a shirt off the hanger. Before he could button it, there was a knock on the door.

He grabbed the knob and swung it open to find Jill standing there. She looked miserable, and he had a feeling he was the cause.

"I can't stay long. I have to pick up Lucas." She took a long breath as if to say more when Rick interrupted her.

"All right, I should have tried harder to call you. I didn't mean to make you worry."

She stared at him. "I'm not someone you have to report to. It doesn't matter, anyway."

He pulled her inside, closed the door. "Stop lying, Jill."

She didn't respond.

"Why is it so hard to say you have feelings for me? We made love. I don't think you do that with just anybody."

Her gaze darted around, her eyes as luminous as a trapped animal. "That was a mistake," she finally whispered.

"No way, *cara*." He cupped her face in his hands. "No way," he repeated, and pressed his mouth to hers. Then he pulled away. "Damn, you have a sexy mouth."

Her gaze lowered and he could see her weaken. "So do you."

He smiled. "What do you want me to do?"

Her hands moved up his chest and she leaned into him. "Kiss me."

He bent his head, his mouth inches from hers. "So you like my kisses?"

"And you like mine." She gave as good as she got.

His hands toyed with her soft hair. "Seeing as we both want the same thing, then we'd better do something about it," he murmured, and touched his mouth to hers. He began nibbling, biting and sucking until she moaned his name and pressed herself against him. Finally his mouth crushed hers. Their tongues mated hungrily as their bodies worked to get closer. He was drowning in her. How had he survived the week without her?

He broke off and placed butterfly kisses along her silken neck. Jill gasped when he reached her ear.

"You're complicating things, Rick. I can't handle it."

"What about me?" he argued. "I haven't had a good night's sleep since the first time I kissed you."

She smiled at that and he decided it was the prettiest sight he'd ever seen. "That's crazy."

"I know I'm going crazy over you. All I can think about is how incredible it was when we made love. The feel of your body, how good it was to be inside you..."

She glanced away. "That shouldn't have happened."

His chest tightened. "No. I can't regret that."

"But we can't let this go any further. I have Lucas and you have your job in Texas."

He raised her chin so she had to look at him. Somehow he managed to speak, "What do you suggest we do?"

She shrugged. "I don't know. I'm no expert at this. Can we be friends?"

A knife went into his heart. "'Friends' wouldn't be my first choice, Jill." But it seemed to be the only option she was offering.

Rick walked into the construction office three days later. He'd put in a week of ten hour days and was exhausted. Now he was being summoned to a meeting. Hell, he didn't want to sit all afternoon while they talked numbers.

He pulled out a chair and sat down at the table next to Angelina.

Tony and Rafe came into the room.

"Good to see you, cuz," Tony said. "I've been wanting to get us all together for this meeting."

"Don't you know that Rafe is a slave driver?" Rick said.

Tony smiled. "To begin with, I want to fill Rick in on what's been happening," he said. "First, we've decided that since we're branching out and becoming property owners, it would be wise to form another company. Actually we're just adding a different name."

Rick nodded. "Good idea."

"Second, I've scheduled an appointment with a loan officer at Bedford Mutual Trust next week. Since we've already been awarded the federal grant, I'm going to attempt to get a loan for the working capital. The figures are all in here." Tony passed out a copy of the development budget sheet.

Rick could handle the amount easily, but with Rafe's stubborn pride, maybe it would be a better idea to hold back the offer until there wasn't an alternative.

"We need to establish credit for this project. Get a good relationship with the bank. It's in their best interest to give us this loan. We'll be bringing them a lot of business in the future."

"How can you guarantee that?" Rick asked.

"We're going to get a return on our money by making the upstairs into low income apartments. Half our investment, in fact, and also a healthy tax break." Tony grinned. "With that money, we can turn around and invest it again in yet more property. And right now, the cost is minimal. Covelli and Sons will be doing all the remodeling."

Rafe leaned back in his chair and smiled at Tony. "Nice to see that your college education hasn't gone to waste."

"We're doing this for more than money, Rafe. We all

want the Covelli name to be associated with something positive again. I want the planned convention center to become a reality and for Covelli and Sons to do all the finished carpentry. The tourist trade between the new hotel and the center could be incredible. Haven Springs was booming back in the twenties. People were drawn to the mineral springs and the beautiful surrounding area. Why can't we have that again?''

Tony glanced around the table waiting for comment.

It was a lot to digest. Rick knew that this operation wasn't just refacing a few homes. It would take a big commitment from everyone. Rick found he was excited about the project.

"Have you met the new owner of the hotel?" Rick asked.

Tony shook his head. "Rossi International from New York. They're going to send someone out late this summer. That's when they'll be taking bids for the renovation of the hotel. You know, Rick, we could use your expert carpentry skills on the Grand Haven job. Have you seen the incredible woodworking inside?''

Rick shook his head. "I can't. I'm an oilman these days.''

"Why can't you do both?" Angelina demanded. "Work with us, then rejoin Tuck's crew on another well.''

Rick tensed. "I have commitments in Texas, but I'll think about it." He knew his brothers wanted him to stick around. He glanced at Angelina.

She smiled. "Please, Rick, think about it. I've missed having you home.''

Rafe laughed. "Yeah, she's looking for someone to side with her when it comes to men. She's attracted some real losers and is sick of hearing about it from us.''

Angelina gasped. "I could pick King Kong and it would be none of your business.''

"As my sister, you are my business," Rafe said, suddenly serious. "I promised Dad."

She stood. "I'm twenty-four. Your job is done."

"A brother protecting his sister is a job that's never done."

Anger flashed in her eyes. "I don't need protection, I have the blasted Covelli curse to keep men away."

Angelina stormed out of the room and Rick heard the door to her small office slam. "I guess that about wraps up this meeting," he said, smiling at Rafe and Tony. Rick stood. "I'll go talk to her."

Rick knocked on Angelina's door but got no response. He pushed the door open and stuck his head inside.

His pretty baby sister was sitting at her desk, arms crossed. She took one look at his grubby appearance and turned up her nose. "The least you could do is shave every few days."

"I haven't had time, sis. All I've been doing is working. You okay? That was quite an outburst in there."

"I'm fine. I shouldn't let them get to me. I know they're doing what they think is right, protecting me." Still, she looked concerned. "What's wrong, Rick? You haven't been by the house. Mom says to leave you alone, and Nonna has lit three extra candles for you at church. Is there something you're not telling me?"

He felt a tug at his heart. He'd told his mother about his feelings for Jill. Of course, Maria Covelli wasn't blind—she could see what was going on. It was strange knowing that so many people cared. "I'm just going through some personal stuff."

"Jill?"

He scrubbed his hands over his face. "Yeah. It's Jill."

"What happened? I thought you'd worked things out."

"I thought so, too."

"Have you tried talking to her?"

''What is it with you women? You think everything is settled by talking. Besides, Jill doesn't want to talk to me.''

Angelina toyed with a strand of her long, raven hair. ''Why not?''

''Jeez, if I knew that I could straighten this all out myself.'' He sighed. ''Maybe it's for the best. She and Lucas ought to find someone more dependable.''

Angelina raised a finely shaped brow. ''You really want someone else in Jill's life? Someone taking your place? Someone kissing her, someone lov—''

Rick jerked up in his seat, anger tearing at his gut. ''All right, I get the message. So I don't want another man sniffing around her. But what the hell am I supposed to do? One minute she's fine about us, and the next she practically tosses me out of her place without an explanation.''

''Well, don't sit around like Rafe and Tony. They use the family curse as an excuse not to get involved with anyone. Those two haven't asked a woman out for way too long.''

Rick thought about his older brother and cousin. The Covelli boys had had their share of female attention. There certainly wasn't anything wrong with their looks. They'd stayed in shape. Rick figured the failing family business was the real deterrent to starting a relationship.

''You and Jill need to get together so you can work out this misunderstanding.'' Angelina nibbled her lower lip. ''I've got an idea. I'll baby-sit while you take Jill out somewhere. It's hard to talk with a baby demanding attention at inopportune moments.'' Angelina wiggled her eyebrows. ''If you know what I mean.''

Rick knew exactly what she meant. He groaned. ''Great, my kid sister is arranging my love life.'' Although he hated to admit it, he was willing to do anything at this point.

''You've got to try, Rick. Jill is a wonderful person. She's had things rough the past few years, and she's a little gun shy. Her parents more or less deserted her when she got pregnant, even after Lucas's father died.''

Rick tensed, hating to think about Jill being all alone and pregnant. What kind of man, let alone her own parents, could walk away from her? He froze. Wasn't he about to do the same thing? Then he realized he couldn't walk away. Now could he convince Jill that he wanted to stay around—for good? Would she give him that chance?

The next evening at the William M. Stewart Park, Rick climbed out of his car. A warm breeze brushed his face as he drew a long breath, trying to ease his nervousness. He glanced around. The park hadn't changed much over the years. It was the main playground in town. The baseball diamond where the Covellis had come to watch Tony play now had bleachers. The rows of swings were still intact and kids filled the seats, pumping their legs to go higher.

Rick stepped onto the grass, searching for Jill and Lucas. Not ten minutes ago Karyn had told him they had come here. He walked past the swings until he saw a sandbox—and Jill sitting on a bench reading a book while her son was busy digging with a shovel.

Rick's heart pounded as he walked toward them. He only had seconds to think of something to say, something to keep Jill from telling him to get lost again.

When he reached the sandbox and hunkered down beside it, Lucas looked up and his blue eyes widened in excitement. Well, one out of two wasn't bad, Rick thought.

"Ree…" Lucas cried. He dropped his shovel and got to his feet.

Jill looked up from her book and pulled off her glasses. Time seemed to stand still as her sapphire eyes locked with his. The reflection of her desire had him mesmerized and aroused.

She broke the spell first. "Rick."

He accepted the little boy's hug. "I came by your place and Karyn said you were here. I just want to spend some time with you…you and Lucas." He swallowed. "As your friend." His heart was in his throat. "I know that what happened between us that night was…too soon. I moved too fast for you…" His words trailed off. He stared at her luscious mouth, knowing he was lying about wanting to be just friends. He wanted this woman like none other he'd ever known.

"Puck…et." Lucas held up his bucket to show Rick.

"I see. You've been digging."

"I dig," the boy said, and went back to his sand pile.

Rick returned his attention to Jill. "I don't want you to feel awkward around me, Jill. You've been avoiding me all week. I never meant for you to feel uncomfortable or to feel you couldn't trust me." He looked off into the distance, hearing the happy chattering of kids playing. "Two years ago when I was probably at my worst and all I wanted to do was drown myself in my misery, you came to me. I felt something even then. I still feel it, and I think you do, too. Then when we made love, we shared something very special. I just wanted to say I was sorry if I pushed you into something you weren't ready for." He stood, waiting for her response, feeling a strange tightness in his chest.

When she remained silent, her face averted, he took it as a dismissal. Struggling to keep his voice even, he told her, "I hoped we could spend some time together, but I guess it won't work. I won't bother you again. Goodbye, *cara*." He had started for his car when he heard her call out his name.

He turned around as Jill and Lucas came rushing toward him. She was holding Lucas's hand. Jill was breathless when they reached him. "It wasn't you, Rick. You never did anything wrong. It's me."

He saw the tears pool in her deep blue eyes and he ached

to draw her close and kiss away the tear drops, but he fought the temptation.

"I've been hurt," she said. "And I'm afraid to…to let myself get involved—with you…with anyone." She brushed her fingers over Lucas's hair. "I need to finish school…and make a life for me and my son. It's important that I prove to myself I can do it on my own."

He nodded. "Jill, I understand. I think it's wonderful what you're doing, raising your son and putting yourself through college. But how about some time for you to relax? I just want to spend time with you and Lucas." He looked down at the boy and smiled. "No pressure. I promise."

Her gaze searched his face, then shyly she said, "I'd like that, Rick. I'd like that a lot."

His pulse surged with excitement and he picked her up and swung her around in a circle. They both began to laugh. When he put her down he placed a kiss on her lips, then immediately pulled back. "Damn, I'm sorry. I shouldn't have done that."

She smiled. "It's okay, Rick, but you need to practice the no-pressure bit."

Rick felt someone pushing against his leg.

"Me, too!" Lucas cried. "Up, high." He raised his arms in the air.

"I can't forget you." Rick lifted Lucas up and swung him around until he giggled, then placed a kiss on the boy's cheek.

Rick looked at Jill. "Did I ever tell you what a nice kid you have?"

She smiled. "You wouldn't say that if you'd seen the fit he threw when he thought we weren't coming to the park."

Rick poked his finger at Lucas's tummy. "Were you giving your mommy trouble?"

Lucas shook his head. "Good boy. Ride horsey."

Jill groaned. "No horsey now."

"Is there a problem with the rocking horse?"

"Only when I try to pry him off. He's been riding it constantly."

"Sorry. I guess I didn't think about that kind of problem. Is there anything I can do?"

"Yes, you can come by the house and show Lucas that his horsey has to go night-night, just like little boys do."

At the invitation to her home, Rick lit up like a Christmas tree. "Sure, I could do that," he replied quickly, lest she change her mind. "Let's go!"

Chapter Eleven

Jill wondered if she was crazy bringing Rick back to her apartment. The place where, only a week ago, they'd made love with shattering intensity.

Rick carried Lucas up the stairs and she unlocked the door. Once inside, he put her son down and together they approached the rocking horse.

As usual Lucas began chattering away while Jill went into the kitchen and made coffee. Soon she heard her child saying, "Night-night, Mr. Horsey."

Surprised it had happened so fast, Jill didn't waste the opportunity. "Okay, time for your bath, Lucas."

Lucas held up his arms to Rick. "Ree…"

"How about I give him his bath?" Rick scooped up the boy and headed to the bathroom.

Jill hurried after them. Inside the bathroom she moved around Rick and grabbed the panties and bras hanging on the shower-curtain rod.

She turned around in time to catch his sexy grin. He mumbled something in Italian as she dropped her unmentionables in the laundry basket in the corner. She was going to have to learn the language. Then again, she might be more alarmed if she knew what he was saying.

Jill filled the tub while Rick stripped Lucas. Once her son was down to his diaper, Rick pushed her out of the bathroom. "We can handle it from here," he said. To her surprise, her son nodded. "Me do, Mommy."

Rick placed a quick kiss on Jill's nose. "Now, go relax. We have everything under control." He gave her a gentle shove.

Sitting on the sofa, Jill listened to the laughter and the sound of water splashing. She was going to have a mess to clean up, but she didn't mind—the important thing was that Lucas was having a good time. Smiling, she blessed Rick for giving it to him.

Abruptly, her smile died. She wasn't all her son needed in his life. As much love as she could give him—even with all the honorary uncles who were part of his world—didn't make up for the absence of a father in his life.

Jill's thoughts turned to Rick. It was unbelievable how Lucas had taken to him, and how well they'd gotten along from the very beginning. But soon Rick would leave. How would his departure affect Lucas? And how could she protect her child from the inevitable hurt Rick's absence would cause?

Nor was it Lucas alone who would be hurt. How could she protect herself when it became harder and harder to push Rick away?

Suddenly the door opened and Rick came out carrying one damp little boy wrapped in a towel.

"Well, I see you didn't drown..." Her words trailed off when she discovered that Rick was shirtless and his hair was wet. His jeans hadn't escaped the spray of water, either. ''Who got the bath here?''

Lucas clapped his hands. ''Ree…''

''This guy has a way of making you realize how out of shape you are,'' Rick said.

Jill tried to avoid staring at Rick's muscular chest. She'd have to disagree. ''He can wear you out, that's for sure.'' She took her son and set him down on the floor.

This time, Rick watched as Jill skillfully put on Lucas's diaper. Then came the pajamas, along with a game of peek-a-boo and numerous belly kisses until mother and son were laughing. It was obvious Jill shared something special with her child.

A knot of envy tightened in Rick's chest. What would it be like to have a family of his own? To come home each night to a woman who was generous with her kisses—and her love. His gaze settled on Lucas. To have a son.

''Ree…'' Lucas's arms stretched out to him.

''Lucas, Mommy will put you to bed,'' Jill said.

''No.'' Lucas started to fuss. ''Ree…go.''

''I can take him,'' Rick said, and lifted Lucas out of Jill's arms. ''He's getting pretty heavy for you to carry, anyway.''

Before she could respond, he carried Lucas into the bedroom. They didn't make it to the crib without a detour to the bookcase, where Lucas convinced Rick to read his favorite book, *Good night Moon*.

Jill left them and went into the kitchen to check on the coffee. She returned minutes later to find her son sound asleep in Rick's lap. The sight triggered a flashback to the night she and Rick had made love, and afterward she'd curled up against his wide, warm chest.

''The kid's all talk,'' Rick whispered. ''He crashed before I got to the end of the story.''

''That's the whole idea.'' Jill came over and gently

scooped up her son. Her hand grazed Rick's hard biceps, sending warm shivers up her spine.

Ignoring them, she carried Lucas to his crib and tucked him in. Rick left the room and Jill followed, closing the door. Silently they went into the kitchen and Jill poured some coffee.

Rick took a sip and sighed. "This is good coffee. Much better than mine."

Jill couldn't hold back a smile. "That's a compliment?"

He leaned against the counter. "Definitely. Tuck says mine can eat away your stomach lining. Guess I should have paid more attention to how my mother made it."

Jill nodded. "There's a lot of things we should pay attention to. Too bad I didn't listen to *my* mother."

Rick saw the hurt flash across Jill's face. He suspected that she and her mother hadn't been getting along for a while. A long while. "Oh, I don't know. Parents aren't perfect. They don't know *all* the answers. Sometimes we have to stumble along on our own."

Her blue eyes met his. "They're only trying to guide us down the right path."

"What if it's not the path you want to take? They can't live our dreams, Jill, just as we can't live theirs." Rick's thoughts turned to the many arguments he'd had with his father about school and going into the family business. "What if you're not happy doing what they think is best for you?" He looked at her. "Shouldn't we get a chance to choose?"

Jill shrugged. "Most of my life I've tried hard to please my mother and father. I was a good student—not the best— but close to the top. Then Keith came on the scene. My parents were devastated by my pregnancy, then Keith's desertion. I broke their hearts, especially my dad's."

Rick could see the pain in her eyes. He wanted to take

her in his arms, but he knew this wasn't the right moment. Wisely he kept his distance.

"Mistakes are a part of life, Jill. Hopefully we can learn from them." Too bad he hadn't taken his own advice.

"I have. It's one of the reasons I've gone back to school to get my degree. Besides the fact that it will lead to a good job, it's always been important to my parents. I want them to be proud of me again."

They should be proud of her now, he thought angrily. "Do your parents put conditions on their love?"

Jill glanced away. "No. I'm also doing it for Lucas and my future. I want to teach school."

He nodded. "You'll make a wonderful teacher. You're already a great mother. I should know—I have the best."

Jill smiled, and Rick was mesmerized by her sexy mouth. He already knew what she felt like in his arms, what it felt like to be inside her, to hear her cries of pleasure, to have her hands on his skin.

His body stirred. "I better be going." He put his mug in the sink and started for the door.

"Wait," Jill said, then walked into the bathroom and came out with his shirt. "Here, you shouldn't go outside without something on. It's still a little damp, but it should be okay until you get home."

Rick reached for the shirt and their hands brushed. He felt her tremble, and his fingers circled her wrist so she couldn't move away.

"I know I promised to give you some room, Jill, but if I don't kiss you... I've wanted to all night." He moved closer. "But if you don't want me to, just push me out the door."

Her eyes widened. "I don't see that one kiss could hurt."

That was all Rick needed to hear. He leaned forward and his mouth covered hers. Tentatively at first, then, testing the waters, he parted her lips and slipped his tongue inside, stroking hers. For the past week he'd ached for her, for her touch. He wanted to crush her to him, to absorb her into him.

No. He had to let her go before things got out of control and she pushed him away. He couldn't bear that again. He broke away and rested his forehead against hers until their breathing slowed.

"I better leave," he murmured.

She nodded. "And I need to study. I have a final tomorrow."

When she didn't back away, he took the opportunity for another kiss. With the last of his willpower, he released her.

"I'm going now before I do something crazy." He opened the door. "Good night, Jill," he said, and walked out into the cool spring night. A soft breeze brushed his heated skin, but did nothing to lower its temperature. This wasn't a temporary condition, either.

When it came to Jill Morgan, nothing seemed to work to get her out of his system. And that terrified him.

The next day Jill rushed into work. Late. She'd had to write her final and that had her running behind. Then Lucas had started fussing. He didn't want her to go to work. He cried for nearly an hour before she got him to sleep.

Thank goodness, she had an understanding employer. Maria had told Jill to take her time, that they'd handle things until she got there.

It was after six o'clock, the busiest time of the dinner rush, when Jill walked in the back door. She stopped in amazement when she discovered who was handling things for her.

Rick. He had on freshly pressed jeans and a blue denim shirt with the sleeves rolled up, exposing his muscular forearms. He had a white apron tied around his waist, a notepad in his hands and was taking a dinner order. The female customers at the table seemed to enjoy the attention of this good-looking Covelli.

Jealousy surged through Jill, but she quickly pushed it aside as she hurried into the kitchen. She put her purse away, grabbed an apron and went to relieve Rick.

"Cara," he said, smiling as she approached the table. "You're here."

"And it looks like just in time," Jill murmured, glancing down at the four young women, most likely college students. "I'll take over now. Thank you."

"But Rick is taking our order," a brunette said with a pout.

"Jill's here now. She's our best waitress," Rick insisted as he soothed the customer.

"But, Rick." One of the blondes picked up her fork and spoon. "You promised to show us how to eat spaghetti. You know, how to twirl it on the fork."

He grinned. "I promise I'll return. Ciao, ladies."

Jill watched as Rick walked away.

There was a collective sigh from the table. "He's gorgeous," one said.

"Wouldn't mind his boots parked under my bed," came from yet another.

Jill gripped her order pad. She didn't want to hear any more women praising Rick's attributes. "Is there anything else I can get you ladies?"

"Yeah, we'll take four of him," the brunette said, and the group broke into laughter.

Now Jill was fuming. All she could do was turn, cross the dining area and storm into the kitchen, angry with herself for letting their comments get to her. She had more important things on her mind than Rick's flirting. Jill handed the order to Maria, then went to the salad area and got out four plates.

So what did she expect from Rick? The man was single and good-looking. He had every right to check out women.

"Hey, good thing you got here."

Jill gave a start, nearly dumping the lettuce. She recovered and glanced at Rick. "Looked like you were doing just fine on your own."

"I was trying to help you out, but I didn't know the dinner specials so I wasn't sure about how to write their order."

"The ladies didn't seem to notice," she said, flinging lettuce onto the plate.

A slow smile spread across his face. He leaned his hip against the counter. "Why, Jill Morgan, I do believe you're jealous."

She gasped. "I am not. I've no ties on you."

He took hold of her hand. She tried to pull away, but he held tight. Then he leaned forward and whispered, "Oh, yes there are, *cara.* You have me tied in a million knots. You have me awake nights, aching for you, remembering how we were together. How sweetly you made love to me."

She swallowed as his ebony gaze bore into hers.

"I just hope that, at night when you climb into bed— alone—you're as miserable as I am." He released her and left the kitchen.

Jill took a deep breath. Oh, God. She closed her eyes, trembling from the words he'd whispered.

She was acting like a crazy woman. There was no excuse for her anger at Rick. So he was flirting. Big deal. No doubt about it, women were attracted to him.

He wasn't the type of man she needed, anyway. She needed a man who was going to be around. A man who wanted only her. Rick obviously wasn't that man.

Pushing through the door, she carried the salads into the

dining room—and found Rick once again talking to the girls.

A pain gripped her heart. She'd told him that they couldn't have a permanent relationship, that he'd never be part of her life. It was her decision. Why did it hurt so much?

Rick climbed the stairs to Jill's apartment shortly after ten. In the past four hours, he'd managed to work as a waiter, bus a few tables and take over behind the bar when the regular bartender had to leave for an emergency. Oh, yeah, he also managed to find time to act like a total jerk.

Most of the night he'd baited Jill, trying to get a reaction. Well, he'd gotten one. Now she'd probably never speak to him again. He should have been tickled that she was jealous and let it go at that. But she was angry at him again. Great.

He paused at the door, holding on to the one red rose he'd plucked from his grandmother's garden and some wine, along with two glasses. He drew a breath and released it, then knocked on the door.

"Who is it?" Jill's soft voice came from the other side.

"It's me, Rick."

He heard the lock click, then she pulled open the door. "Rick, what are you doing here?"

He looked down and saw that Jill was dressed in a bright pink nightshirt that fell just above her knees. "To apologize for giving you a bad time at the restaurant."

She raised her chin defiantly. "Oh, for being a jerk."

He raised his hand. "Guilty." He held out the rose. "A peace offering."

Smiling, she took it. "Thank you."

"I also brought some wine." He pulled a corkscrew from his pocket, opened the bottle and poured her a glass, then one for himself. "Here, come out and have a drink with me. It's a beautiful night. The stars are so bright."

"I'm not dressed."

"You're not naked, either. And I promise you're safe with me. I'll keep my hands to myself."

"Oh, I don't know. Your reputation with the ladies is notorious around these parts. I hear you broke a lot of hearts when you left town."

"An exaggeration. Probably got me confused with my brother." He took her arm and led her to the stairs. They sat on the first step and remained silent for some time.

At least he said, "I'm really sorry about tonight. I was just goofing around."

"You have every right to act any way you want. You and I have nothing going on. We're only—"

"Friends," he finished for her.

She swallowed. "That's right."

He looked up at the night sky, trying to contain his desire for her. Impossible. He hadn't been able to get Jill out of his head since the first time he'd lain eyes on her. "So this friends thing is all right with you."

"It works with Rafe and Tony."

"You feel the same about me as you do my brother and my cousin?"

She glanced away. "Not exactly."

"So you do have feelings for me that go beyond friendship."

Jill refused to look at him. She pulled her nightshirt over her knees. "You know I do."

He sighed in relief. "Thank God. *Cara,* I can't be in the same room with you without wanting you. When I sleep I dream about you…us. What I want us to do together."

"Rick, don't." She started to get up.

He reached for her, preventing her from leaving. "I didn't say I would act on them."

She looked at him with trusting blue eyes.

"I care about you, Jill. If all we can be is friends, I'll

accept that," he agreed, knowing he was dying a slow death.

She nodded and they sat enjoying their wine and the peaceful night.

"So, do you think friends can go out to dinner on Friday night?"

She started to argue when he touched his finger to her lips.

"No buts, Jill. I know that your finals will all be over by then and I've even got a sitter for Lucas. Angelina has made a standing offer to spend the evening with her favorite guy. I thought we'd make it a nice casual evening and go out to the lake for a picnic. I'll bring the food so all you need to bring is a sweater in case it gets chilly. What do you say? Is it a date?"

He saw the hesitation in her eyes. "It's just a picnic, Jill. No more. We'll go about five o'clock and I'll even bring you home early."

A smile lifted the corners of her mouth. "I was just trying to figure out who I can get to switch shifts with on Friday."

He let out a breath. "Maybe I can help you. I have connections with the management."

Rick had just finished showering and pulling on a pair of jeans when the apartment door opened and Tuck walked in.

"Hey, you made it back." Rick came into the living room to greet his friend. "Everything taken care of at the well?"

"The drilling started again two days ago. I waited another twenty-four hours before I handed the reins over to Hal Johnston. Then I hopped in my truck and drove straight through."

Rick grinned. "Bet Hal's tickled to death to be playing boss."

Tuck nodded. "He's always wanted to run things. He's been bugging me about buying in."

"How do you feel about that?" Rick asked, knowing the subject had come up often during the past year. Hal's offer held more interest for Rick ever since he'd begun thinking about staying in Haven Springs.

Tuck shrugged. "It would free up more time for us. And since you're committed here for a while, I have no problem. Hal's proved himself over and over. Besides, I was thinking that maybe there's more to life than waitin' around for the next oil well to come in."

Rick's smile faded as he reached up and put his palm to his friend's forehead. "You feeling all right?"

"I'm feeling fine. I've just realized I'll be thirty-six this year. I've made a sizable sum of money I'd like to make use of before I'm too old to enjoy it."

"And you think you can find some excitement in Haven Springs?"

"It's not a bad place to start," Tuck argued. "Things are going to get pretty interesting when the hotel reopens. I wouldn't mind getting in on the ground floor. Who knows? I might even be able to earn my second million right here in Indiana."

Rick cocked an eyebrow. "That brunette you took home from the barbecue wouldn't have anything to do with your decision?"

Tuck shrugged. "Could be. But mostly I'd like to see how my investments do. I have a few things I'd like to discuss with Tony." Tuck smiled, and the lines around his eyes intensified. "Besides, I want to hang around and see what happens with the Covellis and the curse. Speaking of which, how are things going with you and Jill?"

"We have a date tonight," Rick said, and went back into

the bathroom with Tuck following. He spread shaving cream along his jaw. "I'm taking her out to the lake." He reached into the medicine cabinet and pulled out his razor. "On the Harley."

Tuck leaned against the doorjamb. "She agreed to that?"

"Not exactly," Rick confessed as he took the first run with the blade down his face. "I haven't told her yet how we're getting there."

Tuck laughed. "Like to be there when that happens." He slapped Rick on the back.

"Ouch," Rick said, then looked in the mirror to examine the cut he'd just made. "You drew blood."

"Jill's going to take a lot more."

"No, she won't. She'll love it." Rick stared at his reflection, remembering the night he'd taken Jill home on his motorcycle. He loved the feel of her against him, her arms around his waist, her breasts pressed into his back.

He groaned and closed his eyes. Tuck was right. He was never going to survive the night. But what a way to go.

Jill ran around the apartment, trying to get things picked up for Angelina. She looked at her son playing contentedly on the floor with his blocks. She'd bathed him and changed him into pajamas. All Angelina had to do was read him a story and put him to bed.

She returned to the bathroom and finished fixing her hair. Then she set down her brush and checked her rose colored blouse and the new jeans she'd bought for tonight. A frivolous expense, but she was going to treat herself to celebrate the completion of her finals. And tonight she wanted to celebrate with Rick.

There was a knock at the door and Jill's pulse began to race. He was here. She swung open the door to find Angelina, with Rick behind her.

"Angelina's baby-sitting service," Rick's sister said as

she stepped inside. "Hello, Jill." She and Jill hugged each other.

"Angelina." They were about the same age, and both were finishing up their college term.

"There's my guy. Hello, cutie," Angelina called to Lucas. The child squealed in delight, got up from the floor and ran to her. Angelina swung Lucas in her arms and kissed both his cheeks. She said something to him in Italian.

Jill turned to Rick. He was dressed in jeans and a light brown shirt open at the collar.

"Hi," was all she managed to get out.

"Hi, yourself."

His gaze combed her body, and she tingled as if he'd caressed her with his hands.

"You ready to go?" he asked.

No, I'm not ready for this, she cried silently. But instead, she nodded, then gave Angelina instructions for the evening.

"You'll need a sweater," Rick reminded her.

Jill went back into her bedroom and put on the pink pullover Maria had given her for Christmas. She ran a comb through her hair again and took a deep breath. Grabbing her purse, she kissed her son and headed for the door. Rick caught up with her and they made their way down the stairs. Jill looked around for his Durango, but instead, found the big black-and-chrome Harley parked in the driveway.

She stopped in her tracks. "You never said anything about going on your motorcycle."

Rick walked to the bike and pulled two helmets off the high handlebars. "I rode this bike all the way from Texas. It's perfectly safe, and I'm a good driver. I even bought you a helmet." He went back to her, took her hand and pulled her closer. "I'd never let anything hurt you, Jill."

All Jill could see was the big engine, the spiked wheels, the black leather seat. Excitement raced through her. She trusted Rick. She knew he would never do anything to hurt her. And it would be fun to take a nice leisurely ride around the lake. Suddenly she wanted to go.

She looked up at him. "You won't go too fast?"

"Oh, *cara*. Slow and easy is one of my favorite ways." As she knew—only too well.

Chapter Twelve

Jill loved the incredible sensation of the wind in her face, the soft vibration of the engine beneath her, the feel of Rick's muscular body against hers. The ride down the highway was exhilarating and she realized she didn't want it to end.

Her grip tightened around Rick's waist as she watched the sun slowly set behind the tall maple trees. Wildflowers blanketed the roadside in their vibrant spring colors. Off in the distance, the lake came into view, its water still and silent now that the last of the motorboats had come in for the day.

Rick downshifted, slowing the Harley, and turned off the main road onto a gravel path. They rode by a large picnic area, but didn't stop. Instead, he cut through a thick grove of trees, then came to a clearing at the lake's edge. About a hundred yards away, on the slope of the hill, was a white cottage.

Rick parked the motorcycle and shut off the engine.

"Oh, Rick, it's beautiful," Jill breathed. "But this is private property."

"The cottage is up for sale," he replied. "No one lives here now."

Jill climbed down from the bike. She stumbled a little, her legs wobbly after the twenty-minute ride. She pulled off her white helmet and shook out her hair. "But aren't we still trespassing?"

Rick set the kickstand, then removed his helmet. "We're not hurting anything, Jill. Just using a little of the shore for a few hours for a picnic."

A few hours, Jill thought. Even though it's still daylight, that was a long time to eat.

"But if you'd rather, we could go back to the official picnic area."

Jill's glance took in the breathtaking view, the calm water, reflecting the last of the sun's light. The fragrance of jasmine filled in the air. She looked at Rick. This gorgeous man wanted to spend the evening with her. She'd be crazy to leave.

"I guess if anyone comes by we can say we're thinking about buying the property."

"But that's a lie," he said, then smiled as he reached into his pocket and drew out a key. "Of course, if you had the key to the cottage, it wouldn't be."

She gasped. "Rick, where did you get that?"

He shrugged.

"Rick." She folded her arms.

"I talked to the Realtor today. He said I could come by tonight and check it out."

Rick saw Jill's stubborn look and knew she wasn't going to budge until he offered a more detailed explanation. "Okay, when I was a kid, we used to come to this side of the lake. Yesterday I rode out to pick a spot for us to have dinner. I saw that the cottage was for sale. I was curious, so I went by the Realtor and he showed it to me. He said if I wanted to I could bring you by tonight.''

Rick had left out a lot of the story, but now was not the time to tell it. He grabbed Jill's hand and pulled her toward the cottage before she decided he was crazy and headed back to the road to hitch a ride home. ''C'mon, I want you to see the inside.''

On the big back porch, he fitted the key in the lock, then pushed open the door.

''Rick, you aren't serious. You're really thinking about buying this cottage?''

''Yeah,'' he said, and reached in and flicked on the lights. He took her hand again and pulled her inside.

A weak protest died on her lips as the large living room came into view, complete with a huge brick fireplace and a pile of wood stacked against the hearth. Overstuffed chairs and a sofa circled a big coffee table.

''The Realtor told me the cottage has belonged to the same family since it was built back in the fifties. The parents recently retired to Florida, and none of the kids want to take the place on.''

Rick followed Jill into the kitchen. It boasted a breakfast bar that could seat half a dozen. He examined the handiwork of the built-in pine cabinets. Not bad, he thought as he opened one of the doors.

He noticed that Jill was interested in the doorjamb leading to the back porch. ''Oh, look, Rick. These lines here on the wood must mark how tall the kids were when they were little.'' She pointed to the bottom one, then progressed upward. ''Tommy, age four. Lisa, age seven. John, age ten. Jennie, age twelve. Four kids.'' She sighed. ''I love big families. You're never lonely.''

''And you never get any privacy, either. Believe me, Jill, getting into the bathroom is a production.''

She turned to him, and he saw the sadness in her eyes. "But you'd always have someone to talk to, to share things with. Kind of like having a best friend around all the time."

"Yeah, you're right." Rick shrugged. "Rafe was okay— as big brothers go. He was there when I needed him." Too bad he couldn't say the same about himself.

"It's good that you could come home and help out. I know how much they all missed you." She crossed the room and stood in front of him. "I bet you missed them, too."

He couldn't lie to her. She already knew too many of his secrets. "Yeah, I did." There had been times when he'd thought he'd die from the loneliness. Tuck helped, always able to sense his moods and draw him out. Rick shook away the painful thoughts and turned his attention back to Jill. "How about your family?"

Jill moved away from him.

"Jill?"

After a moment she faced him again. "We were never a close family, but Mother and I are still trying to work things out," she mumbled, then her face brightened as she glanced around the room. "I'd have given anything to be able to spend a summer in a place like this."

"You practically lived next door to Lake Michigan, and your parents never took you there on vacation?"

She went to the window. "My parents didn't do family vacations. Didn't believe in them. If you threw me in the water out there, I wouldn't even know how to swim. I spent my vacations in summer schools or some kind of educational camp. I have no idea where my parents went. They never took me along."

Her expression was so sad that Rick crossed the room and drew her into his arms. "I'm sorry, *cara*." He sighed. "I thought my summers were bad because of my asthma." He pulled back. "I can teach you to swim."

He kissed her forehead. "How about now?"

"Don't you think it's a little cold?" she asked wryly. "Besides, I don't have a suit."

He cocked an eyebrow. "Who said anything about a suit?"

"You're pretty sure of yourself, Mr. Covelli."

"A guy can always dream, Ms. Morgan." This time his mouth found hers in another kiss, and he couldn't resist turning up the heat a bit. When he finally released her, they were both breathing hard.

"Oh, my." She sighed. "I'm still not going into the water."

"You fell right into my plan. I was hoping to have to do more convincing."

She moved closer into his arms, where she fit perfectly.

"I can always handle more convincing." She lifted her face and offered him her lips, an invitation he couldn't turn down. He placed his mouth against hers, then parted her lips with his tongue. His calm was shattered as his hunger grew. A kiss wasn't all he wanted. He knew he should stop. Now. With the last of his control he pulled back.

"How about we go eat?" he suggested, not missing her confused look. "It's that or I'm going to have to jump in the lake to cool off."

She smiled. "Then let's eat."

They returned to the porch and Rick locked the door behind them.

Jill gazed out over the lake. "How can a family sell all these memories?"

Rick turned in time to see her blink back tears. "Sometimes you don't have a choice. And who's to say the memories were all good ones?" He knew for a fact that as wonderful as his family had been, things hadn't always been perfect—especially between him and his father.

Jill looked at him and nodded. "You're right. A beautiful house doesn't guarantee beautiful memories."

Rick took her hand and walked her back down the slope to the Harley. After opening a saddlebag, he pulled out a red plaid blanket. He spread it on the ground, then went back and removed a bottle of Chianti, along with two plastic glasses and plates. Next came the food. From a brown paper bag, he withdrew a container of lasagna and a green salad. Another trip to the bike produced a half loaf of freshly baked bread.

"I take it this meal is compliments of Maria," Jill said.

He pretended to be hurt. "I beg your pardon. I prepared this food myself. Well, almost. Nonna Vittoria was beside me."

Jill sat back on her heels and watched as Rick used a corkscrew to open the wine. It amazed her how this man seemed comfortable anywhere, doing anything.

He poured wine into the glasses, then handed her one. "I wasn't planning on bringing you all the way out here and then feed you hamburgers from the Pixie Diner." He corked the bottle and set it aside. "Mom taught all us kids the basics when we were young. Besides, when I couldn't play outside, I hung around and watched Nonna and Mom a lot. So I know my way around the kitchen."

She knew that wasn't the only room Rick Covelli knew his way around. Her body temperature rose at the thought of their night together.

He lifted his glass. "To a wonderful evening."

"To a wonderful evening," she agreed.

"Salute!"

"Salute!" she repeated, then took a sip of the dry red wine. "I'm not much of a drinker."

"Hey, if you don't care for the stuff…" he said, reaching for her glass. She pulled it back.

"I can handle one glass."

He smiled. "That's all I'm having, too. I'm driving." He grew serious. "I'd never chance harming you, *cara*."

"I know." She could barely get the words past her tight throat. "I trust you, Rick."

An easy smile appeared on his handsome face. "I wouldn't go that far, *bella*." He brought her hand to his lips and kissed her palm.

His gentle caress sent tremors of need through her. Jill closed her eyes. She wasn't going to survive this night. She wanted Rick. Badly. Her gaze met his, and she could see he felt the same.

He eliminated the space between them and took her face between his hands. She thought about pulling away, but the second he touched her, her hunger intensified.

His lips met hers and their passion caught fire. He shifted the angle of his head and deepened the kiss, then thrust his tongue into her mouth. Jill clutched his head and matched him touch for touch, stroke for stroke.

With a groan he pressed her down onto the blanket and stretched out beside her. Quickly his hands went to work on her body, driving her need to fever pitch.

Before she realized it, he had her blouse unbuttoned and was placing kisses along her throat, then moving to her breasts.

"Rick," she gasped when his mouth covered her nipple through the lacy bra. She combed her fingers through his hair and held his head, savoring the sensation. Between the cool breeze and the dampness she found herself shivering. His mouth sought hers again in another searing kiss and she pressed her body against his, quickly drowning in the wonderful feelings Rick created. She already knew what his lovemaking was like. But this time she had to stop before she was lost for good.

"Rick—" she pulled back "—stop, please."

He froze, then buried his head against her neck.

"Rick…"

Leaning on his elbow, his dark eyes met hers. "Jill, I'm sorry. I promised you this wouldn't happen again, and… Damn!" He sat up.

Jill pulled her blouse together and brought herself upright. "Rick, we just got a little carried away. I'm as much to blame as you." She worked to calm her racing pulse. She drew a deep breath and released it slowly. She watched Rick's broad back, knowing he was also fighting for control.

"Can't we just forget about this and eat our dinner?" She glanced at the neglected containers of food. "I can't wait to taste your lasagna."

He turned around, and his raven eyes seemed to melt into hers. Once again she was reminded of their night together. The night they'd made love. And she had no doubt he was thinking about the same thing.

He gave her a pained smile. "You're something, Jill Morgan. And we're an explosive combination. I'm not sure I can keep my hands off you." He stroked her cheek. "I'm trying like hell to keep my promise to you. I don't want you to hate me."

"I could never hate you, Rick." She took a deep breath. She loved him. "Why don't we forget about it. I want to eat."

"Sounds good." He straightened the blanket while she buttoned her blouse. Soon he had the plates filled.

After they'd eaten their fill, they spent the next thirty minutes relaxing. Rick sat against a tree, Jill at his side. She leaned close to him as they drank their wine and watched the lights twinkle along the shore. Jill realized she'd never been as comfortable with anyone as she was with Rick. Had never found anyone else so easy to talk to.

At eight-thirty Rick folded the blanket and put it in the saddlebag. They cleaned the area, then Rick got on the motorcycle. Jill strapped on her helmet and climbed on behind him. They were back on the road in minutes. The ride home was much more reflective for Jill than the ride out.

In her heart she felt that Rick Covelli was everything she wanted in a man. Kind, caring and loving.

In her head she knew that a man like Rick would never fit into her life. He would never settle down and be happy with a wife and family.

Jill's hold tightened around his waist. He might go back to Texas anytime. He'd told her often enough not to count on him.

No matter what happened now, the man was going to break her heart.

The following Thursday morning Rick arrived at the construction office about eight, just as Billy Jacobs walked in.

"Morning, Billy. I hear you've got some news."

The private investigator nodded. "Good news, I hope."

Rafe poked his head into the reception area. "Billy, everyone, come in here."

They all filed into the meeting room. Angelina switched on the telephone answering machine and joined them.

Billy placed his briefcase on the table and opened it as everyone sat down. "We located Adam Kirby." He pulled out a picture and passed it around. "Here's a recent photo of him. He's in Indianapolis, working for a large lumberyard."

"Hot damn!" Rafe roared. "Let's go after him."

Billy raised a calming hand. "I suggest we take it slow."

"And let him get away?" Rafe argued. "I don't think so."

Billy spoke again. "I don't believe Adam Kirby had anything to do with the material switch. But he might know something."

Rafe stood. "Then he can tell us who is responsible."

"You're right," Billy said. "And I think he'll talk, but I doubt he'll testify. With the accident, he might think he's guilty by association. So we're going to have to be careful about how we approach him."

Rick knew that the investigator was right. "What do you suggest, Billy?"

"Well, I think one of you should approach him. Maybe if he's shown the human connection, with the victim being your daddy and all, he might give you some information."

The two brothers exchanged a glance.

"I can go," Rafe volunteered, "but I'm afraid I'll want to tear him apart if he doesn't give me any answers."

Billy frowned. "We definitely don't need that."

"I'll go," Rick said. "Just tell me when and where."

"I don't think we should wait too long," Billy said.

"How about Monday?" Rick suggested. "We've got the Covelli and Sons picnic this weekend. Mom would get suspicious if I left town and missed it." Rick also had a date with Jill for that picnic. He didn't want to miss spending the day with her and Lucas, either.

"Monday it is," Billy agreed. He closed his briefcase and started to leave.

Rick caught up with him in the reception area. "Thanks, Billy."

"No problem. Just doing my job."

"And an excellent one at that." Rick glanced around to be certain no one overheard. "Make sure your bill is sent to my address in Midland." He reached into his wallet and pulled out a business card.

Billy nodded and headed for the door. When Rick turned he discovered Tony standing only a few feet away. His cousin shook his head. "Rafe isn't going to like what you just did."

"What? I'm only helping out until the company gets

back on its feet. Don't tell me you haven't fed money into the business a time or two."

Tony shrugged. "We all have, including your mother. But we do it openly and not because we feel guilty." He turned and went into his office.

Stunned, Rick followed Tony in and closed the door. "What gives you the right to judge my motives?"

"I'm worried about the people who'll get hurt when you decide to take off again."

"Whoa. Slow down. I've made a life for myself in Texas."

Tony sat on the edge of the desk. "And a good life." He gave a knowing smile. "It's surprising how easily you can find out business info when you know how to do it. You have an excellent credit rating, Rick, and impressive financial assets. Why have you kept your millionaire status a secret?"

Rick stopped cold, then shrugged. "I've never intentionally kept that a secret. No one ever asked."

"That's because we already know."

"You do?"

"Your father used his business connections to keep tabs on you. He wanted to make sure you were surviving out there on your own." Tony smiled. "You should have seen his pride showing when he confided your success to us. He told the family just before the accident."

"So Dad knew I'd done well for myself?"

"Yes. That was a comfort to him—your happiness and success. But he always wished you'd stuck around. And it would have been nice to hear from you over the years. Aunt Maria was the only one who ever got news."

Rick glanced away. "I tried at first. But it's hard staying in touch when you know your dad doesn't want you around."

Tony folded his arms over his chest. "Uncle Rafael

wasn't any stubborner than the other Covelli men. I heard it's an inherited trait.'' He grew serious. ''Just don't push us away. We want you to be a part of the family again.''

Rick wished that honesty was all it took to be considered a true Covelli. ''I want that more than you'll ever know.''

It had rained Sunday morning, but by one in the afternoon the sun had dried everything nicely for the picnic. The park and baseball diamond had been reserved for the annual Covelli picnic. The staff of Maria's Ristorante were all included, too.

Rick helped set things up at the park and hung the banner. It had been a long time since he'd attended the function. This year he was really looking forward to it. Maybe because he'd be able to take Jill and Lucas. Teach the kid how to play baseball.

He drove over to Jill's apartment and found her waiting for him. She was dressed in a pair of white shorts and a navy polo shirt, white tennis shoes on her feet. Lucas wore jean shorts and a red T-shirt. He also had on white tennis shoes.

''You ready to go to the picnic?'' Rick asked as he came through the door.

''Go…pic.'' Lucas rushed to him. Rick scooped him up and kissed both his cheeks. Then he reached for Jill with his free hand and placed a lingering kiss on her mouth. This had been their routine for the past week. He'd spent nearly every free moment at her place.

''You look too good to take out in public and let other men ogle you.''

She smiled. ''Why, Mr. Covelli, don't tell me you're a possessive male.''

''I'm a *normal* male, Jill. I don't want to share you.''

''I don't say anything when other women ogle you.''

He cocked an eyebrow. "Oh really? That's not how I remember the night I waited tables at the restaurant."

"I shouldn't have let you know. Your ego doesn't need any more stroking."

He whispered in her ear that he needed a lot of stroking and he wasn't talking about his ego. Jill blushed and punched him playfully in the stomach.

"Carry these things down to the car," she said. "I need to get the baked beans from the oven."

"Oh, my. Beautiful and she cooks, too." He looked at Lucas. "Did you know that your mom was so talented, squirt?"

Lucas nodded and grinned.

"Smart boy." Rick grinned back. "C'mon, we need to get these things into the car." He put Lucas down and handed the boy his baseball cap and sand bucket to carry. Rick grabbed the cooler, and together he and Lucas managed to negotiate the stairs. Rick opened the door and tossed the things in the back.

He turned as Jill came down the steps. It took his breath away just to watch her. No makeup, her hair pulled into a ponytail, she was downright adorable.

God, he wanted her. Not just for sex, although he knew he was dying a slow death from craving her this past week. But he'd also discovered he liked just being with her.

Ten minutes later they arrived at the park. Nearly fifty people, including kids, made the day's activities. It wasn't as big a group as in past years, but considering what the business had gone through, it was a good turnout. The women arranged the food and drink while the men and kids headed to the baseball diamond.

Rick took Lucas and joined the others. They had plastic balls and bats for the little ones to play first. When Rick took Lucas up to the plate, Tony tossed him the ball, and Rick helped the bat make contact, then he grabbed Lucas' hand and they ran around the bases together as everyone cheered.

Jill watched the game from the picnic table with the other women.

"This is the best time, when the men take charge of the kids," one of the young mothers said. "Enjoy it. Once the big game starts, they'll forget about everything else except winning."

"We can take turns watching the kids," Jill suggested.

"Rick Covelli, is he your man?" the young mother asked.

Jill swallowed at the brunette's bluntness. "I'm his date, yes," she answered. And his lover, she thought. Not wanting to answer any more questions, she busied herself setting up the tables. Soon the men and kids lined up for lunch. It was amazing how much food they could eat.

Rick stayed close to her side during the meal, helping her with Lucas. Her son did a pretty good job of putting away the food and afterward went off to play in the sandbox. Two twelve-year-old girls had been put in charge of watching the little ones.

At three o'clock it was time for the big game. Rafe was already warming up as pitcher while Tony practiced at bat. A few of the women went out to join the men, but Jill hung back, helping with the cleanup.

Rick called to her to come out onto the field.

She shook her head. "I've never played baseball before."

"Then it's time you learned," he yelled back.

Angelina came up to her. "Here, use one of the extra gloves. Just don't let my brothers bully you."

Rick finally ran in to get her.

"You'll be sorry you wanted me out here," she warned.

"Never."

He hugged her.

"Okay, it's time to choose teams."

"Captains," Rafe said, looking around. "Tony and how about…Rick."

They both agreed, then picked the players for their respective team. Jill went with Rick. When the game got under way, she was sent to the outfield while Rick pitched and Angelina played first base. Luckily none of the balls were hit Jill's way and she just stood there until Rick waved her in. She wasn't as lucky, though, when it was her turn to bat.

Rick showed her how to choke up on the bat, and instructed her to keep her eye on the ball. He gave her a pat on the bottom for good luck and sent her to home plate.

The first ball sailed by. "Strike one," the umpire called.

Jill glanced back at Rick. He cupped his mouth and yelled more encouragement to her. Determined not to make a fool of herself, she stepped up to the plate again. Eye on the ball, she repeated to herself over and over again.

Smiling, Tony began the pitching motion and threw the softball toward her. Jill's heart pounded in her chest as she waited, then swung at it. To her amazement, she made contact. Without seeing how far the ball went, she started to run toward first base. Her team cheered when she made it safely. Rick came out and praised her efforts.

"Lucky bunt," Tony yelled.

"We planned it that way," Rick said as he walked up to the plate for his turn. "Get ready to run, Jill," he said, then aimed his bat to center field. "I'm going to hit a long one right out there."

"In your dreams," Tony mocked.

"I'm your worst nightmare, cuz." Rick took a few practice swings. Then with a cocky smile, he winked at Jill. Her heart soared just at the sight of him. In his jean shorts and T-shirt, he was a beautifully built man.

He stepped into the box and exchanged a few words in

Italian with his cousin. "C'mon, just send one over the plate."

Tony served up the first pitch, and Rick hit it sky-high. Jill watched as it went all the way to the fence.

"Home run," the umpire called.

Jill began to run with Rick close on her heels. When she crossed home plate, he came up behind her and lifted her into his arms.

"You did great, Jill." He put her down.

"That was fun."

"I'll have to show you more. Maybe next time you'll keep your eyes open."

"I didn't shut my eyes," she argued.

Rick grinned and Jill realized she liked baseball, after all.

When the game ended, Rick's team had beaten Tony's team ten to eight. But the best part was they'd all had a great time.

Jill returned to the tables to find that the Ashmores had shown up for the festivities. Bob was talking with Rick. Karyn looked uncomfortably large. She was due in two weeks. Jill sat down next to her friend. "I'm glad you made it."

"Beats sitting at home waiting for labor pains to start."

"Ah, I remember it well." Jill laughed. "I take it Bob isn't giving you a moment's peace?"

Karyn frowned. "I have to lock the bathroom door to get any privacy. If he goes to work, I get a call every hour on the hour. He drives me nuts."

Jill smiled. "Don't knock it. The man loves you."

Karyn gleamed. "Speaking of love, you and Rick look like you're getting along pretty well."

"We're just fooling around."

"One of my favorite former pastimes. Tell me all about

it. Since there's been no sex in my life this last month, let me live vicariously through you.''

"Karyn!'' Jill glanced around to see if anyone was listening. Luckily no one was.

"I'm just kidding. But he's a good-looking guy.''

"So is Bob.''

"And I'm eight and a half months pregnant and big as a house.'' Karyn's eyes suddenly filled with tears. "I'll never look like I did before.''

Jill spent the next ten minutes soothing her friend, remembering how hard that last month was. Now with summer coming, Karyn had to be miserable with the heat and anxious for the baby to arrive.

"It'll get better,'' Jill said, looking over her shoulder to where Lucas was asleep in the portable playpen. "Then you get one of these cherubs. And you won't have another full night's sleep for years.'' She leaned over and stroked his golden curls. "He sure played hard today.''

"So did his mama,'' Karyn said. Then she nodded toward Rick, who was talking to Rafe. "Seriously, how's it going with him?''

"We've decided to take it slow.''

"Then how come he looks like he wants to devour you?''

Jill blushed. She didn't need to think about Rick wanting her. Things were tough enough already. "We're friends.''

"Right,'' Karyn mocked, rubbing her rounded stomach. "And I'm Mother Goose.''

They were both laughing when Rick walked over and sat down next to Jill. "Hi, Karyn. How are things going?''

"I'm a little uncomfortable. Anxious for the baby to get here.''

He turned his attention to Jill. "After we clean up here, everyone's heading over to the Whistle Stop in Bedford. Angelina said she'd watch Lucas.''

Jill wanted to go with Rick. "Doesn't Angelina want to go, too?"

Rick shook his head. "She said no and offered to baby-sit."

Angelina came over and picked up Lucas. "I'm not in the mood to go out." She kissed the boy's cheek. "I'd much rather spend time with this little guy." She looked at her brother. "I'll take your car because of the baby seat and you can take mine. Now you need to load up the play-pen and his diaper bag and anything else he might need to spend the night with his Auntie Lina."

"Sounds like a plan," Rick said. "Jill?"

"I guess it's all right."

Rick leaned down and kissed his sister's cheek. "I owe you one."

"A big one," she teased.

Rick hugged Jill to his side. "It's worth it."

The Whistle Stop was next door to the train station in Bedford. It reminded Jill of the television show *Cheers*. The hardwood floors were scarred but gleaming. So was the oak bar, and the high stools were filled with patrons. A jukebox sat next to a small dance floor. Pool tables and dartboards were in the crowded back room.

The group made their way to a corner near the jukebox and pulled a few tables together. One of the guys dropped money into the jukebox, and the room came alive with music. Some of the couples got up and began to dance. A few minutes later Rafe and Tony arrived with four pitchers of beer and a tray full of glasses.

They passed them around and Rafe raised his glass. "To the Covellis. *Salute!*"

Everyone raised their glass and shouted, *"Salute!"*

Rick looked at Jill. "You having fun?" he asked.

She grinned and nodded. "I haven't been out like this in

a long time. The whole day's been fun. Thanks for taking us."

"You're welcome." His eyes locked with hers. "I had a great time, too." The music changed to a soft ballad and Rick pushed back his chair. "C'mon, it's not over yet. Let's dance."

She didn't hesitate as he took her hand and led her to the floor. He pulled her into his arms and gently pressed her head against his shoulder. They began to move to the music of Mariah Carey's "Hero."

Rick savored the feel of Jill against him, her soft curves, her thighs brushing his. Never wanting to let her go, he tightened his hold and slowed his steps. He took a deep breath, but it didn't help calm his racing heart. When her fingers touched the base of his neck, a warm shiver ran down his spine and he grew hard.

Somehow he managed to dance her into a secluded corner. A little privacy would be nice, he thought. They hadn't been alone all day. He whispered in her ear, "Just holding you close does unbelievable things to me. Your body feels so good next to mine."

Jill pulled back, her blue eyes dark with longing. "Oh, Rick."

He savored the feel of her body against his. "I feel the same way, *cara.* I lose all my willpower when you're this close."

"So do I," she whispered, and he heard her breathing increase. "Take me home," she murmured.

His heart sank. Had he pushed her too far?

Suddenly her hands moved up his arms. "I want you to make love to me."

He needed no further encouragement.

Chapter Thirteen

Jill was trembling with anticipation by the time Rick pulled up in front of her apartment. He helped her out of the car and they silently walked up the stairs. She unlocked the door and stepped aside. Rick followed right behind her. He took hold of her arm and drew her to him, then brought his mouth to hers.

Jill released a groan and dropped her purse and keys. She threaded her fingers into his hair.

Rick pulled back. "Tell me to leave now before it's too late. I want you so much I can't handle—"

She pressed her finger to his lips. "I don't want you to leave, Rick. Make love to me. Now."

The moonlight streamed through the open door, and she could see his hungry look.

"You mean it?"

"Yes." She placed a trembling hand on his chest, feeling his heat, reveling in his rapid breathing. "I want you."

He closed the door. At the sound of the lock catching, Jill's heart went into a tailspin. She didn't have time to think anymore as Rick swung her up in his arms and she wrapped hers around his neck. Her lips found his as he carried her toward the bedroom. He used his foot to push open the door. The room was dark, except for the moonlight coming through the window.

He lowered her to the floor, letting her body slide down his. She gasped, feeling every rock-hard inch of him. He cupped her jaw and kissed her again, taking his time to taste, to nibble, tease her mouth. When he stopped she was whimpering in need.

"I'm going to love you, *cara,* so slowly and thoroughly that we'll both die a little from all the pleasure."

"Rick, I'm dying now."

"You're not ready." He reached over and flicked on the small light next to the bed. "Soon," he promised.

Rick took the hem of her shirt and tugged it over her head, all the while telling himself to go slowly. Next he unbuttoned her shorts, then fumbled with the zipper until Jill helped and they dropped to the floor.

Real smooth, Covelli, he thought, cursing his own nervousness.

Then his attention turned again to Jill. She stood in front of him in only her panties and bra.

He took a calming breath. "Take your hair down," he said.

She smiled shyly. "Only if you take off your clothes."

He jerked his T-shirt off over his head, then kicked off his shoes. Next came his shorts.

Jill reached out and touched his chest. "You are so beautiful," she breathed. "So hard, yet your skin..." She stopped speaking and pressed her lips to his flesh. Dear, Lord. He thought he'd die. His fists clenched as her tongue glided over his nipple, driving him wild.

He leaned down and kissed the soft skin at the base of her neck as his hands roamed over her body. He released the clasp of her bra and pulled it off her shoulders. Soon his hands were caressing her breasts, his mouth closing over her nipple, teasing, suckling, until she moaned in pleasure.

He pressed her down on the bed and lay next to her. His mouth covered hers, drinking in her heavenly taste, her hunger.

"Oh, Rick!" she cried.

With a downward stroke his hand moved over her slim waist seeking the fevered dampness between her thighs. She cried out again as his fingers tested her readiness.

He couldn't wait any longer, either. He jerked off his briefs, then reached for his shorts and pulled out his wallet. In moments he managed to put on protection and was back in Jill's arms.

He gazed down at her beauty as he moved over her, and nearly lost it. She reached up and cupped his face. He turned to place a kiss on her palm. She was so sweet and, in so many ways, very innocent.

"I want you, Jill. More than I ever thought possible." His voice quivered as he pushed inside her. Then he slid his hands beneath her bottom and plunged in even more.

"Oh." The surprised cry rushed out of her.

"Ah, *cara*," he whispered as he pulled back, nearly withdrawing, only to push in again, completing the miraculous sensation.

Another cry of pleasure escaped her, causing him to increase the pace. He bent his head and took a nipple into his mouth, feeling the bud harden against his tongue.

When her legs tightened around his waist, he knew she was close. "Let it go, Jill," he encouraged her. He wanted to make her explode with passion. He moved his hand between their bodies and touched her. Almost at once, Jill arched against him, then moments later cried out his name.

He braced his hands on either side of her face and absorbed her convulsions as he slowed the tempo. He gazed into her deep blue eyes and was lost…forever. Leaning down, he brushed his lips against hers.

She took hold of his face and used her mouth and tongue to drive him over the edge. His grip tightened on her as his thrusts grew stronger and faster again, finally rocketing him into oblivion. He cried out her name just as she moaned his.

Perfect. Nothing could be so perfect. Rick tried to slow his breathing. He'd never felt so close to anyone. He raised his head and saw the tears in Jill's eyes, and he had trouble holding back his own emotions. It was then he knew he could never let her go.

She had buried herself in his soul.

Rick woke up the next morning, felt Jill curled up against him and smiled. Memories from last night flashed through his head, and he immediately grew hard. He guessed three times hadn't been enough. The last time they'd made love had been at dawn. As the morning light caressed her skin, they'd both found ecstasy in each other's arms. And now he wanted her again.

Jill made a purring sound and moved against him. Rick tightened his hold, leaned down and placed a light kiss on her head. She stirred again and opened her eyes. Her sleepy, blue-eyed gaze locked with his.

"Rick," she said hoarsely.

"You were expecting someone else?"

That made her smile. "No, but I usually don't wake up with a man in my bed."

He moved against her naked body. "Well, as I recall, last night you woke up next to me twice."

She blushed. "I guess we got a little carried away."

"I'd say we got a lot carried away. What about trying for going-out-of-our-minds?"

She glanced at the clock. "We need to think about Lucas's arrival. Angelina could be here soon. I'd better get up and shower."

"Sure," Rick said. He wasn't going to push her. Not after the closeness they'd shared last night. "How about you shower and I'll fix breakfast? If you have pancake mix, we're all set."

"There's a box in the cupboard."

She hugged the sheet closer to her chest, looking for an escape route. "Then I'll just go and take my shower."

Rick smiled, knowing that with the double bed against the wall, she had to climb over him or wait until he got up. He wasn't moving.

Jill finally made her move to exit the bed, but when she swung her leg over his, their bodies touched. Rick couldn't resist, drawing her against him. Their eyes met and so did their mouths, in a kiss that relayed hunger and need.

"Oh, *cara,*" he whispered, "I want you again."

"Rick, we can't," she pleaded. "There isn't time." She broke his hold and climbed out of bed. She managed to hang on to the sheet, but Rick was stripped of any covering. His desire for her was evident.

"I'll be out in a few minutes." She turned and rushed into the bathroom, the sheet trailing behind her.

Jill made it into the bathroom and shut the door, listening to Rick's laughter. She brushed her hair from her face as she replayed last night's lovemaking.

Oh, God. What had come over her to act that way? And this morning she'd wanted him again. She turned on the faucet and climbed in, letting the cool water wash over her. Soon the water warmed and Jill felt the spray begin to stimulate her skin. Her thoughts returned to Rick, recalling how his skilled hands had caressed her body. How he'd brought her to heights of pleasure she'd never believed possible.

Her reverie was interrupted when Rick knocked and poked his head in the door. "Jill, there's a phone call for you."

Dread overtook her and she wrapped a towel around herself. She jerked back the shower curtain. "Who is it?"

He frowned. "Your mother."

"Oh, God."

"I'm sorry, Jill. I only answered the phone because I thought it was about Lucas."

"It's okay," she said. But it wasn't. Dealing with Claudia was never easy, but this time... Jill didn't even want to think about it. She grabbed the silk robe off the back of the door and slipped it on as she hurried into the kitchen.

She picked up the receiver. "Hello, Mother."

"Jillian, what's going on there?"

"Nothing."

"You entertain men early in the morning?"

"Of course not, Mother. That was Rick Covelli. He's a...friend." Jill glanced at Rick. He was standing across the room, shirtless.

"It's barely eight o'clock in the morning."

"Mother, I know—"

"What will the neighbors think?" Claudia interrupted her. "I warned you about this. How can you expect to get any respect if your behavior isn't any better than... You should know that letting a man spend the night in your bed doesn't guarantee he'll stick around. Haven't you learned anything from your experience with Keith?"

"Mother, stop," Jill said, trying to hold back tears. She refused to cheapen what had happened between her and Rick.

She looked at him and could see the concern in his eyes. But was her mother right? Had last night only been about sex? There had been no vows of love exchanged, no commitment made. And he'd been telling her all along that there never would be. She would be left once again. Alone—to pick up the pieces of her shattered heart.

"Mother, can I call you later?"

"What good would it do? I thought you wanted to work things out with your father. You know he's been thinking about coming to your graduation, but if he finds out about this it will break his heart again."

Jill squeezed her eyes shut and tears ran down her face. "I'm sorry." She hung up the phone and immediately Rick hurried to her side.

"Are you all right?"

She nodded and pushed him away.

"What did your mother say to you?"

"She was upset because you're here."

"Jill, you're an adult. Your mother can't run your life."

Jill swung around and glared at him. "I'm not like you. It's important to me what my parents think."

She saw the flash of pain in his eyes and regretted her words, but she had to make him understand. "I have been trying to bridge the gap between us since I had Lucas." Her fist clenched in frustration. "My father has never even seen his grandson. I was hoping he'd come to my graduation. That would be a start. They were coming, Rick. She'd called to tell me my father finally agreed. Now they... Oh God, this hurts."

"I'm sorry." He tried to hold her. "It'll be okay."

"You don't understand." She avoided his touch, knowing she had to stay strong. How could she trust another man—love another man—only to have him walk away from her? She couldn't take that again. Her heart wouldn't survive.

"They'll come around, Jill."

Even Rick didn't believe his words. He hated to see her

so miserable. They'd just shared an incredible night together. He'd never cared about a woman so much. Now the best thing he could do for her was let her go. She needed her family now, not him.

"I think you should call your father. Try and work things out. It's the only way." He knew from his own experience that he and his father never had a chance to work things out. Rick had waited too long and now his father was gone. He couldn't let that happen to Jill.

"And what should I tell him? That my relationship with you is different from the one with Keith?" She stared at him, pain evident in her eyes. "We don't want the same things, Rick. Like you said before, you'll be leaving town soon."

"What if my plans change?"

Her back straightened. "Well, mine haven't. My first concern is my son. I can't have men walking in and out of our lives. It's not fair to either one of us."

Pain gripped his chest, and Rick went into the bedroom. He got his shirt and put on his shoes. When he returned, Jill was still in the kitchen. "I think it's best if I leave town."

She didn't say anything, but a lone tear found its way down her cheek. They both knew his leaving was for good.

"God, Jill, the last thing I want is to hurt you." He ached to hold her in his arms, but his dad's words echoed in his head. He wasn't able to stick around for the long haul. He had to get out of there. He reached out and touched her cheek. Big mistake. The need to hold her in his arms nearly killed him. He wanted her more than his next breath. She was a burning in his gut he knew would never go away. Jill Morgan was his dream. A dream he could never have. He leaned down and placed a tender kiss against her mouth, then drew back. "Ciao, *cara*."

After walking to the door, he paused, thinking about

turning back, trying to convince Jill that they belonged together. Instead, he walked outside and started down the steps.

Angelina was coming up, carrying Lucas. "Ree..." the boy called, his arms outstretched.

Rick greeted his sister, then took the child into his arms. "How you doin', squirt?"

"Ride horsey."

"Good idea," he said. "But I can't. I have to go somewhere."

"Ree...pay," Lucas said stubbornly.

"Can't today, son," he choked on the last word, never realizing until this minute how much he wanted Lucas as his son. The idea shook him to the core. "Jill's upstairs." Rick ignored his sister's curious look.

"You're not going to be around?"

Rick shook his head, avoiding eye contact with Angelina. "I've got to go to Indianapolis today, so can you do me a favor?"

"Sure."

"Will you be there for Jill? She's having a rough time with her parents."

"I would think you'd want to be there for her," Angelina said.

"Believe me, I'm the last person she needs messing up her life." Rick kissed Lucas goodbye, handed the boy back to Angelina and hurried down the steps, listening to the child calling for him to come back.

Rick ached to stay, but fate wasn't on his side. Wouldn't he ever get the girl, or the family, he'd longed for?

At eleven o'clock that night, Rick walked into the kitchen of the Covelli house. He'd dropped Billy Jacobs off at the motel after their two-hour drive from Indianapolis.

Rick was exhausted, but he and Jacobs had gotten what they wanted. The name of the man who signed the receipt for the faulty building materials.

Rafe walked into the kitchen. "Hey, you're back."

He hugged Rick. For the first time in a long time, Rick didn't feel uncomfortable with the touch. He needed his family now more than ever.

Rafe pulled out a chair for both of them. "Sit down and tell me what happened."

Rick sat. "We found Adam Kirby. He's living in Greenfield with his wife and working for a construction company there."

"I need coffee for this." Rafe poured them both a cup and moved back to the table. "Did he remember anything about the time he worked at Hardin's?"

"Yeah, but he was pretty reluctant to talk about it."

"But he finally told you?"

Rick nodded. "Did you have a man working for you by the name of Adler? Sam Adler?"

"Sure, Sam was with Dad for five years." Rafe's dark eyes narrowed. "You mean Sam was responsible for the accident?"

"We're not sure. All Kirby could tell us was that Sam and Pete Hardin, Jr. always worked together on any ordering of supplies. Kirby wasn't eager to reveal too much, but he said that a lot of strange things went on while the owner's son, Pete Hardin, ran the lumberyard those six months. Looks like we've got a lot more digging to do before we reach the conclusion to this."

Rafe grinned. "You've done so much, Rick. We have names to work with now. In time we'll get the guy. I just know it."

Rick wished he could share the optimism. "I'll keep Billy on the job until we find Adler. Billy can contact me in Midland."

Rafe looked puzzled. "Aren't you going to stick around to see this through?"

"I'm not sure it's such a good idea." Rick suddenly noticed Nonna Vittoria standing in the doorway, her face ashen. She was dressed for bed in a rose-colored robe and slippers. Her white hair hung in a long braid.

Anger tinged Rafe's voice. "Why? I thought you were going to stay around awhile."

"I have responsibilities in Texas. You know that."

"What about Jill?"

Rick's head jerked up. "It's better this way."

"Damn!" Rafe smacked his fist on the table and stood up. "That girl thinks you hung the moon. How can you walk away?"

The two men exchanged glares, then Rafe turned and walked out of the room.

Rick sat there staring into his coffee cup. He finally glanced at his grandmother. "Well, aren't you going to yell at me, too?"

"You don't need me to do anything but love you." She walked across the room and sat down next to her grandson. "Why, Rick? Why do you punish yourself?"

"You punished yourself for everything that went wrong between you and your papa. You both were stubborn Covelli men and wanted different things out of life. I regret that you didn't resolve your problems before the accident, but you blame yourself for everything."

Vittoria reached out and touched his cheek. "You are so much like your *nonno* and your papa. Those two didn't always get along, either. And maybe if Rafaele hadn't been so stubborn, you would not have stayed away so long."

"Dad didn't want me here," Rick said, still feeling the hurt. "Nothing I did was ever good enough for him."

"Your papa had no right to ask so much of you." She shook her head. "I should have smoothed things out between you two. But I thought that Rafaele would understand why you had to leave. He was a good son, and I will miss him until the day I die, but that doesn't mean he should have pushed you away."

Rick took her hands in his. "No, Nonna. If I'd come home and worked with Dad in the business, none of this would have happened. He might still be alive."

"No, Enrico. Your *padre*'s fate was in the hands of another."

"But maybe—"

Vittoria touched a finger to his mouth. "When you left, it was to find your own way—just like your *nonno* did when he came back to Italy for me. Then with me, his new bride, he moved here and started the business. His family needed him to stay in Pennsylvania and work in the factory, but Enrico wanted a better life. He had his dreams, just like your papa—and just like you deserved yours."

Rick wanted to believe his grandmother's words so that the guilt and loneliness he felt would disappear. "I caused Dad and the family so much trouble, and I didn't finish college."

"Children are never easy to raise. They all cause some sort of hurt, but as parents, we forget about it." Tears came to her eyes as she pressed her hand to her chest. "Because you make my heart full with so much love."

"And you make my heart full, too."

Maria's voice rang out.

Rick turned to find his mother in the doorway. "Mom…"

Maria walked to the table and Rick pulled out another chair. "It is hard being the second son, Rick," she began. "Your brother knew he wanted to be a carpenter when he started kindergarten." She rested her hands on her son's arm, her dark gaze on his. "But you were different. Even as sick as you were in your childhood, you were never set on anything. You wanted to test everything. But we, your *nonna* and I, were so afraid to allow you to do anything.'' A sad smile appeared. ''We tried to fill your time with games and books, but you couldn't understand why we wouldn't let you out to play.''

''I did later,'' Rick said, wanting her to know he understood.

''But it put a strain on your relationship with your father. Once your asthma went away, you were like a tiger—you wanted to make up for all the time you lost. We couldn't hold you back. And your father didn't know how to handle your…freedom.''

Nonna added, ''And Rafaele wanted you to accept everything he told you. All you wanted was to experience life. And you had a right.''

Maria exchanged a look with her mother-in-law. ''Our only regret is that you and your father never made peace.''

Rick glanced away. ''I wish…''

''Listen, son, your father was proud of you,'' Maria said. ''He may not have liked you going away from home, but he bragged about you all the time. He loved you, Rick. Just as I love you.''

''And I love you, too.'' He pulled her into an embrace. This would keep him going, knowing his family loved him.

She drew back. ''Please, Rick, won't you stay here where you belong, with your family?''

He hesitated, thinking about Jill. He couldn't stay around here, knowing he couldn't be a part of her life, knowing he couldn't be what she needed. ''I don't think it's a good idea.''

''Why?'' Maria's eyes grew intense. ''Because of Jill?''

Rick walked to the counter. ''I'm wrong for her.''

''Good heavens! It didn't look that way at the picnic.''

He couldn't meet his mother's eyes. He turned to his *nonna,* then glanced away. ''We were just horsing around.''

''Rick, why is it so hard for you to say you love her?''

Oh, Lord. A pain tightened his chest. ''Okay, I love her. But I'm not what she needs in her life.''

Maria crossed the room and Vittoria followed. ''What she needs is a man who loves her and her son. And Jill loves you.''

Hope sprang to his chest, and he found it difficult to breathe.

Maria patted his hand. ''Have you told her how you feel?''

Rick shook his head.

''*Uomini!* Men!'' Vittoria gasped. ''Have you said that you want to stay in Haven Springs? That you've started making plans?''

Ashamed, Rick lowered his head. ''No.'' He'd spent most of his time with Jill telling her not to expect him to be around.

''Rick, are you going to stay?''

His excitement died. ''I'm not sure if I'm capable of staying in one place.'' He thought about his small apartment in Midland, Texas. He could have easily afforded a house, but never had any desire to buy one. ''I guess I'm not the type of man who settles down.''

''That's crazy,'' Vittoria said. ''Who tells you this?''

Rick shrugged. ''Dad once said I wasn't capable of sticking to anything. That I was a wanderer.''

Vittoria muttered something in Italian. ''Your *nonno* Enrico was a wanderer, as were his parents. A man needs to find someone to make him feel that he's home. Your *nonno* came back to Italy and fought for me. He took me away from another man. Even braved the curse to keep me. Do you love Jill that much? Enough to want to fight for her?''

Rick was surprised how easily he could answer. ''Yes, I love her that much. I want to make a home here with her and Lucas.''

''God bless you,'' Vittoria said, looking heavenward.

"He finally admits it. Now I can go to sleep." She kissed them both and left the room.

Maria turned back to her son. "If you love Jill so much you should be honest with her. She will come around." She smiled. "Oh, she loves my handsome son. Just be honest with her. Tell her how you feel. From the heart. Tell her you will always take care of her and her child."

Rick's eyes narrowed at his mother's knowing look. "How did you know how I felt?"

"It's a mother's job. Sit down," she said, and they both moved to the table and sat.

A wide smile transformed her face. Maria Covelli was so beautiful, Rick could understand why his father fell in love with her. "Now," she said, "you and I have to figure out a way to make Jill realize you are the perfect man for her."

Rick looked down at himself. Black jeans and T-shirt. And shaggy hair. "Perfect" wouldn't be the word he'd use for himself.

Maybe it was time he came out of hiding.

Thursday afternoon Jill rushed through the hospital doors. An hour ago she'd received a call at the restaurant from Bob, saying that Karyn had gone into labor.

As soon as Jill had gotten Angelina to baby-sit for Lucas, she'd left for the hospital to help out. She'd promised her friend she'd be there for her, just like Karyn had been when Jill had given birth to Lucas.

When the elevator doors opened, she hurried to the desk to ask where to find Karyn Ashmore. When the information was given, Jill headed for the room. She stopped short at the door when she took in the intimate scene.

Bob was rubbing Karyn's back and soothing her with his voice, telling her how well she was doing and how much he loved her for carrying his baby. And how lucky their child was to get a mother like her.

Jill stepped back before being seen. She needed to compose herself. Maybe Karyn didn't need her. She had Bob. After all, wasn't this a special time to share with the one you loved?

Her thoughts immediately went to Rick. She covered her eyes, but the image didn't go away. The look on his face when she told him to leave her apartment. He'd been physically gone for two days now, but that didn't erase him from her thoughts—the memory of his kisses, his touch, his lovemaking.

No! She couldn't think about Rick. He wasn't in her life anymore. She had to move on. Jill smoothed her hair, pasted a smile on her face and stepped inside.

This time she interrupted her friend in the throes of a heavy contraction. Jill went to Karyn's side and took her hand, hoping to talk her through the pain.

Bob wiped his wife's face with a cool damp cloth. "That was a good one," he said.

"Like you could feel it," Karyn said flippantly.

Bob exchanged a quick glance with Jill and shrugged.

"Hey, Bob, how about I take over for a while and you run out for a bathroom break and get something to drink?"

Bob hesitated.

"Go on," Karyn encouraged. "Believe me, I'll be here when you get back."

"All right." He kissed his wife and took off.

"Oh, Jill, I've been so hard on him the past two hours." Tears filled Karyn's eyes. "It's like someone has taken over my body and I can't control it. I've heard stories about women getting mean during labor but…"

Jill wiped her friend's face. "Believe me when this baby is born, Bob isn't going to care about anything you said to him during labor. So rest."

"I can't. Talk to me. Oh…" she groaned, taking Jill's hand, "here comes another one."

"Okay, take a big breath. That's it. Now breathe… slow…and easy." Jill held the watch and eyed the second hand. "Okay, you're coming out of it. Keep breathing. The pain should be easing up…about now."

Karyn relaxed and rubbed her stomach. "That was a strong one. Now give me an update on your life—take my mind off the pain."

So Jill had no choice but to tell her about school and how Lucas liked being in day care. Even though Karyn knew about her breakup with Rick, that didn't stop her from giving Jill a lecture on how crazy she was to let a man like Rick Covelli get away. Jill tried to tell her friend that she didn't let him go—he decided to leave on his own.

Then she straightened Karyn's pillow. "Hey, you just concentrate on having this baby."

"Remember, friend," Karyn said, "If you need to talk I'm here."

"And at the moment you're a little busy. Besides, some things I have to handle on my own."

"Did you give the guy a chance? Or do you just think your parents won't approve?"

Jill looked away. "It doesn't matter anymore. Rick's probably on his way back to Midland."

"And you're miserable— Oh, here comes another pain."

Jill talked her through it, relieved that she didn't have to answer any more questions. Someone like Karyn, someone secure in her husband's love, wouldn't understand.

Jill eased her through the contraction, then spooned slivers of ice into her friend's mouth and gave her some chapstick for her dry lips. "This reminds me of when I was in labor with Lucas. I was so afraid, but you kept me focused, telling me that everything was going to be just fine. That as long as I loved my baby, he'd grow up happy and healthy.'' Jill looked at her fatigued friend. Karyn's face was flushed, her hair damp and straight. "You were right."

Another pain started, this time more intense, and Karyn had to begin her panting breaths to stay in control. By the time the contraction ended, Bob had reappeared. Then the doctor came in to examine Karyn. Exhausted, Jill left and went out to the waiting room—only to discover Rick sitting on the vinyl sofa.

"Rick," she whispered as all the air rushed out of her lungs in a long sigh. It had been only three days, but it felt like an eternity. He looked so good. He wore his familiar black jeans, but with a denim shirt.

He stood. "How's Karyn doing?"

"About as well as can be expected during labor. What are you doing here?"

He smiled. "I thought I might stand by for support." He picked up a paper sack from the table. "Nonna sent over some *berlingaccio*. For the new baby, a blessed medal for the crib."

He started to give her the sweet bread and medal. Their hands touched. Immediately Jill pulled back.

"I'm sorry," she said. She didn't need this now. Her emotions were too close to the surface.

"Maybe it would be better if I go," he said. His gaze searched her face as if waiting for her to decide.

She had trouble with her own anguish when she saw the pain in his eyes. Had she caused it?

"Please stay," she said. "I mean, if you have the time. I don't think Karyn's going to last more than a few hours. I'm sure Bob could use some male support. Someone to hand a cigar to." She tried to smile, fighting the urge to take comfort in his arms. No matter how much she needed him, she had to resist. It would only make things harder later on.

A commotion in the hall drew their attention. Bob came running toward them.

"They're taking her into delivery. The baby's coming." He grinned, although his voice was tense and ragged. He hugged Jill. "Thanks for coming." He looked at Rick and they clasped hands. "Thanks to you, too, man."

"Anytime. I'll go buy the cigars."

Bob smiled and took off down the hall.

Rick watched in envy as Bob hurried to his wife, kissed her and held her hand as she was wheeled down the hall.

Rick turned to Jill and saw her tears. "Are you all right?"

"Yeah. I just know how much Bob and Karyn want this baby and how hard it's been to get to this point. They've been married seven years and Karyn had trouble conceiving. I'm so happy for them."

"They're a lucky couple to have each other." Rick watched Jill, and love swelled in his chest. Somehow, some way, he and Jill were going to have the same thing. He just had to find a way to convince her he belonged in her life—and that this time he would stay.

Chapter Fourteen

Rick parked his car along a tree-lined street in a quiet suburb of Chicago. From under the shade of a large maple, he looked around the upper-middle-class neighborhood, two-story brick homes with perfectly manicured lawns and clipped hedges.

Jill grew up here.

He pulled in a calming breath and released it as he ran his fingers through his recently cut hair. Feeling the short strands, he grimaced.

"This had better work," he muttered.

Steeling himself for the upcoming confrontation, he straightened his tie and climbed out of the rental car. He shrugged into his navy suit jacket and reached back inside for his briefcase, thinking about the seemingly impossible job ahead of him.

But if he and Jill were to have a chance together, this was the only way. His chest tightened; he didn't want to think about a life without her. He loved her so much he was willing to try anything. Even if that meant flying to Chicago to convince Jackson and Claudia Morgan to work things out with their daughter.

He stepped up on the curb and double-checked the number on the Tudor-style home. Taking another breath, he opened the wrought-iron gate and walked up the long brick walkway. He arrived at the door and, before he lost his nerve, rang the bell.

Seconds ticked by as the pounding of his heart grew louder. Finally the door opened and an attractive middle-aged woman appeared. Rick saw the resemblance to Jill immediately. Claudia Morgan's skin was fair, her blond hair streaked sparingly with gray. She had blue eyes that mirrored her daughter's.

Her gaze combed him. "We don't allow solicitors," she said, her nose tilting up a bit.

Oh, Nonna, I hope you're saying that rosary for me. Rick's hand shot out to stop the door from being shut in his face. "I'm not soliciting, Mrs. Morgan. I'm a friend of Jill's. My name's Rick Covelli."

A glimmer of pain flashed in the woman's eyes, but she quickly masked it. "You were the one on the phone…"

"Yes. I answered that morning you called," Rick admitted. "I've spent a lot of time with both Jill and her son, Lucas." He turned on his smile. "And he looks a lot like you."

That seem to render her speechless.

"Jill needs you, Mrs. Morgan."

Before she could respond, a man appeared at the door. "Who is it, Claudia?" asked a gray-haired man with brown eyes. He nodded at Rick. "May I help you?"

Rick held out his hand. "Yes, Mr. Morgan, I'm Rick Covelli. I'm here to extend an invitation to you and your wife to attend your daughter's college graduation."

* * *

Saturday morning Jill sat in Karyn's kitchen. She couldn't believe she was actually graduating from college. Today. After all this time, she was finally getting her diploma. So why wasn't she more excited about it?

Because of Rick. She hadn't seen him in a week, not even a glimpse in the last seven miserable days. Maria said he'd gone out of town on business. Jill couldn't help but wonder if he'd gone back to Texas and no one had told her. The only thing that gave her hope that he'd return was his Harley, which she'd seen in its usual parking spot behind the restaurant.

God. Why couldn't she get the man out of her head? They were no longer together. He didn't want her enough to hang around. All she could do was watch as he walked away. She loved him but couldn't hold him. But had she really tried? The day he left her, she just stood there and let him go. Maybe if she'd told him how she felt, he would have stayed.

How was she going to move on with her life when she didn't want to head anywhere but to Rick? Maybe she should go to Texas and talk to him. Tears welled in her eyes, threatening to shatter the last of her control.

Karyn walked into the kitchen and set the baby monitor on the table. "Well, I got Emily fed and to sleep."

"Good." Jill brushed away the moisture from her eyes. "You know, Karyn, you don't need to go to the ceremony today. It's only five days since you had the baby."

"Hey, I have a lot invested in this graduation. I helped you cram for finals. I watched Lucas. No one wants to see you get that diploma more than I do."

They were both teary-eyed now. "Oh, Karyn, how can I ever thank you and Bob for all you've done for me?"

"By going out there and fulfilling your dream, making a good life for yourself and your son. When you get your first teaching job, I'm going to personally help you move into a bigger place.''

Panic surged through Jill. ''Move?''

''I'm not kicking you out. But when you start teaching you'll be able to afford a house so Lucas can have his own bedroom. You both can use more privacy.'' Karyn looked thoughtful. ''The Hayes place on Ash Street is for sale. Needs fixing up, but I bet you could get it for a good price.''

''Wait a minute.'' Jill held up a hand. ''This is happening too fast. I need to get a job first and pay off my student loan.''

Karyn dabbed at her eyes with a tissue. ''Just so long as you find one around here. I don't want you to move away.''

Jill was shocked her friend thought she would leave Haven Springs. ''Where else would I go?''

Karyn shrugged. ''Back to Chicago.''

Jill shook her head. ''Not a chance. My mother has made it perfectly clear that I've let her down for the last time.'' It struck Jill that now, after everything, she'd lost her parents...and Rick.

''I'm sorry, Jill. I know how much you wanted to reconcile with your parents.''

Jill smiled despite her pain. ''My true family is here. Lucas and you and Bob...and my new godchild, Emily.''

''What about Rick?''

Jill's chest tightened with longing. ''He'll be gone.''

''You sure about that?'' her friend asked. ''When Maria came to visit me in the hospital, she said Rick is thinking about staying in Haven Springs.''

Suddenly there wasn't enough air in the room to breathe. Jill's lungs felt like they were about to burst. Rick was staying here? No. She refused to let herself hope. She'd already blown it. She never gave him a chance...

Her misery was like a knife, piercing her heart. She

needed him desperately. "We'll have to stay out of each other's way."

"In a town of less than ten thousand people? Impossible. Maybe you two can work things out."

Jill shook her head, unable to fight her emotions. She burst into tears. "Oh, Karyn, I hurt him. I can't expect him to want me back. I've pushed him away too many times."

"Love can survive a lot of obstacles," Karyn said.

Before Jill could argue, the doorbell rang.

"I'll be back to finish this discussion," Karyn warned, then left the kitchen to answer the door.

There were voices and a few moments later Karyn returned. "Jill, you have visitors. They're in the living room."

She frowned. "Me? Who?"

"Come see."

Jill took a few seconds to pull herself together and then walked out of the kitchen. When she arrived in the living room, she froze. Standing there were her parents, Jackson and Claudia Morgan. For the longest time the three of them said nothing, did nothing. They just stood where they were as the years seemed to fade away.

"Isn't this a surprise, Jill?" Karyn said, breaking the silence. "Your parents came all this way to see you graduate."

Jackson Morgan finally spoke. "Hello, Jillian."

Hearing her father's voice, a huge ache formed in Jill's chest. Until that moment she hadn't realized how much she'd missed them, how crushing their decision not to come had been.

"Mother! Father!" she cried, and rushed first into her father's arms, then her mother's.

Although the Morgans had never been very demonstrative, they didn't seem to have the problem today.

"I didn't think you were going to come," Jill said as she pulled back.

Claudia was dressed in a navy tailored dress and her blond hair was cut short and fashionably styled. She glanced at her husband, then back at her daughter. "I may have been a little hasty in my decision." She sighed. "It was time to reconsider. That nice young man of yours explained how important it was for us to be here for your graduation. So here we are."

"My young man?" Jill repeated. "Mother, who are you talking about?"

Claudia sighed. "Why, Mr. Covelli, of course. You work for his mother, Maria."

Rick? Jill couldn't breathe as excitement raced through her. Rick had gone to her parents?

"Your dad and I were quite impressed. He was such a gentleman." Claudia smiled. "And so handsome in his dark suit. We seldom see young men dress neatly. And his clean-cut look, manicured nails and short hair made a welcome change from the ruffians one usually sees today."

Jill's heart sank. It hadn't been Rick. It had to have been Rafe.

"It was his plans for the future that impressed me," Jackson added. "He also told me about his father and how they never had the chance to solve their differences." Jackson drew a deep breath. "I don't want that to happen to us."

"The entire Covelli family has been wonderful to me," Jill said. "You'll meet them today."

Claudia looked a little ashamed. "They've been your family these past couple of years."

Jill nodded and gestured at Karyn. "So have Karyn and Bob Ashmore."

Claudia toyed with her pearl necklace nervously. "I

know I've been hard on you, Jill. The other morning I said some things…you didn't deserve. I'm sorry.''

This was the first time Jill could remember her mother ever apologizing for anything. She had always been a controlling type of person. Although there had been a lot of hurt over the years, Jill didn't want to dwell on the past. ''It's okay, Mother. I know you were trying to protect me.''

''Sometimes we forget our children are grown-up.'' Claudia smiled. ''Do you think we can put it all behind us?''

Unable to speak, Jill swallowed hard and nodded.

''Good, now can we see our grandchild?''

''Yes,'' Jackson put in. ''I hear he's quite the bright little boy.''

Jill's heart raced. Her father looked forward to meeting his grandson. ''Sure. Lucas should be awake from his nap about now. I'll go check.'' She headed to the small bedroom off the kitchen. Tears threatened and she quickly blinked them away. She wasn't going to cry today. Not when everything was perfect—or nearly perfect.

In the bedroom Jill found her son jabbering in his crib. ''So you are awake,'' she crooned. ''There's someone here to see you.''

The boy stood up. ''Ree…!'' he cried excitedly.

''No,'' Jill said. ''It's your Grandma and Grandpa.''

Lucas shook his head. ''No! Ree…'' he cried stubbornly.

''Is something wrong, Jill?'' Claudia came into the room, then hesitated upon seeing her grandchild. ''Oh, my, he's growing into such a handsome little boy.''

Her words caught Lucas's attention and he turned on his best grin.

''Lucas, here's your Grandmother.''

''Na…na…''

Claudia gasped. ''Did you hear what he called me?''

Jill nodded. She lifted Lucas out of the crib and carried

him to the dressing table to change his diaper. "Ever since Lucas was born, I've talked about you and Father a lot. I wanted him to know his grandparents."

Her mother gazed at the child and smoothed his curls back from his forehead. "He doesn't look anything like...Keith."

"Mother, you seem surprised," Jill said, continuing her chore. "You were there when he was born, and I've sent you pictures of Lucas since his birth."

Claudia couldn't seem to take her eyes off the boy. "There's a strong resemblance to my father."

"Heaven forbid." Jackson Morgan strode into the room and examined his grandson. "I'd say this child looks like...Lucas. You gave him a good solid name, Jill."

Jill finished dressing Lucas. "It's Lucas Jackson Morgan."

She could see that her father was touched. "May I hold him?" he asked.

Jill nodded.

"May I hold him?" he asked.

Jill had waited for this since her son's birth. She swallowed back the lump in her throat. "I think Lucas would like that." She looked down at her son, who was now seated on the table. "Lucas, this is your grandpa."

The boy's chubby finger pointed to Jackson's gray hair. "Pa...pa."

Everyone laughed as he lifted his grandson into his arms. Jill watched, her heart full, not caring how or why her family had come. The important thing was that they were here for her. At last.

After two hours in the hot June sun, the graduation ceremony came to a conclusion. Bob and Karyn, with baby Emily, stayed long enough to take pictures, then went home to feed Emily, promising to be at the party later. Lucas had spent the entire ceremony with his grandparents and the Covellis.

When Jill arrived back at the restaurant, she was greeted with cheers and applause by friends and customers who wanted to share her special day. Maria ushered everyone into the back room where she had set up a buffet for the celebration.

Jill was overwhelmed by everything, her parents coming today, her extended family, the Ashmores and Covellis, and Lucas. Everyone was here to share her joy—except Rick.

"Oh, Jill, have you tried these wonderful hors d'oeuvres?" her mother asked.

"I'm too nervous to eat. But enjoy the *taralli* pastry ring. Maria makes the best."

Claudia Morgan smiled. "I'll have to diet when I get home—this stuff is too wonderful to resist."

Jill found she was looking for Rick, hoping he might show up. But he wasn't there. Did she really expect him to be?

"Where's Lucas?" Jill asked.

Her mother took another bite of pastry. "Your father has him. I think I'm going to have trouble separating those two."

Jill smiled. "I think it's wonderful."

"I better go check to see if they need anything." Her mother hugged her. "Enjoy your party," she said, and walked away.

How can I when the man I love isn't here? Jill wanted to scream. Instead, she smiled again when Maria Covelli came up and kissed her on both cheeks. "I'm so proud of you."

"Thank you. I couldn't have done it without your help."

"Nonsense!" Maria waved her hand. "You had the desire. You will be a good teacher. Although I will hate to lose you here. You are like my daughter."

Jill blinked at the threatening tears. ''You'll never lose me, Maria.'' *But I've already lost,* Jill thought. *I tossed Rick's love away.*

''Don't look so sad,'' Maria said. ''You have everything today. Your mother and father are here. Your friends…your future.''

Jill could no longer hold back the tears. ''Oh, Maria, I made a big mistake.''

''No, child, don't cry. Whatever is wrong can be fixed.''

Jill shook her head. ''Not this. I ruined everything. I sent Rick away. Now he's gone.'' She brushed away her tears, not wanting anyone to see her.

Maria smoothed back Jill's hair and smiled. ''Are you so sure he's gone?''

''He hasn't been around in a week. I wanted him to be here today so I could tell him I'm sorry and how I really feel.''

''So you love my Enrico?''

Jill looked Maria in the eye. ''Yes, very much.''

Maria patted her hand. ''Everything will work out, you will see. Come, we will open some presents.'' The last thing Jill wanted was to draw attention to herself, but Maria had gone to a lot of trouble. So Jill agreed and the group gathered around the table as she opened a card from her parents. Inside was a sizable check for her and a savings bond for Lucas. She smiled with each card and gift she unwrapped until she came to the last. One more package, wrapped in white paper and without a card.

Inside the first box was a smaller jewelry box. Her pulse pounded as she lifted the lid and found an exquisite gold watch. She gasped, along with the guests.

''Who's it from?'' Karyn asked.

''I have no idea.'' Jill glanced around the room of thirty guests, but no one claimed responsibility.

''Maybe it's engraved,'' someone suggested.

Jill lifted the watch out of its holder. She turned it over and her heart almost stopped when she read the inscription: *Till the end of time, cara mia. Love, Rick.*

''Rick...'' Her hand shook as she looked up and searched the room again, at last spotting a tall man with neatly trimmed hair and a piercing dark gaze standing behind everyone. Rick.

With all eyes on her, the crowd parted, and knees shaking, she walked across the room. She stopped in front of the man who'd made her laugh, who'd spent hours repairing a rocking horse for her son, who'd taught her how to play baseball...who'd taught her how to love again.

Now she understood. ''You *were* the one who went to my parents. Why?''

His beautiful dark gaze locked with hers. ''It was important to you,'' he said. ''I wanted your graduation to be special. Everything you wanted it to be. Best wishes, Jill.'' He turned and left the room. Stunned, Jill felt her heart breaking.

Her mother hurried over, holding Lucas. ''Jillian Marie Morgan, are you going to stand there and let that wonderful man walk out of your life?''

Jill swung around. ''No, I'm not. Lucas and I love him very much.''

Lucas pointed at the door. ''Ree...''

''Then go after him,'' Claudia urged her. ''That young man has a future and he loves you.''

Jill kissed both her son and mother and then took off down the hall. Outside in the sunlit parking lot she saw Rick next to his motorcycle. ''Rick,'' she yelled. ''Wait.''

Rick's heart pounded with excitement as he saw Jill hurrying toward him. Damn. Maybe all those rosaries had paid off. He yanked off his suit jacket and stuffed it into his saddlebag. When she reached him, he had to fight not to drag her into his arms.

"Don't go," she said.

Stay cool, he told himself. He needed more from her. He shrugged. "Why should I hang around?"

She took a step closer. "Because I want you to stay. I need you to stay."

Rick pointed to his short haircut and white dress shirt. "This isn't me, Jill. I only did this so your parents would listen to reason."

"I know, Rick. I always loved your hair." She reached out and touched his temple. "Long or short."

He grabbed her wrist. "What do you want, Jill?"

She pulled her wrist free and put her arms around his neck. "I want you. I've always wanted you." She stood on tiptoe and kissed him on the lips. He froze. He tried to stay still, but he was too hungry for her touch, the feel of her soft skin. Unable to resist, he crushed her to him and deepened the kiss.

When he tore his mouth away, he had trouble catching his breath. "I want it all, Jill."

But before she could answer, he climbed on the Harley and handed her a helmet. "C'mon, I need to show you something."

She looked down at her long flowered skirt, then at the encouraging crowd that had gathered at the back door. She shoved the helmet on her head. Grabbing a handful of her skirt, she swung her leg over the bike and wrapped her arms around his waist. "This better be good, Covelli."

"It's going to be the best ever, *cara*." He started the engine and turned down the alley as the crowd cheered them on.

Rick prayed there was going to be something to cheer about.

Jill held on tight as Rick sped along the road to the lake. Twenty minutes later they arrived at the same place he'd taken her for their picnic. He parked the bike under the tree and Jill climbed off.

The light was fading as day turned into evening. It was still warm, however, and there were people and boats on the water. It was peaceful, too, and from where they stood under a grove of trees, very private.

"It's so beautiful here," she whispered.

He finally smiled. "I'm glad you feel that way." He looked out at the lake. "I like it here, too. In fact, that's why I bought this place."

Jill blinked. "You bought the cottage? Why?"

He looked at her, and she felt a catch in her throat. "I'm staying in Haven Springs. I'll go back to Texas when I'm needed, but between Tuck and our foreman we can manage. Then eventually I'm going to sell out." He caressed her cheek with his thumb. "I want to be here. I'm going to help Covelli and Sons get back on its feet and clear my father's name. I promised the family."

"Oh, I see. And you need a place to stay. But why out here?"

"Because you fell in love with the cottage the night I brought you here." He sighed and turned toward her. "That was the night I realized I was in love with you."

Jill's trembling hand went to her mouth as hope and longing seized her. "Oh, Rick...."

He raised a hand. "I know I'm not what you planned, Jill. But if you give me a chance I can make you happy. And Lucas, too. I'm crazy about the little guy."

She saw the truth of what he said reflected in his eyes.

"He's crazy about you, too." She drew a long breath. "So am I, Rick. Even when I had this silly idea that you were all wrong for me, I loved you. I've loved you so much that I thought I'd go out of my mind. You and the times we were together was all I thought about. How it was to be in your arms, for you to make love to me. Oh, Rick, I'm sorry it took me so long to realize—''

''Shh,'' he whispered, then kissed her and kissed her again. ''It's okay, *cara*. We're together now.'' He hugged her closer. ''We'll have the rest of our lives together.''

''Rick, what about your job in Texas?''

''Don't worry about it. I've got it under control.'' His mouth covered hers again in a searing kiss.

Jill broke off. ''But…can you just leave Tuck?''

''Lord, woman,'' he groaned. ''Will you give a guy a chance to propose?''

Jill was rooted to the spot as her blood pulsed through her veins. ''Propose?''

He grinned, then walked to his bike. When he returned he held a small box. ''Jill Morgan…'' He hesitated. ''I'm not very good at this kind of stuff.''

Her gaze searched his handsome face while her fingers caressed the watch he'd given her earlier. He was wrong. He was very good at this kind of stuff. ''Say what's in your heart, Rick.''

He nodded. ''It would take a lifetime to show you how much I love you. I can't believe I found someone as beautiful and good as you are. You're a generous woman. A great mother. I want to make a life for you and Lucas. I want us to be a family. Jill, will you marry me?''

''Oh, yes, Rick. Yes. Yes. I'll marry you.'' She went into his arms. ''I love you so much.''

''I love you, *cara*.'' He lowered his mouth to hers in a kiss that swiftly turned fiery. His arms circled her waist and pulled her against him so she could feel his desire.

He tore his mouth away, rested his forehead against hers. ''Whoa, I'm getting carried away.''

''I don't mind,'' Jill murmured.

''I need to give you this first to make it official.''He opened the box and displayed a diamond engagement ring.

He slipped the large stone in its Tiffany setting onto her finger.

"Oh, Rick, it's beautiful." The ring glowed in the twilight.

He raised her hand and kissed the finger where he'd just put the ring. He lifted her in his arms and carried her up the steps to the porch. "Now, I want to show you how much I missed you."

Jill laid her head on his shoulder. "This is so romantic. I'm going to love living out here."

"I'm glad," he said, and she could see he'd been worried. "The night we came out here for dinner, I wanted to make love to you. I wanted this place to be special for us."

"Oh, Rick. I wanted you that night, too. And you made it more special tonight when you proposed." Her gaze met his. "I want you," she whispered.

"Hold that thought," he said as he opened the cottage door and stepped over the threshold. The room was dimly lit and filled with fresh-cut flowers, their beauty and fragrance almost overwhelming her senses. Four hurricane lamps were lined against the fireplace, along with a bottle of champagne chilling in a bucket.

"My, you've been a busy man," she murmured, touched that he'd made everything so special.

"June is too warm for a fire, but I wanted the effect." He took her to the rug in front of the hearth.

"You had this planned."

"I was hoping you'd be willing to come out here with me. This is where I wanted to begin things—where I fell in love with you." He shook his head. "No, the cottage is where I *admitted* to myself that I loved you. The first night I came home and saw you in the restaurant was when I believe I fell in love. From then on I couldn't get you out of my head."

Jill gazed into the ebony eyes she loved so much. "I felt

it, too. But I wouldn't let myself believe it. I was afraid of getting hurt.''

''Since we're talking about personal admissions, there's something else I need to tell you.''

A slight look of panic crossed Jill's face.

Rick cupped her cheek in the palm of his hand and smiled. ''Don't worry, *cara*.''

Jill gave Rick a curious look. ''Whatever it is, I don't care, I'm yours. Totally.''

''It's nothing bad. It's just that...I've done very well in Texas, in fact I'd say well enough to be called a millionaire.''

Her eyes widened. ''A millionaire.''

He nodded. ''A couple of times over, even. You and Lucas will never want for anything again. I promise.''

A bright smile spread across her face. ''And I figured the oil business must be in a slump, considering all the time you've spent hanging around Haven Springs,'' she teased.

Rick embraced Jill and laughed. ''You were the biggest reason I stayed around.'' Then he lowered her to the blanket in front of the fireplace and lay down beside her. ''And I'm going to spend the rest of the night convincing you that I'm going to stay. And how much I love you.''

Smiling, her hands moved up his chest and circled his neck. ''That'll be my favorite part.''

''Mine, too. And I'm going to prove that our love is strong enough to handle anything, even *la maledizione*. The curse.''

''Just promise me you'll let your hair grow out again.''

''Anything for you *cara mia*,'' he promised as he brought his mouth to hers.

Jill let the delicious feeling of being in Rick's arms wash over her. Her only thoughts were of love and forever after with the bad boy who had turned out to be the perfect man for her.

Epilogue

Rick and Jill had wanted a simple affair for their July wedding, but the families had had different ideas. To keep everybody happy, Jill and her mother had taken care of all the wedding details, while Rick and Maria had arranged the reception.

The day of the wedding, Jill managed to stay calm as she dressed in her tea-length ivory satin dress with its fitted lace bodice and gathered skirt. Her hair was pinned up and adorned with a wreath of white flowers and a short veil. Karyn was her matron of honor and Angelina a bridesmaid. They both wore mauve dresses and carried bouquets of baby rosebuds.

Rick had been persuaded to wear a slate-gray morning coat and dark trousers. A white pleated shirt showed off his olive skin. As promised, he'd been letting his hair grow. The wavy dark strands were now curling across his forehead. Now he stood by the altar with Tuck and Rafe, waiting for Jill to come down the aisle.

From the back of the church, Jill couldn't take her eyes off her husband-to-be. Rick was her anchor, her strength. His love had changed her. He'd made her believe that she could do anything. With his encouragement, she'd applied for a teaching job at Haven Springs Elementary and was delighted when she got the job. Rick planned to work part-time for Rafe while Lucas was in nursery school. He wanted to adopt her son, to make him a Covelli.

Once again tears filled her eyes as she took her father's arm. She was so lucky she had Rick's love. And to think she'd nearly let this wonderful man walk out of her life. Well, things would be different now. She was going to let him know every day that she returned his love and was grateful he'd been willing to take a chance on her.

The music swelled and Jill and her father started down the aisle. Families and friends turned to watch, but her eyes were on her man. It was all she could do to keep herself from running to him.

Lucas sat in the front pew with Maria.

She let go of her father's arm and leaned down to kiss her son. "You're going to get a daddy, Lucas. Just like I promised."

"Ree…" the little boy said as he pointed and smiled. "Da…Da."

"That's right. Real soon." She straightened and continued toward the altar and Rick. Her father took her hand and placed it in her future son-in-law's.

Rick raised it to his lips. *"Mia bella cara."*

His words were like a caress as a warm shiver moved down her spine. *"Mio amore.* My love," she whispered.

They turned and faced the altar, where the priest stood waiting for them, and the ceremony began.

The reception was in full swing. The band was playing love songs and couples were dancing. Rafe and Tuck had toasted the bride and groom several times, as had other friends and family. Rick wasn't paying much attention anymore. His gaze was on his beautiful bride, and he was thinking about sweeping her away from all this and starting their honeymoon immediately.

After the day he'd put the ring on Jill's finger at the cottage, she'd asked him to wait until they were married to make love again. Reluctantly he'd agreed, not realizing how difficult the promise would be to keep. But that all ended tonight. He checked his watch. In less than thirty minutes they would take off for the cottage and their wedding night. Tomorrow they'd take a flight to the Bahamas for a week together. Alone. No interruptions.

When the music stopped, Rick went out to the dance floor and rescued his bride from an elderly partner. He pulled her into his arms and danced her around the crowd of people.

"Can we blow this joint?" he teased. "I've just about had enough."

Her blue eyes sparkled. "I'm ready any time you are."

Rick took her hand and together they went to the front of the room. He grabbed the microphone. "Attention, friends and family. Jill and I want to thank you all for coming and sharing our special day. But now we're leaving." There were groans and chuckles. "So all you single ladies step up here, because Jill's going to toss her bouquet."

The women giggled and gathered around. With a kiss from Rick, the bride turned her back and threw the bouquet. Squeals filled the air and the bouquet landed in a surprised Angelina's arms. Rick's younger sister blushed as she cradled the flowers.

Again he grabbed his new wife's hand and they hurried out the door as the guests showered them with rice. The limousine was their refuge, and the moment they were in, the driver sped off.

Rick watched Jill with pleasure. She was the most beautiful woman he'd ever known.

She glanced over and smiled. "What?"

"I was just thinking how lucky I am." He drew her closer and kissed her. "And now I've finally got you all to myself."

"You always had me all to yourself."

He arched an eyebrow. "But now you're legally mine, Mrs. Covelli."

"Oh, my gosh. That's my name now."

"Jill Covelli." He smiled. "I like the sound of that."

She curled up against him. "The best part is that you come with the name. Oh, Rick, I love you so much."

"You better, after everything I went through today. Especially wearing this monkey suit." He smiled.

"Poor guy," she murmured, then her mouth met his. He groaned and deepened the kiss. Somehow he managed to pull her onto his lap. "God, Jill, I want you so much."

"What's stopping you?" she teased.

His mouth went to her neck. "Hold that thought a few minutes. I don't want our wedding night to be spent in the back of a limousine. But, *cara,* when I get started with you, we're not moving from the bed."

She touched his lips with a fingertip. "Promise?"

Luckily the driver had pulled off the highway onto the road to the lake or Rick might have challenged her. Soon the cottage came into view and the limo stopped and the driver let them out. Rick thanked and tipped the man, and sent him on his way.

Then he swept his bride up in his arms and carried her up the steps of their vacation home.

They had decided a while back that if she was going to teach in Haven Springs, they should live in town. They'd bought the Hayes place, a block from the Ashmores'. Rick was going to remodel the old Victorian for them. The cottage would be used as a weekend getaway.

They crossed the threshold. "Here we are, Mrs. Covelli."

The place had had visitors. All the flowers from the wedding had been placed around the room, and there was a note saying there was food in the refrigerator along with several bottles of wine. Then they went upstairs to the only room that had been redecorated—the master bedroom. Last month they'd painted the room a color called Morning sun; they'd also purchased furniture, including a king-size bed.

This room had been invaded by the flower fairies, too. As well, there was a bottle of champagne on ice next to the bed. Rick picked up the card. Congratulations To You Both On Your Special Day. With All Our Love, The Family.

Jill walked to the window. Rick followed and slipped his arms around her waist as she leaned against him. Together they stared out at the lake. "It's all so perfect I don't want it to end."

He turned her to face him. "Our love is never going to end, *cara*. It's only going to grow stronger."

Rick's mouth inched toward her tempting mouth until their lips met in a tender kiss, but soon it changed to one of hunger and need. Jill slipped her arms around his waist and drew him close, and he knew he'd found what he'd been looking for all along. The angel who came to his rescue that night in the garden.

He knew that with her, he was finally home.

* * * * *

Turn the page for a preview of
HER SURPRISE FAMILY

by
Patricia Thayer

the next book in her emotional miniseries
WITH THESE RINGS

September 1999
Only from Silhouette Romance

Rafe stopped his truck in front of Stewart Manor and peered at the woman standing on the porch. It looked like he was about to meet Haven Springs's newest resident, Ms. Shelby Harris.

Grabbing his clipboard, he climbed out of the cab. He made his way through the overgrown weeds in the front yard, up the long walkway, to the steps.

"Ms. Harris?" He tipped his baseball cap with the Covelli and Sons logo. "I'm Rafe Covelli."

The young woman appeared to be in her late twenties. She nodded. "Thank you for coming by, Mr. Covelli."

"No problem. I've been working in the area. We're doing the facade restoration on the houses up the street."

When Rafe went up the steps onto the porch, he was surprised to find himself nearly eye-to-eye with the woman. He was over six feet, so Shelby Harris was at least five-ten. A quick glance told him her height was all in a pair of long slender legs, which were now encased in a pair of nicely fitted jeans. His gaze moved to her narrow waist and the cotton T-shirt that did little to hide her full breasts. His pulse began to race in appreciation. It had been a while since a stranger this appealing had come to town. The last had been Jill Morgan, who recently married his younger brother, Rick. Rafe's gaze raised to her face, framed by short brown curls, and his heart did a somersault as he met the most incredible green eyes he'd ever seen.

His scrutiny seemed to make her nervous and she glanced away. "As I told you on the phone, I plan to turn Stewart Manor into a bed-and-breakfast inn."

Rafe let out a low whistle. "And I explained that was going to take some work—and money."

"I'm not afraid of work, Mr. Covelli," she said. "But if you can't handle the job…"

The woman was as prickly as a cactus. "I didn't say I couldn't handle the job. How much time and money do you have, Ms. Harris?"

"That's what I wanted to talk to you about."

The look on her face told him he was in trouble. Damn. He'd seen that same expression on his sister's face too many times. This was serious. Something was up and he wasn't sure he wanted to know that. "Okay, talk."

Her back straightened stubbornly. "Most of my ready cash went into buying this house. It will be a month or so before I have more available. Right now I need to be a little frugal. I thought maybe we could work out some sort of deal."

Rafe knew he should turn around, climb back into his truck and drive off. He had enough of his own problems without giving away his time. But something kept him rooted to the spot. Maybe he was curious why a single woman wanted to buy this old house and turn it into a bed-

and-breakfast. And the longing in her green eyes made him ask, ''What do you have in mind?''

''I've seen your work around town. You're very good. But I also need more done. I wanted to ask you to check the roof and have a look at the inside. Tell me how much it would cost to fix it up—'' she hesitated and took a deep breath ''—a little at a time. The bare necessities—enough so I can open for business.''

There was that stubborn look again. Her full mouth drew into a pouty bow and something stirred in Rafe's gut. Damn.

''Let's have a look, then.'' He returned to the porch and walked to the heavy oak door with the oval-cut-glass center. He opened it and stepped across the threshold into a huge entryway. A coolness greeted him as he stood on the bare hardwood floors. A cut-glass chandelier hung from the high ceiling, edged with oak crown molding. The long majestic staircase across the hall made its way to the second story. There were several missing spindles in the banister, and a few of the steps were missing.

''You'd better stay off the stairs until I've checked them out,'' he said as he turned to his left and entered the front room—what used to be called a parlor.

Shelby stood back and watched the cocky Mr. Covelli move around her house. So he thought that she was helpless. That she had to be warned about obvious dangers. Well, she had news for him. She'd spent her entire life taking care of herself and could do just fine.

She'd asked around and knew he was her best chance for a fair deal. She knew it. Worse, he knew it, too.

He was now standing at the three double-hung windows and eying the frames. She joined him there as he glanced down at the dark ornate woodwork along the baseboards, then squatted for a closer look. She couldn't help but notice the nice curve of his rear end, his muscular thighs strained against the fabric of his worn jeans. Her gaze moved to his chambray shirt as the muscles of his broad shoulders and back flexed. A shiver of awareness raced through her. She quickly raised her eyes to his face and found him in deep concentration. His olive skin told of his Italian ancestry and the fact that he worked in the sun.

His eyes were coal-black and mesmerizing. His dark hair was cropped short around the ears. He pulled off his cap and she saw that his thick mane was still neatly combed. She somehow knew that was the way Rafe Covelli's life was. All in neat, organized order. Everything cut and dried. Black or white.

The complete opposite of hers.

She doubted he would go along with her idea. It was beginning to seem crazy even to her.

''Well, Ms. Harris,'' he said as he stood and faced her, ''there's bad news. You've had a water leak around these two west windows. I'll have to replace these frames and tear out the plaster.'' He pointed out the spots.

Rafe walked into the hall again. She hurried to keep up. ''The stairway needs to have some steps and several spindles replaced.'' He kept walking until he was finally in the living room.

This was the room where Shelby had taken up residence. She'd cleaned and put up curtains, then arranged her furniture, which consisted of a sofa and chair, along with a portable television and bookcase. Her desk and computer were against the far wall. The only other rooms she'd used since moving in three days ago, had been the small servant's quarters off the kitchen, consisting of a bedroom and bath.

Rafe approached the huge stone fireplace and began to check out the carved-oak mantel. She held her breath when he stopped and eyed the framed photographs lined up along the top.

He looked at her. "Family?" he asked.

Shelby hesitated, then answered, "Yes."

He smiled. "I didn't think anyone had more family than I do."

He studied the assortment of pictures, and a wave of envy washed over her. Like most people, Rafe Covelli seemed to take his relatives for granted. *But there are those of us who don't have a real family to claim,* she thought.

She shook away the rush of loneliness. "You have a big family, Mr. Covelli?"

He nodded. "A grandmother, a mother, a brother and sister, but there's also a large assortment of aunts and uncles and cousins. Our reunions are a madhouse." He smiled as his gaze met hers. Like a magnet, he held her captive with his midnight eyes. She couldn't breathe until finally he turned away and moved on to finish his appraisal of the house.

He leaned down and examined the floor, then wrote some more notes on his clipboard. "Do any of your family live around here?"

"Uh, no," she said. "They're farther south."

He glanced over his shoulder. "Why didn't you buy a house there? Then maybe your family could help you."

"I'd rather do this on my own. Besides, I could afford this place."

"I'll go have a look upstairs." He started out of the room and she followed him again. When they arrived at the staircase, he stopped. She didn't, and ran into him. He reached out and grabbed her by the arms before she could lose her balance. "You better stay down here. These stairs aren't safe. And until the repairs are done I don't want you using them."

Shelby felt a sudden heat from his surprisingly gentle touch and lost any desire to argue. Then he turned and continued up the stairs. She watched as he moved with an easy athletic grace over the broken steps. Finally he disappeared from view, and she returned to the living room.

Shelby crossed to the mantel and studied the row of pictures. Her family. Uncle Ray and Aunt Celia, along with an assortment of cousins. They were spread all across the country, of course. That way people didn't ask why they never came to visit. All she had to do was make up stories about them. And she was really good at make-believe—she made a living at it. Shelby drew a long breath and released it. She glanced around the room, feeling a flood of contentment.

She finally had her home. And soon it would be filled with people, and she wouldn't be all alone anymore.

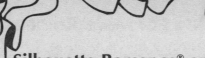

**Silhouette Romance® and
Silhouette Special Edition®**
welcome you to a heartwarming
miniseries full of family traditions,
scandalous secrets and newfound love.

*With These
Rings*

by
PATRICIA THAYER

THE SECRET MILLIONAIRE (June '99)
Silhouette Special Edition®
A sweet-talkin' Texas oilman is just itching to transform this
sexy single mom into Cinderella!

HER SURPRISE FAMILY (September '99)
Silhouette Romance®
To this bachelor, marriage is The Great Surrender. Will he
wage war with his feelings…or give up his heart to the new
lady in town?

THE MAN, THE RING, THE WEDDING (December '99)
Silhouette Romance®
Would a shocking family secret prevent two star-crossed
lovers from making their own family…together?

Available at your favorite retail outlet.

V *Silhouette*®

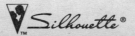

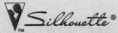

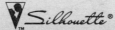

*This June 1999, the legend
continues in Jacobsville*

Diana Palmer

LONG, TALL TEXANS
EMMETT, REGAN & BURKE

This June 1999, Silhouette brings readers
an extra-special trade-size collection
for Diana Palmer's legion of fans.
These three favorite Long, Tall Texans
stories have been brought back in
one collectible trade-size edition.

*Emmett, Regan & Burke are about to be led
down the bridal path by three irresistible women.
Get ready for the fireworks!*

**Don't miss this collection of favorite
Long, Tall Texans stories…
available in June 1999
at your favorite retail outlet.**

**Then in August 1999 watch for
LOVE WITH A LONG, TALL TEXAN
a trio of brand-new short stories featuring
three irresistible Long, Tall Texans.**

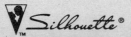